P9-CDF-597

ELLERY ADAMS

MURDER IN THE BOOK LOVER'S LOFT

Kensington Publishing Corp.
www.kensingtonbooks.com

KENSINGTON BOOKS are published by

Kensington Publishing Corp.
119 West 40th Street
New York, NY 10018

All Kensington titles, imprints, and distributed lines are available at special quantity discounts for bulk purchases for sales promotion, premiums, fund-raising, educational, or institutional use.

Special book excerpts or customized printings can also be created to fit specific needs. For details, write or phone the office of the Kensington Sales Manager: Attn.: Sales Department. Kensington Publishing Corp., 119 West 40th Street, New York, NY 10018. Phone: 1-800-221-2647.

The K and Teapot logo is a trademark of Kensington Publishing Corp.

First Printing: August 2023
ISBN: 978-1-4967-2950-7

ISBN: 978-1-4967-2951-4 (ebook)

10 9 8 7 6 5 4 3 2 1

Printed in the United States of America

For Wendy.
Thank you for adopting this series when it
needed a home.
Like Muffet Cat, it has thrived in your care.

What is that feeling when you're driving away from people and they recede on the plain till you see their specks dispersing? —it's the too-huge world vaulting us, and it's goodbye. But we lean forward to the next crazy venture beneath the skies.

— Jack Kerouac

Welcome to Storyton Hall!

OUR STAFF IS HERE TO SERVE YOU.
Resort Manager—Jane Steward
Butler—Mr. Butterworth
Head Librarian—Mr. Sinclair
Head Chauffeur—Mr. Sterling
Head of Recreation—Mr. Lachlan
Head of Housekeeping—Mrs. Templeton
Head Cook—Mrs. Hubbard
Spa Manager—Tammie Kota

SELECT MERCHANTS OF STORYTON VILLAGE
Run for Cover Bookshop—Eloise Alcott
Daily Bread Cafe—Edwin Alcott
Cheshire Cat Pub—Bob and Betty Carmichael
Canvas Creamery—Phoebe Doyle
La Grande Dame Clothing Boutique—Mabel
Wimberly
Tresses Hair Salon—Violet Osborne
Pickled Pig Market—the Hogg brothers
Geppetto's Toy Shop—Barnaby Nicholas
Hilltop Stables—Sam Nolan
Storyton Outfitters—Phil and Sandi Hughes
The Old Curiosity Shop—Roger Bachman

RESIDENTS OF OYSTER BAY
Olivia Limoges
Francis Belvedere
Bartenders Sammi and Reggie
Rachel Wilcox
Trent Little
Officers Lorna Locklear and Art Henniger

AUTHORS MENTIONED (FICTIONAL)
Angel Sanchez
Justin St. James
Heather O'Grady
Winston Hall

Chapter 1

Jane Steward stood in a small, secret room in the attic turret of a sprawling manor house called Storyton Hall, a world-famous resort catering to readers, and tried to come to a decision.

The old mansion was a repository of books. Thousands of them. Entire rooms were dedicated to books. They lined the walls and filled the shelves. They marched across mantelpieces and were stacked on tables.

A guest of Storyton Hall could spend a lazy morning cocooned in one of the soft chairs of the Daphne du Maurier Drawing Room, sipping coffee and nibbling a buttery croissant while they turned the pages of a well-loved paperback. They could while away a rainy afternoon reading by the fire in the Isak Dinesen Safari Room or borrow a book from the Henry James Library and carry it outside to the Anne of Green Gables Gazebo.

When it was time for a reading break, guests could swim in the Jules Verne Pool or take a long walk on Tennyson's Trail. There was almost always a croquet game in progress on the Lewis Carroll Court or one could sign up for a falconry or archery lesson.

Such activity was bound to rouse an appetite, but no one stayed hungry for long at Storyton Hall. There was casual dining in the Rudyard Kipling Café, formal dining in the Madame Bovary Dining Room, and afternoon tea was served daily in the Agatha Christie Tea Room.

In this attic space high above those public areas, Jane knew that the tea service had already started, and she was unlikely to make it in time to savor a cup of Earl Grey and one of Mrs. Hubbard's pumpkin scones. As much as she'd liked to take a break, she had important work to do first.

Her current task was to review the inventory list of what the literati would surely dub the Eighth Wonder of the World, and to select several items to sell, donate, or, if possible, return to the descendants of the original owner.

Hundreds of priceless literary treasures were housed in this fireproof, climate-controlled vault. There were drawers of manuscripts, scrolls, maps, and books. Works of fiction and nonfiction by some of the best-known authors of the ages were wrapped in layers of white paper and tucked into archival boxes like babies in their cradles.

The drawers also contained obscure and frightening propaganda by authors whose sole purpose was to negatively impact humankind's future. The goal of their work was to twist the truth and transform the sacred into the profane. These materials had been handed over to the Stewards to be forever hidden.

The Steward family had served as Guardians to this

strange and wonderful collection for centuries, and the august role often came with a steep price. Ever since Uncle Aloysius had passed the mantle on to her, Jane's life had been marked by violence and strife.

Like all Guardians before her, Jane had sworn to protect and preserve the contents of the secret library. Fortunately, she was not alone in this endeavor. She had her Fins to keep her safe. Named after the fletching on an arrow, the Fins were four men of unwavering loyalty and specialized skill sets who worked as employees at Storyton Hall. They were as much a part of Jane's family as were her twin sons, Fitzgerald and Hemingway.

Not long ago, Jane had decided it was time to put an end to her guardianship and to empty the secret library. Without it, there would be no reason for thieves and other miscreants to come to her resort. After hundreds of years, the Stewards would finally be safe, and Jane could focus her energy on her family, friends, and business.

However, the process of selling or donating the collection was proving to be a slow one. Some of the most incredible items, like an undiscovered Shakespeare play and the sequel to *Jane Eyre*, had already been re-homed, but a king's fortune of literary treasures still remained.

Jane selected a notebook filled with prose written by Nathaniel Hawthorne. A tag on the archival box described how, in this unseen draft of *The Scarlet Letter*, Hester Prynne had had an affair with a freed Black man named Jacob Strong instead of the Reverend Arthur Dimmesdale. A member of the Hawthorne family had asked Jane's ancestor to hide the notebook. This individual had offered no explanation but had paid a hefty storage fee.

"What should I do with you?" she said out loud, addressing the box containing the notebook.

Hawthorne's work could be found in the archives at Yale, Harvard, the Library of Congress, and in three museums. He had dozens of living descendants, and Jane could hardly pull a name out of a hat and surprise one family member with a piece of literary history that was not only worth a king's ransom but would also invite a torrent of media attention.

In the end, she decided to reach out to her contact at the Library of Congress. Through this contact, she could donate Hawthorne's notebook, as well as a poem attributed to William Cullen Bryant. Not only would Jane's anonymity be guaranteed but the library would share its new acquisitions with the world.

"Books are meant to be shared," she told the room at large. When she paused to consider a slim volume in the bottom drawer that touted the attributes of eugenics, she amended her comment to, "Most books are meant to be shared."

As for a folio of studies by Mary Cassatt she'd found in a case near the door, this would be sold. The trio of unfinished drawings of a young mother bathing in a river with her children—all in the nude—would bring in enough money to pay for the new furnace and steam boilers.

Storyton Hall was a five-star resort, and if Jane wanted it to stay that way, she had to continuously improve its facilities. The funds from the sale of the Cassatt folio would go toward finishing the work on the new folly, the sculpture Uncle Aloysius had commissioned for the reflection pool, and, most importantly, a pay raise for the groundskeeping crew.

Jane carefully placed the Hawthorne notebook, the poem, and the Cassatt folio into a padded box and left the library. She locked the door, descended the narrow spiral staircase, and slipped through the gap in the wall behind her great-aunt's china cabinet.

Aunt Octavia had already gone down for tea and was no doubt drifting through the kitchens in search of treats and new tidbits of gossip, so Jane returned the cabinet to its proper place and exited the apartment.

She'd just pressed the button to call the service elevator when her phone buzzed.

"Ms. Steward, it's Abby at the rec desk. I have a guest here who signed up for a trail ride at Hilltop Stables that starts in fifteen minutes. She didn't think she wanted to go but just changed her mind. The problem is there's no one to drive her to the stables. Mr. Lachlan is running a falconry lesson and my archery class starts in ten minutes. All the drivers are either at the train station or with other guests."

"I'll drop her off. I'm going to town anyway, and I don't want her to miss her ride. It's so beautiful on the trails right now. Can you ask her to meet me on the front steps?"

Forgoing the elevator, Jane took the stairs to the ground floor and walked briskly to her office. After depositing the box on her desk, she locked the office and headed for the garages.

Storyton Hall owned a fleet of vintage Rolls-Royce sedans, which were all in use. The only available vehicle was a mud-splattered pickup.

"Sorry about the dirt," Jane said to her guest as she pulled up in front of the main doors.

Her guest, a lovely young woman with a corona of

blond hair and a winsome smile, didn't mind one bit. After telling Jane that she was grateful for the ride, she chatted amiably the whole way to Hilltop Stables.

When Jane turned onto the road leading to the stables, the woman confessed that she was incredibly nervous, and that her desire to impress her boyfriend had taken precedence over her fear of horses.

"Don't worry. Sam is used to beginners," Jane assured her. "He's been taking people on trail rides for years. His horses are so gentle and calm that my sons have been riding them since they were knee-high. Try to relax and concentrate on the foliage. It's peak leaf-peeping season around here, and the woods are putting on quite a show."

Jane pulled into the dirt lot in front of the smaller of Sam's two barns and turned to the young woman. "Sam is probably giving your group a quick orientation in that building with the green roof. Let's see if we can get you there before it's over."

Inside the building, one of Sam's assistants was addressing the group.

Jane waited until the young woman had joined her boyfriend before heading back outside. She was a few feet from her pickup when a Sheriff's Department SUV crested the top of the hill.

Sheriff Evans parked in an empty spot and exited the vehicle. He waved at Jane and said, "I didn't expect to bump into you here."

Jane smiled at the man she'd come to think of as a friend. "The last time I saw you, you said you'd been binge reading Westerns. Are you here for a ride? And did you bring your spurs and your lasso?"

"I'm not a horse guy. I like to keep my feet planted firmly on the ground." Adjusting his utility belt so it rested more comfortably on his hips, he glanced around. "Do you know where Sam is?"

"No. I was just dropping off a guest and didn't look for him. Is everything okay?"

The sheriff rubbed the salt-and-pepper bristle on his chin. "Sam found a body in the woods, not far from that rental cabin with the view of the river. Sam thinks the guy's been outside for a while."

Startled by the news, all Jane could think to say was, "That's awful."

At that moment, Sam appeared from around the corner of the barn. He jogged over to Jane and the sheriff and pointed to one of the trail heads. "He's that way. Is Doc Charles coming?"

"Should be here any minute now," said the sheriff.

Sam pushed a wave of sandy brown hair off his forehead and looked between Jane and the sheriff. "I don't think the guy's local. I don't recognize him."

A knot formed in Jane's stomach. "We're not missing any guests. At least, no one's reported someone as missing."

Hearing the growl of an engine, all three of them turned to watch a yellow Bronco emerge from around a bend in the road. The sheriff signaled to the driver, and Doc Charles parked his dust-coated car.

"Sorry to keep you waiting," he said as he grabbed his field kit from the back seat. "There's a nasty bug going around, and half of the third grade was in my office today. If you haven't had your flu shot yet, you should get it."

Sheriff Evans said, "I've had mine, but my wife hasn't. I'll remind her when I get home. Sam? Can you show us the way?"

"Sure."

When Sam began walking, Jane fell into step beside him. When an unusual death occurred within the town limits, Storyton Hall always seemed to be involved, which was why Jane didn't think twice about accompanying the men.

"I thought Edwin might come for a ride this morning," Sam said as they headed for the north trail.

Jane's partner, Edwin Alcott, was Sam's best friend, and she often referred to them as Mr. Bingley and Mr. Darcy. Sam was blue-eyed and fair-haired, while Edwin had dark hair and eyes, but they had similarly wide shoulders and square jaws. Both men were lean, muscular, and heartstoppingly handsome.

"He had to meet a repairman at the restaurant," Jane replied. "The oven's acting up again."

Sam shook his head. "Ah, the joys of being a small business owner. I'm glad you two are finally taking some time off. I can't remember the last time I saw the ocean. What's it like? This place on the coast?"

Jane sensed that Sam wanted to be distracted from thoughts of a dead body, so as they climbed the uphill trail, she told Sam what little she knew about Oyster Bay, North Carolina. She was in the middle of describing a museum she wanted to visit when Sam put a hand on her shoulder.

"Sorry to interrupt, but we're almost there," he said. "This guy's been exposed to the elements for hours, so it's not a pretty sight. You might want to hang back."

Though Jane wasn't squeamish, she'd seen what a day or two in the woods could do to an animal carcass and decided to heed Sam's advice.

Sam pointed to a group of five boulders so similar in size and shape that they reminded Jane of Yahtzee dice. "He's behind these rocks."

"One sec." Doc Charles opened his kit and removed a disposable mask and nitrile gloves. He then passed out masks to the rest of the party before following after Sam as he left the trail.

The men disappeared behind the boulders, which were easily twenty feet tall, but Jane could hear them speaking in low murmurs.

Why do we whisper in the presence of the dead? Jane thought. *Is it because their voices have been silenced and it feels wrong to speak when they can't?*

From farther down the hill, she heard a bark of laughter and assumed that the guided trail ride had gotten underway.

The riders were lucky. They had sunshine, a forest ablaze with fall colors, and crisp air that smelled of pine trees and woodsmoke. Their horses would carry them at a leisurely pace for an hour, and when their peaceful walk was over, the guests would dismount, say goodbye to their well-behaved animals, and be treated to hot cider and apple doughnuts.

For some reason, the disparity of their experience compared to that of the man lying on the other side of the boulders compelled Jane to pull up her mask and step off the trail.

Peering around the rough edge of the formidable rock, she took in the scene. Sam stood off to the side, his hands plunged deep into his pockets. Sheriff Evans was in a catcher's squat and Doc Charles was on his knees, next to the body.

Because the dead man's face was turned away from Jane, all she could see was the curve of a moon-pale cheek. As for the rest of him, her initial impression was of the color brown. His head was covered in thick, shaggy brown hair that merged into an equally shaggy brown beard. Leaf and pine needle fragments clung to his heavy brows and mustache, the legs of his brown work pants, and the soles of his tan boots. His coat, the only thing that wasn't brown, was shale gray.

"No sign of trauma," Doc Charles told the sheriff.

"I wonder if he's staying in the Shaws' rental cabin." Sheriff Evans straightened and gestured at the hill rising behind him. "It's the only reason I can think of why he'd be out here without ID or a phone. I'll give Jimmy a call as soon as I'm back in the office."

Doc Charles was examining the man's fingers. Without looking up, he said, "He's been dead for a couple of days. His clothes and the drop in temps at night have kept him fairly well-preserved."

"He's dressed for a hike. His boots are worn. He's no tourist from the city who got lost out here. Maybe he popped back here to relieve himself and, I don't know, had a stroke or his heart gave out." Taking notice of Jane, Sheriff Evans said, "Do you recognize him?"

"I can't see his face very clearly, but I don't think so."

Sam turned to her. "Don't get any closer. His body might look okay, but his face isn't pretty."

Jane stayed where she was.

"I'll call the EMTs." Sheriff Evans put his phone to his ear and locked eyes with Sam. "Would you walk Ms. Steward back to the stables? There's nothing else you can do for this gentleman. I'll let you know when he's been moved, and when you can use this trail again."

Sam and Jane made their way back to the parking lot in silence. When they reached her pickup, Jane said, "If you learn his name, would you let me know? I want to think of him as Bill or Hank or whoever he really was, instead of the dead man behind the boulders. As long as someone speaks his name, he won't be forgotten."

Inside the big barn, a horse whinnied. This was immediately followed by another, louder whinny.

Sam smiled. "That's Honey. She knows I left a bag of carrots in the tack room. They're her favorite."

"You'd better give her one before she starts a rebellion." Jane got into the car and rolled down her window. "What can we bring you from the beach? A T-shirt, or some saltwater taffy?"

"No, thanks. I have way too many T-shirts, and I like my candy salt-free. Just forget about everyone else and focus on yourself for once in your life. Okay?" As he walked away, he called back over his shoulder, "But if you see any mermaids, put in a good word for me!"

Jane drove to La Grande Dame, the clothing boutique owned by her friend, Mabel Wimberley. She pushed open the door and paused in astonishment. It looked like a bomb had gone off, scattering skeins of yarn and bolts of fabric over every surface.

The stack of shopper's baskets Mabel kept by the door had toppled over, creating a domino effect by striking the spinner displays of ribbon. All three of these had fallen, causing ribbon rolls in every color to launch across the shop like confetti from a cannon.

Picking up a roll of red ribbon whose loose end made it look like it was sticking its tongue out at her, Jane laid the roll on top of a bolt of blue silk.

"Mabel?" she yelled over the whir of a sewing machine. "Are you alive back there?"

The machine didn't stop. "Barely!"

Jane wanted to tell her friend about the dead man. Seeing his body in the woods had unsettled her, and it would be a comfort to confide her feelings to a friend.

However, the mess in Mabel's shop made it clear that her friend had enough on her mind as it was, so Jane decided to keep the incident to herself.

"May I pass through the curtain, Oh Great and Powerful Oz?"

"Get in here, woman. I don't have the energy to shout."

Jane parted the purple velvet curtains leading to Mabel's sewing room. If the shop was untidy, this space was utter chaos. Several clothes racks stuffed with costumes had been shoved to one side of the room, while Mabel's sewing table and a three-way mirror occupied the other side. Her worktable, which hugged the back wall, was covered with an assortment of paper patterns, scissors, pincushions, and spools of thread. Tape measures were coiled like snakes at Mabel's feet and the floor was littered with fabric scraps.

"I know, I know. It's bad. But *you're* the one who decided to host a masquerade party on Halloween, and all of my customers want to be the belle of the ball." She paused to examine her stitching. "I'd prefer to have more beasts."

"Finish what you're doing. I'm going to make you a cup of tea."

Mabel nodded tiredly and resumed her work.

Jane entered Mabel's kitchen, which was in a similar state to her workroom, and put the kettle on. She didn't have time to tidy this space and the shop, so she settled for transferring the dirty mugs and plates from the sink to the dishwasher and starting a wash cycle. She then wiped off the counters and emptied the overflowing garbage into a can in the alley.

When she came back inside, the kettle was singing. She used the last clean mug and the last bit of milk for

Mabel's tea. She was carrying the steaming mug into the workroom when two ladies entered the shop.

"Hello!" Jane greeted them with a friendly smile. "Come on in. I just need to give Rumpelstiltskin his tea and then I'll be back out to straighten up and assist you if I can. It's been a wild couple of weeks for La Grande Dame."

"I prefer the Oz reference," grumbled Mabel.

Jane placed the cup next to the sewing machine and gave Mabel's shoulders a squeeze. Her friend's muscles were tight as bowstrings, and though she groaned, she continued to change the thread in her sewing machine from white to gold.

"Tell me when you're ready," Jane said. "For now, I'll see if these ladies need any help."

The ladies in question had gravitated over to the wall of yarn. While they handled a skein, comparing its type, weight, and shade to another skein, Jane righted the shoppers' backets and returned all the ribbon rolls to the spinner rack. By the time she'd finished scooping bolts of fabric off the floor, the women had selected four skeins and a beechwood yarn bowl and put them down on the checkout counter.

Luckily, Jane knew how to use Mabel's register, so she punched in her friend's password to unlock the screen. She then aimed the handheld barcode scanner at the yarn bowl and said, "Are you visiting Storyton?"

"Just for the day," replied the first woman. "We live in Lexington, but we like to pop over here to have lunch and do a little shopping. We love your little market."

The second woman grinned. "I just adore the name. The Pickled Pig! But I miss seeing their precious mascot. That tiny, spotted pig has to be the cutest animal on God's green earth."

Jane grinned. "He sure is. But he was getting overwhelmed by so much attention, which is why Tobias and Barbara keep him at home now."

"Tobias is such a sweet man. He signed copies of his book for me. I'm going to give them to my grandchildren for Christmas."

The other woman handed Jane her credit card. "Even though we've spent enough money today, we might get some coffee from the Canvas Creamery. But only if that annoying whistling person isn't there."

Jane gave her a quizzical look. "Whistling person?"

The woman rolled her eyes. "Someone with a song stuck in their head. We've heard them whistling the same tune over and over all over town. It's gotten under my skin."

"We heard them in the market, and again on the street after lunch," her companion added.

Her friend uttered a self-deprecating laugh and said, "We're just old and cranky. The silliest things can set us off, which is why we should go get a coffee *and* a nice gelato. We could both use a little sweetening. Right, Vera?"

Vera grudgingly agreed, and the two women thanked Jane and left.

A few minutes later, Mabel parted the purple curtains and shuffled into the shop, her hands pressed against her lower back. "Thanks for being patient. And for the tea. And for taking care of this mess. Are you ready to try on your costume?"

Jane rose to her tiptoes in excitement, and for the moment, the dead man was forgotten. "I can't wait!"

In the workroom, Mabel wheeled the clothes rack to the side to reveal a second rack. The items hanging on here were secured in garment bags and labeled with each customer's name and phone number.

Mabel removed one of the garment bags and laid it down on the worktable. She then gathered up the fabric bolts piled on an empty chair and said, "Slip into that while I put these away."

When Jane eased the garment bag off and caught sight of her costume, she gasped. "Mabel! This is . . . it's incredible!"

"Not gonna lie—I'm mighty pleased with how it came out. Don't try to zip it by yourself. Let me know when you've got it on and I'll zip you up."

A few minutes later, Jane said, "I'm ready."

Mabel found Jane standing in front of the full-length mirror in the corner. After pulling up the zipper, she took a step back to assess her work. "How's the length? Can you move around?"

Jane took a turn about the crowded room. "I feel like a queen. It's perfect."

"I am *loving* this on you. I can already picture how you're going to look with your hair and makeup done. You're going to outshine all the belles at the ball. What made you pick this costume?"

Strolling back to the mirror, Jane said, "I've always tried to be one of the good guys. Every day of my life. For just one night, I wanted to be a villain."

Mabel grunted. "Well, don't let it go to your head. This world has plenty of villains as it is. And for whatever reason, they tend to end up at Storyton Hall."

Chapter 2

Jane had never been on vacation without her sons. She'd taken day trips and the occasional overnight stay at an area B and B with Edwin, but she'd never been away from her boys for five whole days.

"I know it's not normal," she told her book club friends over dinner. "But think about it. For the first ten years of their lives, my time was divided between Fitz and Hem, running Storyton Hall, and making sure Uncle Aloysius and Aunt Octavia were okay. I didn't have time to go away, and I didn't have anyone to go with."

Jane's best friend, Eloise, feigned offense. "So, *this* is how chopped liver feels."

"Stop it. You know I would've traded my signed copy of *A Man Called Ove* to go on a girls' trip with all of you, but I was raising the twins on my own and running a resort. I'm sure the managers of big chain hotels have time for girls' trips, but I didn't. There's always a crisis with old manor houses—a leaking roof, a broken boiler, and, in my case, a murder or two."

"More like twenty-two," scoffed Eugenia Pratt, the oldest and loudest member of the Cover Girls.

Mabel nudged Mrs. Pratt in the side. "Forget about murders. Don't we have more important things to discuss?"

"Yeah, like Jane's engagement ring," said Phoebe. "Everyone's talking about it—or the lack of it. I'm going to tell my customers that Edwin gave you a Ring Pop just to put an end to the speculation."

As proprietor of the Canvas Creamery, which was part coffee and gelato shop and part art gallery, Phoebe heard all the latest gossip. If there was something she didn't know, Violet or Anna could fill in the gaps.

Violet ran the only salon in the village of Storyton and Anna was an assistant pharmacist. They both agreed that the absence of a ring on Jane's left hand had the whole village guessing.

People usually dropped by Eloise's bookshop, Run for Cover, in search of their next read, but she'd also overheard several theories as to why her older brother hadn't literally "put a ring on it."

Some of the theories were pretty wild, while others were downright insulting.

Eloise shook her head. "You and Edwin have always danced to the beat of your own drum. If you don't want to wear an engagement ring, then don't."

"I want to wear one," Jane said testily. "I just can't find one that feels like *me*. I didn't have this problem when William proposed. We were in college at the time, and William didn't have any money. My parents had been gone for years, so he called Uncle Aloysius and

Aunt Octavia to ask for their blessing. Not only did they give it to him but Aunt Octavia mailed him a ring that had been in my family for decades. I wore it because I loved William, but I never would've chosen it for myself."

The only Cover Girl who hadn't weighed in on the ring topic was Betty. She was listening attentively, her head cocked slightly to one side, until she noticed that Jane's wineglass was almost empty. She might not be working at the Cheshire Cat Pub tonight, but she'd been a publican for so many years that she reached for the bottle of Spanish red and began to top off everyone's glasses without even thinking about it.

After doling out the last of the wine, Betty set down the bottle and put a hand on Jane's shoulder. "Honey, don't sweat the small stuff. You love Edwin and he loves you. You're going on a romantic vacation together tomorrow. Don't spend that time worrying about a ring, or wedding plans, or clogged gutters. Just enjoy yourselves. Walk on the beach. Eat amazing food. Stay in bed as long as you want."

Mrs. Pratt, a zealous reader of romance novels, nodded in agreement. "That's exactly why *I* wanted us to discuss something written by Nicholas Sparks. You're off for a passionate interlude on the North Carolina coast, and Nicholas Sparks is the expert when it comes to coastal Carolina love affairs. Even though I got outvoted, I *still* want you to drive over to New Bern and ask that man to sign all of my books. I have his address, and it's only forty-five minutes out of your way."

Eloise laughed. "I don't think Jane wants to spend her weekend behind bars for trespassing."

"Oh, please. Doesn't every successful author expect a little healthy stalking?"

Mabel wagged her finger like a windshield wiper. "There's no such thing as healthy stalking. Speaking of authors, are we ready to talk about this week's pick? Because I want to fangirl over Ruth Ozeki."

Violet laid a hand on Mabel's copy of *The Book of Form and Emptiness*. "Before we start, can we reconsider next week's pick? I know we decided to read *Dracula* so we could kick off our Halloween weekend with a vampire-themed cocktail, but most of us have already read it, and there are so many other spooky books to choose from. *The Haunting of Hill House, Something Wicked This Way Comes,* or like, a dozen Stephen King novels. Can't we read a different book and still have the cocktail?"

"I'd be willing to trade Dracula for another vampire. As long as it's not Edward Cullen. How about Lestat?" suggested Phoebe.

Eloise pointed at the bookshelf in Jane's living room. "Let's ask Mr. Predicto."

Anna frowned. "The Magic Eight Ball? We'll be here all night. Can't we just read a spooky ghost story? Darcy Coates writes books that won't have me sleeping with the lights on."

"Never fear—this is not your mama's Magic Eight Ball." Eloise got up to fetch the white ball. "Mr. Predicto has thirty answers, and he *speaks*! The color changes too. I bought a case to sell in the shop and they went so fast that I had to order two more cases."

Jane smirked. "Fitz asked for an advance on his allowance for this thing. He used it for all of five minutes, and now, there it sits, collecting dust."

"If Hem buys one, you'll have a cute pair of book-ends," teased Betty.

Fitz and Hem, short for Fitzgerald and Hemingway, were Jane's identical twins. Her sandy-haired, freckled, high-spirited imps had been born and raised at Storyton Hall. Like generations of Stewards before them, they'd grown up wandering its numerous rooms and labyrinthine corridors. They'd played on its vast lawns, searched for bugs in its gardens, and explored the woods surrounding the estate. One day, they would oversee a hundred staff members and ensure that a steady stream of guests continued to patronize the family's five-star resort.

In the meantime, Fitz and Hem were cheerful and carefree twelve-year-old boys. They liked graphic novels, Dungeons & Dragons, video games, and action films. They were skilled in archery, martial arts, photography, poaching treats from the kitchens, and worming their way out of predicaments of their own making.

Eloise handed the toy to Violet. "You're in charge of Mr. Predicto. Ask of him what you will."

Violet shook the ball and said, "Should we read a Stephen King book next?"

Lights inside the white ball flashed and then its surface turned wicked-witch green, and a sonorous male voice declared, "*THE SIGNS SAY NO.*"

When Mabel asked if they should just stick with *Dracula,* Mr. Predicto replied, "DEFINITELY NOT."

The fortune-telling gadget also rejected Ray Bradbury and Shirley Jackson.

Finally, Mrs. Pratt gave it a good shaking. She wanted to know if Mr. Predicto wanted them to read *The Haunting of Ashburn House.*

"EVERYTHING POINTS TO YES," he replied.

Mrs. Pratt looked pleased. "Apparently, Mr. Predicto likes it a little rough."

Phoebe pointed at her empty wineglass. "I want to ask him if we should open another bottle."

When the reply was "YES, IT IS CERTAIN," the woman cheered.

Jane glanced at her watch. "Should we switch to dessert wine? It's about that time."

The Cover Girls followed her into the kitchen and helped themselves to the selection of desserts on the center island. In between bites of pumpkin cake with cream cheese frosting, a toffee apple tart, and chocolate hazelnut brownies, they wrapped up their book discussion and circled back to Jane's upcoming trip.

"I googled your hotel," said Mabel. "The Admiral's Inn has to be one of the prettiest hotels I've ever seen. I love how you can rent a private bungalow if you don't want to stay in the main house."

Anna let out a wistful sigh. "I looked it up too. Your bungalow has an entire wall of books. Floor to ceiling. And it faces the harbor. Doesn't it have a super-cute name too?"

Jane nodded. "The Book Lover's Loft. Apparently, it's where authors stay when they're in town for events at the local bookstore. And guess who'll be there this weekend? Heather O'Grady, Winston Hall, and Justin St. James. They'll all be under one roof for an afternoon of thrills and chills."

Violet's jaw dropped. "No way! I am *totally* in love with Justin St. James! Not only are his books really good but he is *smoking* hot. Jane, can you please pack me in your suitcase, or let me ride in the truck? I'm dying to meet my number one author crush!"

"Go ask Mr. Predicto if Jane will wait in line to get all of your St. James books signed," Anna said.

Violet returned to the living room. A few seconds later, she glumly called out, "HIGHLY DOUBTFUL."

Eloise grinned at Jane. "I guess you have *other* things planned that day."

Jane's cheeks turned pink. "We haven't made any firm plans."

"Firm, eh? Sounds like you *are* going to spend lots of time in bed," cackled Mrs. Pratt. "Violet, ask Mr. Predicto if I'm right."

"He said, 'YOU CAN RELY ON THAT.'"

The Cover Girls howled with laughter.

"Okay, okay!" Jane shouted over the hubbub. "It's getting late. Who wants to read their favorite quote from *The Book of Form and Emptiness*?"

Her ploy to distract her friends succeeded. By the time everyone had opened their books to a page marked by a bookmark, sticky note, or, in Mabel's case, a grocery store receipt, it was after nine. They continued talking until Eloise stood up and announced that the discussion was finished.

"We're going to load the dishwasher and leave you to finish packing," she told Jane. "You're heading out first thing tomorrow, right?"

"Edwin wants to be on the road by seven."

After collecting Jane's dessert plate, Mrs. Pratt leaned over and whispered, "You should have oysters for dinner tomorrow night. It'll set the tone for the rest of your trip."

Mabel rolled her eyes. "Eugenia, you're incorrigible. Let's clean up and get out of Jane's hair."

When the kitchen was spotless, the Cover Girls said their goodbyes and left.

It would be at least another hour before Edwin closed his restaurant for the night and came home, and because the twins were supposed to be asleep, Jane locked the front door and turned off most of the lights downstairs.

In the living room, she scooped up Mr. Predicto and said, "I'd like to put on my pajamas and read. Should I finish packing instead?"

The toy blinked, turned purple, and said, "YES, IT IS CERTAIN."

"You're no fun, you know that?" she told Mr. Predicto. "But I'm going to have a fun vacation, aren't I?"

She shook the toy, eliciting a response of, "IT'S BEST NOT TO SAY NOW."

Jane turned the ball upside down in search of the Off switch. "What do you know anyway? Of course it's going to be fabulous. We'll have the beach, beautiful sunsets, new shops to explore, new places to eat. No demanding guests and not a single dead body. Right?"

"NOW IS NOT THE RIGHT TIME TO TELL YOU," Mr. Predicto intoned.

"Tell me what? It's a vacation. There will be *no* murder or mayhem. *No* unnatural deaths. *Am I right?*"

Jane immediately regretted the question. Suddenly she didn't want to hear Mr. Predicto's answer and was careful not to shake the ball.

In the darkness, she fumbled with the power button, trying to flick it from On to Off, when the light inside the toy suddenly flashed.

Without warning, the innocuous white changed to siren red. The color seemed to leach from the globular shape, spilling out over Jane's palm and oozing over her wrist. Her hand looked like it was coated in paint. Or blood.

"There won't be any dead bodies. Not a single one," Jane insisted as her thumb found the power button.

In the split second it took for her to toggle the switch, Mr. Predicto's voice rumbled out of the orb like a train bursting out of a long, black tunnel. Every hair on Jane's arms stood on end as his words echoed through the room.

"HIGHLY DOUBTFUL."

The next morning, Storyton Hall's senior staff members lined up in the driveway to see Jane and Edwin off. It reminded Jane of a scene from *Downton Abbey*.

"It's only five days!" She laughed as she was drawn into Mrs. Hubbard's pillowy embrace.

The head cook of Storyton Hall gave her a firm squeeze before releasing her. "It's just that I'm so used to our daily chats in the kitchens. I guess I'll have to give all of your treats to the boys."

"You spoil them enough as it is. And me too. Is that a picnic basket I see in the back seat?"

Dimples appeared in Mrs. Hubbard's apple cheeks. "As if I'd let you spend hours on the road without a hearty breakfast and plenty of snacks."

Sinclair, Storyton Hall's head librarian, gave Jane a paternal kiss on the forehead. "Enjoy yourself, my girl, and don't give this pile of bricks another thought. If there are any problems, Mr. Butterworth will sort them out. That's what butlers do best. They sort out problems and fetch drinks."

Butterworth, a giant of a man with a stern face, scowled at his coworker. "Someone must be accountable. After all, certain librarians have their noses buried so deeply in their books that they wouldn't know if a meteor crashed through the roof and landed in the middle of the lobby."

Jane said, "You two sound just like the twins. Try not to bicker the whole time I'm gone."

Sterling, the head chauffeur, gestured at Fitz and Hem. "Maybe you should put them in charge."

The twins loaded the suitcases into the truck and then turned to call their puppies, Merry and Pippin, who were wandering off toward the garages. On command, the poodles trotted over to their young masters and sat on their haunches. Their tails thumped against the gravel as they gazed adoringly at the boys.

Fitz and Hem had outgrown public displays of affection, but they each allowed Jane a quick hug.

Edwin tousled their hair, clapped their backs, and said, "Gentlemen, I'm counting on you to keep an eye on things. Your mom and I can relax knowing this place is in good hands. When I get back, we'll plan our next men's trip."

"Camping?" asked Fitz.

Hem shook his head. "Nah, we did that last time. How about rafting?"

Jane saw the corner of Edwin's mouth twitch, a telltale sign that he was keeping a secret.

"How about an outdoor adventure involving lots of snow?"

"Skiing!" the boys shouted in unison.

"In Colorado. Or Utah. Just for a few days over winter break. Do some research while I'm gone and when I get back, you can tell me where you want to go."

Fitz and Hem were giddy with excitement.

"What will I be doing while you and the boys are hitting the slopes?" Jane asked as she slid into the SUV's passenger seat.

"Whatever you want. You could have four book club meetings in a row."

Jane laughed. "You say that like I wouldn't but I totally would."

Edwin turned on the car, honked the horn, and headed up the long driveway. In Jane's side mirror, Storyton Hall slowly receded. The massive clock tower in the center and the two guest room wings stretched out like a pair of open arms grew smaller and smaller. The windows of her great-aunt and -uncle's apartments winked in the sunshine, and just as Jane was wondering if Aunt Octavia and Uncle Aloysius were watching her leave, the road took a sharp curve, and she saw nothing but trees and hedges.

Edwin drove through the massive iron gates marking the entrance to Storyton Hall and turned left onto the main road.

"To the beach we go," he said, reaching over the center console to squeeze Jane's hand.

She smiled at him. "You're so different from that brooding, scowling, short-tempered man who nearly ran me over with his horse all those years ago. You still look like my modern Mr. Darcy, but you act more like Mr. Bingley now."

Edwin pulled a face. "I'd rather you didn't compare me to an Austen character."

"Why not? It's the ultimate compliment," Jane said, kicking off her shoes and getting comfortable. "But if you'd rather I compare you to another dark, handsome, brooding, and authoritative literary leading man, I could go with Aragorn. Or would you prefer Severus Snape?"

Edwin pointed at Jane's phone. "Let's start that audiobook you downloaded."

"Okay."

"What's it called?"

Adopting a deadpan expression, Jane said, "*Alone with Mr. Darcy.*"

Edwin's look was one of abject horror. "You didn't."

Jane burst out laughing. "No, I didn't. We're listening to *The Lincoln Highway*. It's the perfect book for our road trip. It's long enough to last our whole journey and exciting enough to keep us riveted without being too distracting. You liked *A Gentleman in Moscow*. This book is by the same author."

"Sounds good, but if you try to sneak in that Darcy book on the sly, I'm going to drop you off at the next rest stop."

"If you do that, who'll feed you goodies from Mrs. Hubbard's basket?"

Edwin pretended to consider the question. Finally, he said, "Okay, I'll drop you at a rest stop after the basket is empty. Now, hit the Play button. I'm ready for a story."

Six hours later, Jane and Edwin passed a sign welcoming them to the town of Oyster Bay.

"'The Sailing Capital of North Carolina,'" Jane read.

Edwin cracked his window and drew in a deep breath. "I can smell the ocean."

Jane put down her own window and felt a rush of warm, salt-tinged air. She smiled in delight. "I haven't been to the beach since I was a kid. Are we too old to hunt for shells and make sandcastles?"

"Never. We can eat Popsicles and use the sticks as flags. And we definitely need a moat. And ramparts. Oh, and a high wall with arrow slits."

"Okay, Arthur of Camelot," teased Jane.

The subject of sandcastles was forgotten as they drove through downtown Oyster Bay. Jane and Edwin took turns pointing out eclectic boutiques and charming sidewalk cafés.

"This place could give Storyton a run for its money. Look at that adorable hardware store."

Edwin pointed at a restaurant on Jane's left. "That diner is called Grumpy's. We *have* to eat there."

The business and shopping district occupied less than ten blocks, and it wasn't long before they'd passed through town and turned onto a crushed shell road lined by palmetto trees. Jane rounded a bend, and suddenly, the harbor came into view.

"Oh, wow," she breathed, taking in the glittering water, the boats bobbing on their moorings, and the elegant white building with the wraparound porch waiting to welcome them.

"According to their website, we should be just in time for tea. The Admiral's Inn is known for its excellent breakfasts, afternoon teas, and happy hours," Edwin said.

"I say we drop our bags in our room and skip right to Happy Hour."

Edwin planted a kiss on her hand. "How I love you, Jane Steward."

The manager of the inn greeted them like they were family.

"Francis Belvedere, at your service," he trilled merrily as he shook Jane's hand. "Ms. Limoges has told me all about you, but of course I already knew who you were. To think—Jane Steward of Storyton Hall, one of the grandest hotels in the world, is to be my guest! I've stayed at your fabulous resort, you know. *Two* times! I'd love to make it three, but this place keeps me way too busy."

He turned to fetch a key from the glass case behind him. When he turned back, his smile was for Edwin. "I don't know if it's the same for you, but my partner is horribly jealous of the Admiral. He says he has to play second fiddle to an inn, and third fiddle to a boat. He's not wrong, but one day I'll retire, and then he'll beg me to go back to work!"

His laugh was so infectious that Jane and Edwin both joined in.

"Let's get you settled, and then you can come back here for tea, or at five for the start of happy hour. We have a limited cocktail menu, but every drink is made with the best ingredients and a touch of panache. If you'll follow me, we'll take a short stroll to your bungalow."

Francis walked with a short, quick gait. As he pointed out the widow's walk on the roof of the main house, he spoke of how the admiral and his wife were the socialites of their day.

"They hosted costume balls and stargazing parties and all sorts of wonderful events," he said, dabbing his shiny forehead with a folded handkerchief.

Jane didn't think she'd ever met a man who reminded her so much of Agatha Christie's fastidious Belgian detective, Hercule Poirot. Francis didn't slick back his dark hair. Nor did he have a mustache, but he had an egg-shaped head and clever, observant eyes.

"We have six bungalows—all built within the last decade—but only three face the harbor. The Book Lover's Loft is the closest to the water and has a private garden. Many authors have stayed with us, and I like to think that our quiet, lovely space has been an inspiration."

He paused at a garden arbor and held out the room key. "Your bungalow is just up this path. If there's anything I can do to make your stay more marvelous, please don't hesitate to call the front desk."

After a quick bow, he headed back to the main house.

Jane and Edwin followed the flagstone path over a brief expanse of lawn until they reached a tiny white cottage with a teal-blue door.

Edwin unlocked the door and held it open for Jane.

Stepping into the room, her eye went straight to the bank of windows overlooking the harbor. Her gaze then traveled to the king-size bed done up in crisp white linens with yellow throw pillows. All the furniture was white, as were the rug and the framed prints of seashells. The wall opposite the bed was floor-to-ceiling bookshelves. When Jane examined them more closely, she saw that the books were an eclectic mix of genres and formats. They filled the room with color and warmth, and Jane couldn't help but run her fingers over several spines.

"It feels like home," she said.

Edwin strolled over to one of the bookshelves and picked up a starfish. "At home, we don't have petrified sea creatures staring at our bed."

"Do starfish have eyes?"

"Yep. On the ends of their arms."

Jane gently plucked the starfish from Edwin's hand. "In that case, we'll just turn him around while we're here."

Edwin said something else, but Jane was too caught up in the beauty of the bookshelves to register his comment. He gave her arm a soft squeeze and said, "I can see you're going to need a moment with the books. I'll go back to the car and grab our bags."

Jane examined titles and picked up a few of a dozen shells placed here and there on the shelves. She recognized the pink conch, the sand dollar, and the scallop, but the others were foreign to her.

Turning away from the bookshelves, she walked over to the pair of sun-yellow chairs positioned in front of the windows. The chairs were separated by a round table that was just big enough to hold one of the board games stacked in one of the nooks under the windows. The other nooks were crammed with yet more books.

Jane could already picture how she and Edwin would use the area each morning. She'd sip her coffee and watch boats come and go, while he'd work the crossword puzzle in the local paper. There'd be no rush to get to work. No to-do lists. No crisis that needed solving.

"Vacay," she murmured happily to herself.

The glass door leading to the back patio was locked, and Jane decided to wait for Edwin before exploring the little side garden. Instead, she walked past the bed and a tall dresser and opened the bathroom door.

Her first impression was of gleaming white. White tiles. White towels. A white claw-foot tub. White cabinets and a white marble countertop. But there was something on the mirror above the double sinks. Something red.

Jane took a few steps closer to the mirror. The red streaks were letters. Someone had written a message on the mirror.

Moving even closer, Jane tried to decipher the letters, but there wasn't enough natural light for her to see clearly.

She flicked the wall switch, and the fixtures above the mirror instantly chased away the shadows.

This time, when Jane looked at the mirror, she didn't see the letters. She saw something else. A reflection that made her go stiff with fear.

Behind her, perched on a ledge in the shower, was a human skull.

Chapter 3

Jane let out a shriek and spun around, hoping what she'd seen was a trick of the light.

It wasn't. The skull was still there.

It stared at her from the corner shelf—a shelf meant for shaving cream or shampoo bottles—and Jane stared back. She didn't move until Edwin called her name.

"I'm here," she said, stepping out of the bathroom.

Edwin cupped her chin in his hand. "I thought I heard a scream. What happened?"

Jane jerked her thumb at the bathroom. "I got spooked. You'll see why."

While Edwin investigated, Jane sat down on the edge of the bed and called the front desk.

"The Admiral's Inn, this is Francis speaking. How may I be of service?"

"Francis, it's Jane Steward. I found something unusual in our bathroom. I think you'd better come see."

The manager softly moaned. "Oh dear. I *so* wanted to

impress you with our humble hotel, and nothing ruins a first impression like a creepy-crawly."

"It's creepy, but it isn't a bug. It's more serious than that."

Francis told Jane that he'd be there directly.

Jane hung up just as Edwin emerged from the bathroom.

"The message in the mirror says, 'YOUR STORY IS OVER.' " He sat down next to Jane and took her hand. "It's not lipstick but some kind of marker. There was probably condensation on the mirror when it was written, which is why some of the letters lost their shape."

"And the skull?"

Edwin shook his head. "I didn't open the shower door because—"

"You didn't want to tamper with a possible crime scene," Jane finished for him.

"Exactly."

"This has to be a mistake, right? That message can't be for us. Other than Olivia and Michel, no one knows us here. Olivia's a friend, and even though I only got to know Michel on a superficial level when he took part in the cooking competition at Storyton Hall, he's a good man. So, who's the story thief? And whose stories have been stolen?"

Edwin's gaze swept over the bookshelves. "Honestly, I don't know what to think."

There was a gentle knock on the cottage door, and Francis announced himself.

When Edwin invited the flustered manager inside, Jane pointed toward the bathroom and said, "There's a human skull in the shower and a strange message on the mirror. We didn't touch anything other than the light switch."

A tiny squeak escaped Francis's lips, and his hands flapped around his face like a pair of startled birds. Quickly regaining his composure, he gave his suit coat a sharp tug and strode into the bathroom like a soldier marching into battle.

When he reappeared a few minutes later, he was noticeably more relaxed.

"I don't think the skull is real. In fact, I believe it's a prop belonging to the previous guest. We place a very high value on privacy, as I'm sure you do, but I see no harm in telling you that this particular guest is an author. He writes crime novels and I believe he carries this prop to all his events. If you don't mind, I'll give him a call right now to see if we can't solve this little mystery."

Jane and Edwin nodded in agreement, and Francis retreated outside to make the call. Because he'd closed the door behind him, they could hear his voice rise and fall but no distinct words.

When Francis returned, his hands were folded in front of his chest as if in prayer.

"The skull, which is a prop, does belong to Mr. St. James. However, he has no idea how it ended up in this cottage. He says he put it in a box in the trunk of his car at home and hasn't thought about it since. He just checked the box, and his skull is indeed missing."

"How can we be sure that the skull in our shower is his?" Jane asked.

Francis gazed at her in admiration. "You have the mind of a detective, Ms. Steward. But I was told to look for a name written on the bottom of the skull. Apparently, the skull is called Septimus."

"We shouldn't handle it," Edwin warned. "Just in case it's not a prop."

"I'll use a towel," Francis assured him.

Jane and Edwin followed Francis into the bathroom and watched as he gingerly stepped into the shower. After draping a bath towel over the skull, he plucked it off the ledge. When he turned it over, they could all see the black letters on the bottom.

"Hello, Septimus," Jane said, her voice light with relief.

Edwin took the skull from Francis and carried it to the table by the windows. He spread out the towel and began examining the skull. "This is very well done. I wouldn't have known it wasn't real until I felt its weight. It's too heavy to be bone."

Jane wasn't interested in how the skull was made. She wanted to know why it was in their bathroom.

"When did the previous guest check out?" she asked Francis.

"Around eleven this morning. Which means someone got inside this room after the housekeeper left and before you arrived." The manager's cheeks reddened. "I'm terribly sorry about this. I have no explanation, but I *will* get to the bottom of this. I'm afraid we don't have any available rooms at the moment, but if you'd rather not stay with us after this, I can call my friend over at the Harbor Inn to see if he has any."

"We don't want to leave," Jane said. "Once the mirror's cleaned, it'll be like it never happened. All I ask is that you keep us in the loop. Otherwise, I'll spend our whole vacation fixating on this mystery."

Francis scooped up the skull and covered it with the towel. "Oh, that won't do at all. You're here to relax and unwind." He walked to the door and motioned to the sign hanging from the handle. "Just put this out whenever it's convenient for housekeeping to come in and clean the bathroom. In the meantime, order whatever food or beverages you'd like from the bar, compliments of the Admiral's Inn."

As soon as Francis left, Jane flopped down on the bed. She spread her arms and legs like a snow angel and said, "Is this an omen? Is our vacation doomed from the start?"

Before Edwin could respond, Jane's phone rang. Seeing the name on the screen, she smiled. Olivia Limoges was calling.

Storyton Hall had hosted thousands of guests during Jane's tenure as manager, and she'd had plenty of interactions with the rich and famous. She wasn't impressed by wealth or celebrity status. As long as a person loved to read, they belonged at Storyton Hall.

Unlike most guests, Olivia Limoges hadn't booked an extended stay to whittle down her TBR pile but to find a way through a prolonged case of writer's block. Not only had she been the first guest to occupy one of the newly renovated cottages on the grounds, but Olivia had been the first guest to share her lodgings with a dog. Jane quickly learned that Olivia didn't go anywhere without her canine companion, a standard poodle named Captain Haviland.

At first, Jane had found Olivia standoffish. But when a murder forced the two women to work together, Jane warmed to the heiress from Oyster Bay, North Carolina, and by the time the investigation was over, she and Olivia had become close.

By the time Olivia left Storyton, she had a troop of new friends, including Jane, the twins, and several staff members. Butterworth was a particular fan. He was sorry to see her go and eager for her to return. And while Jane knew that he and Olivia spoke on a regular basis, she had too much respect for Butterworth's privacy to ask if he was hoping his relationship with Olivia would develop into something more serious.

Scooping up her phone, Jane said, "Hello! We're in Oyster Bay."

"What do you think of the Book Lover's Loft?"

Jane gazed around the beautiful space. "It's amazing. And it'll be even more amazing once the fake skull's been removed from our bathroom."

In the background, someone called Olivia's name. This was followed by a loud crash. "A skull, eh? I want to hear the whole story, but judging by the look on Michel's face, it'll have to wait."

"I thought you sold the restaurant to Michel."

Olivia let out a dry laugh. "I did. And yet I keep finding myself here. That sound you heard was Michel telling the new manager his opinion of the wineglasses he ordered without Michel's permission. See you at seven?"

"Looking forward to it," Jane said.

Edwin pointed at the closet. "Let's put our clothes away and then take a walk."

"Good idea. That'll give housekeeping a chance to tidy up while we get some exercise. You know we're going to be treated to a four-course meal at the Boot Top Bistro, and it's not like Michel makes light fare. I'm pretty sure he uses a stick of butter in every dish."

"I remember Michel telling the other chefs in the competition that he believed in three food groups: butter, wine, and chocolate. I wanted him to win from that moment on."

Jane and Edwin finished unpacking, hung the housekeeping sign from the door handle, and headed down a path leading down to the harbor.

The sea breeze ruffled their hair, and their bodies

were warmed by the October sun. They walked toward the downtown shopping area, pausing to point out a particular boat or marvel over the size of the luxury yachts tied up at the public docks.

"I love reading the names," Jane said. "See the blue boat in between those two white ones? It's called *Smurf's Up.*"

"If I had a fishing boat, I'd call it *Baits Motel.*"

Jane laughed. "If I had one of those giant yachts, I'd call it the *Great Gatsea.*"

Edwin winced. "That's awful."

Grabbing his hand, Jane led him away from the docks to the downtown shopping area. The tree-lined street had wide sidewalks and small green areas with benches and tidy beds of seasonal flowers. Every storefront was shaded by a colorful awning, and the display windows were packed with enticing wares.

Jane and Edwin passed a souvenir shop, two clothing boutiques, and a bakery before pausing in front of an antique store called Circa.

"Look at all this cool vintage Halloween stuff," Jane said. "That clown mask is downright terrifying."

"What about the devil?"

Jane hadn't noticed the devil before. She liked his pencil mustache and toothy grin. "I wonder how many devils will come to the All Hallows' Ball?"

Edwin used his index fingers to mime a pair of horns over his head. "It's Halloween, so I'm sure there'll be a few. I'm glad you decided to throw another Halloween party. It's been years since the last one."

"Considering a guest was killed the first time I hosted one, I haven't been too keen to repeat the experience."

Taking her hand, Edwin said, "Do you know what else happened that October? I came back to Storyton after being gone for ages and saw you. From the moment our eyes met, I was lost."

"Would you still love me if I looked like that?" Jane pointed at a witch mask.

He pretended to shudder. "Absolutely not. I'm only attracted to women with strawberry-blond hair and freckles. Do you want to go in?"

"I do."

Inside, Jane was immediately drawn to the display of old books. While she examined a Victorian book of fairy tales, Edwin meandered over to a jewelry case filled with antique brooches and rings.

A white terrier padded out from behind the counter and sat on its haunches a foot away from Edwin's left shoe. Bending down to pet the little dog, Edwin said, "Hello there. Aren't you a little short to be running this place?"

As the dog's tail thumped against the wood floor, a man in his early seventies appeared from the back room.

"Don't give him any ideas," the man whispered. "He's dying to stage a coup. I'm Fred, and my four-legged security guard is Duncan. Let me know if you have any questions."

Fred moved off to the far corner of the store where he began to dust a stack of blue Staffordshire plates.

Jane gravitated to a display case of nautical items. Her attention was immediately caught by an array of old compasses.

"Do these compasses work?" she asked Fred.

Joining her at the display case, he said, "Absolutely. They range in price based on age, condition, and whether or not they're engraved. Would you like to take a closer look?"

"I would, but from the lower end of the price point, please. I'm looking for souvenirs for my twin boys, and they don't need Lord Nelson's compass."

Fred chuckled and removed a brass compass from the case. "This one is forty bucks. It's from the early 1980s and belonged to a ship's engineer. I've also got this Stanley standing compass from London. It's fifty dollars and has a mirror for more accurate navigation."

"That's perfect." Jane's eyes scanned the case. "Do you have another one that's just as cool but slightly different?"

Fred smiled. "I do. I have another Stanley pocket compass with a black face. It's sixty dollars, but I'll let them both go for an even hundred."

"Sold!" Jane exclaimed.

She exited the antique shop in high spirits. And when Edwin spied a sign for Bayside Books, all thoughts of the bathroom scene in the Book Lover's Loft were forgotten. Here she was, in a charming seaside town, with the man she loved. And she was about to visit the local bookstore. Her day was getting better and better every minute.

Inside, Jane gazed around in wonder. "Look how the books are displayed in different wardrobes. It's like having a dozen portals to Narnia. I need to take a video of this place for Eloise. Run for Cover will always be my favorite bookstore, but this is pretty amazing."

While Jane took her video, Edwin walked over to a sign announcing upcoming events. When she was done, he waved her over.

"Want to see a photo of the guest who occupied our room before us? And his skull?"

Jane hurried over to the sign. She saw a man in his midforties with sun-kissed brown hair and a square jaw holding the skull named Septimus. According to the sign, the author was Justin St. James.

"I know him," she said. "I mean, I've read one of his books. He writes gritty crime novels that appeal to a huge range of readers."

Edwin nodded. "His photo is a bit much. He's gazing at that skull like it's Yorick and he's Hamlet."

"Don't look now, but the Prince of Denmark is standing by a green wardrobe in the fiction section," Jane whispered.

"If you tell me not to look at something, then I *have* to look."

In person, Justin St. James was of average height and build. His tortoiseshell glasses amplified his cornflower-blue eyes, which were presently narrowed in anger. He wore a pinched expression as he jabbed a finger too close to a petite redhead's face. Though he spoke in a heated whisper, certain phrases floated over to where Jane and Edwin stood.

St. James's Southern drawl sounded exaggerated, and his dulcet tones were pure arrogance. When Jane heard him say, "You're being irrational," and "Don't get hysterical," she wanted to shove a sock in his mouth.

The redhead exhibited no signs of hysteria. She stood perfectly still, her arms folded over her chest, glaring at St. James. Her eyes blazed with indignation, and Jane could see the tightness of her jaw, but she seemed determined not to let him rattle her.

When she finally got a word in, she didn't bother to whisper.

"One day you'll pay for what you've done. And when you're dead and buried, I'll dance on your grave."

St. James barked out a laugh. "That would make a good title. You should write that down, sweetheart."

"You're laughing now, but I'm going to make people see who you really are," the redhead said as she brushed past St. James. He tried to grab her by the wrist, but she pivoted out of his reach and stormed off to the back of the shop.

"That one's no prince," Jane muttered to Edwin.

Edwin seemed to be taking the measure of the man and, with a frown of disapproval, he marched over to where the writer stood.

"Mr. St. James? I'm Edwin Alcott. We don't know each other, but I met a friend of yours earlier today."

St. James's brow clouded. "Which friend?"

"Septimus."

Sounding bored, St. James asked, "Are you from the inn?"

"My fiancée and I are staying in the Book Lover's Loft. When we checked in, we found *your friend* in the bathroom. Did you leave him there?"

St. James looked affronted. "I did not. I thought he was in my car."

"And the message on the mirror? Was that meant for you?"

"What message?"

Edwin produced his phone and held it out to St. James.

The author squinted at the screen. "I can't read that. What does it say?"

"'Your story is over.' Any idea what that means?"

St. James shrugged. "Probably a jealous aspiring author. I get messages like that all the time. Most are online, but I do get the occasional note in the post. A message on a hotel mirror is a new one."

"How would this person get into your car?"

Another shrug. "I'm always forgetting to lock the car." His face lit up with hope. "Do you have Septimus?"

"No. Francis does."

Justin St. James gave a satisfied nod. "Excellent. I'll give him a call right now." Putting his phone to his ear, he breezed out through the front door.

"Why'd you give him the third degree?" Jane asked Edwin.

"I wanted to confirm that the mysterious message was meant for him. Judging by his interaction with the redhead, insulting people comes naturally to him."

Jane picked up a book from the new release table and flipped to the back flap of the dust jacket. She tapped on the photo of Justin St. James and said, "He might not know who inked the mirror or took the skull out of his car, but I doubt it was a jealous writer or a dissatisfied fan. He made someone angry."

"That someone can deliver any future messages in person. After all, everyone knows where St. James will be tomorrow."

Jane followed his gaze to the poster advertising the Triple Thrills event. "Signings, swag, and cocktails? We should go. Olivia's part owner of this store, so we should support her."

"I thought we were trying to avoid intrigue and drama, but if you want to go, we'll go." Edwin took out his wallet. "While I'm getting the tickets, would you buy me an iced tea from the café? The sea air makes me thirsty."

Jane entered the café and ordered an iced tea for Edwin and an iced caramel macchiato for herself. While the barista prepared the drinks, Jane examined the books lining the top of the pastry display. The covers all had that crime novel look. Dark backgrounds with shadowy figures. Titles written in bright red or shocking white. Many of the titles used similar words. *Girl, wife, missing,* or *lost* seemed to be the most popular.

"If you like thrillers, this is one of my faves," the barista said, pointing at a book called *The Night She Couldn't Sleep.*

Jane's TBR pile was already massive, but she removed the book from its acrylic stand and opened to the blurb. The story, which was about a young woman whose childhood nightmares were coming to life, sounded compelling, and as Jane turned to the author bio, she was surprised to see that she recognized the female writer. It was the redhead who'd argued with Justin St. James.

When Edwin joined her in the café, she showed him the book.

"I think drama is definitely in tomorrow's forecast. This is Heather O'Grady, and she's part of the Triple Thrills event."

Edwin studied the photograph and then closed the book. As his eyes moved over the cover, which featured a bloodied knife sticking out of a pillow, he muttered, "Books, booze, and a bunch of people obsessed with murder. What could possibly go wrong?"

Chapter 4

"What exactly is a boot top?" Edwin asked Olivia Limoges as the hostess showed them to their table.

Olivia pointed at a framed sailboat print on the wall behind Edwin's seat. "If you turn around, you can see a line painted on that boat's hull. That's the waterline. Everything below that line is underwater. The boot top is, in a way, a divider of worlds. The world above and the world below."

Jane gazed around the dining room, which had a clean, modern vibe. Chairs upholstered in orange leather surrounded square tables with white linen cloths. The small ship lanterns in the middle of each table filled the dining room with just the right amount of light, and nautical art added a splash of color to the creamy white walls.

Removing the knotted jute napkin ring, Jane unfurled the creamy cotton rectangle and said, "The décor makes me feel like we're safely above the waterline. Nothing but clear sailing."

Olivia grinned. "That's exactly what Michel was going for—bright skies and calm waters. The bar area used to have wood-paneled walls and heavy furniture, but he wanted less Herman Melville and more Leanne Ford." Seeing the blank look on her guests' faces, she added, "She's a designer known for using lots of white."

"Do you miss being a restaurateur?" asked Edwin.

"At times. How are things at the Daily Bread?"

Edwin's eyes traveled around the dining room. "Compared to this, it's super-cramped. Maybe I should redecorate."

Olivia shook her head. "I love the Bohemian vibe of your place. All of those conversation pieces transport people to exotic ports of call. But I understand the need for change. Especially when it comes to the specials on the menu. It's good to change those on a regular basis, and it looks like this month's cocktail special is heading our way."

Their server arrived carrying a tray of martini glasses.

"Spiced pear martinis, compliments of Chef Michel," he said. "I'll be back in a moment with your appetizers."

Olivia raised her glass and smiled at Jane and Edwin. "May your time in Oyster Bay be like a library—packed with stories, but also blissfully quiet."

After touching her glass to Olivia's, Jane took a sip of her cocktail. Her eyes widened as she tasted the infusion of ginger and pear. "That's lovely. Now, about that story I promised to tell you. It involves Justin St. James."

The corners of Olivia's mouth turned down. "That doesn't surprise me at all. He's the kind of man who always wants to be in the spotlight."

"Do you know him well?" asked Edwin.

Olivia grimaced. "Well enough to dislike him. St. James

believes that the only good writer is a male writer. He's often quoted saying that he only reads works written by his *brothers in crime*. He's very fond of women and, judging by his many ex-girlfriends and legion of female fans, they're fond of him too. But he only likes women who fawn over him. He sells lots of books whenever he does an event, which is why he's participating in ours, and even though I know he'll line our coffers, I'm not an admirer."

Their server delivered several plates of appetizers, including grilled oysters, cranberry crostini, and marinated olives, and Jane told Olivia about the skull and the message on the bathroom mirror. When she was done, Olivia pressed her napkin to her lips and pushed back her chair.

"Excuse me for a moment."

Jane and Edwin watched her walk across the dining room. As she moved, heads turned and conversations faltered, and it wasn't until she passed through the swing doors leading to the kitchen that the business of eating and talking resumed.

Oliva was tall and slender, with a shock of pale blond hair. She carried herself with the erect posture and unflinching gaze of a monarch, and people often assumed she was cold or arrogant based solely on her bearing.

She reminded Jane of a Greek goddess. Not a maiden goddess like Aphrodite or Artemis, but an older, more world-weary deity. She was more like Hera—a handsome and powerful queen whose heart had been deeply scarred by grief and loneliness.

Edwin gave Jane a gentle nudge. "I think your story hit a nerve. Maybe Olivia's feelings for St. James are stronger than she's letting on."

"I wonder what happened between them. No way

he's a former lover. I can't picture them together at all. I *can* imagine Olivia feeding him to the sharks."

Edwin reached for an oyster. "Speaking of lovers . . ."

Jane threw him a dirty look just as Olivia reemerged from the kitchen.

"Sorry about that," she said, sliding into her chair. "In general, I'm not an emotional person. But talking about St. James opened an old wound."

She picked up her drink, drained its contents, and stared at the empty glass.

As if he'd been anticipating her need, their server materialized with a bottle of wine. He showed Olivia the label, uncorked the bottle, and poured her a taste. After obtaining her approval, he filled everyone's glasses and drifted away.

Olivia pinched the stem of her wineglass between her fingers. "As you both know, my husband was Oyster Bay's chief of police. He died on the other side of those doors, in the kitchen."

Jane darted a glance at the swing doors before turning back to Olivia.

"Sawyer saved Michel's pregnant wife that day. He also saved me. Three lives in exchange for one. That would've pleased him. Sawyer never hesitated. He saw danger and reacted. That's who he was." She smiled wistfully. "I never wanted a hero, but I got one anyway."

Jane reached out and squeezed Oliva's hand.

"When I said I wasn't an admirer of Justin St. James, that falls very short of how I really feel." Olivia lowered her voice to an angry murmur. "The truth is, I hate the man. My manager is new to Bayside Books, and it was her decision to include St. James in tomorrow's event. By the time I heard about it, the authors were booked and tickets had already been sold. I don't work regular hours at the store and could always stay home for the whole thing, but I refuse to hide from that louse. However, if I make it through the day without killing him, it'll be a miracle."

"What did he do?" Edwin asked.

Olivia's eyes narrowed as she fixed her gaze on the ship's lantern in the center of the table. "He wrote about Sawyer. He set the story in South Carolina and changed enough details to make it seem like an original work of fiction to most people, but when I read *By the Dark Water*, I knew that St. James had turned the worst day of my life into a novel."

Jane said, "I haven't read it."

"I hope you never do." Olivia let out a sigh. "The detective is based on my husband. Sawyer had more integrity than any person I've ever known, while St. James's cop is a broken man who accepts bribes, commits adultery, and drinks on the job. He's an unlikable character who did only one thing right—he died saving his wife and a pregnant woman. St. James used Sawyer's story, but in turning him into Detective Roland, he disgraced my husband's memory. That's why I'd like to dig a deep hole in the sand and drop St. James into it."

Two servers carrying heavy trays approached their table. Olivia moved her wineglass aside and apologized to Jane and Edwin for putting a damper on their meal.

"Don't worry," Jane said. "If St. James so much as looks at you wrong, I'll help you dig that hole."

As the first server placed a platter in the center of the table, he said, "We have three entrées for your enjoyment. The first is pan-seared scallops with brown butter and lemon. Next, we have balsamic-and-fig-glazed pork chops served with wild mushroom and parsnip ragout. Finally, a roasted butternut squash risotto with thyme and crumbled chèvre."

The food was an instant mood booster. For the moment, St. James was forgotten and the subject turned to poodles. Olivia talked about Captain Haviland's crush on a police dog named Greta, and Jane told Olivia how the twins' puppies had gotten loose and run amuck during a guest wedding.

"Luckily, the bride and groom were both dog lovers. It was a rainy day, and those puppy escape artists were covered in mud. So was the bride's dress by the time they'd finished congratulating her. And by congratulating, I mean leaping, pawing, and drooling."

They were all laughing when Michel came out of the kitchen to say hello.

"*Mes amies!* Welcome, welcome!" Michel shook hands with Edwin and enveloped Jane in a bear hug. "It's such a joy to see you. I hope you're loving every bite of your meal, but I also want to be sure you save room for dessert. My beautiful wife insisted on making something special for my friends, and she's a *very* talented chocolatier."

Jane jokingly pushed her plate away. "That does it. I'm done."

"You must eat more than that, *ma chérie*. After all, if you overindulge tonight, it does not matter. Olivia will have you over for a swim and a long walk on the beach so you can burn off this dinner like that!" He snapped his fingers. "For now, you should live in the moment. Drink the wine. Eat the chocolate. Be happy."

"He's the most cheerful chef I've ever met," said Edwin.

Olivia poured the last of the wine into Edwin's glass.

"As an experienced travel writer, you must've met your fair share. Do you have your next trip lined up?"

"I'm sticking close to home until after we're married. Where we go next will be up to Jane, which means I'll probably be writing about a tearoom near Jane Austen's birthplace or a quaint pub in Beatrix Potter's town."

"I'm sure readers would love to hear your take on Lake District eateries," Jane said before turning to Olivia. "How's the writing going?"

A twinkle appeared in Olivia's deep-sea-blue eyes. "Thanks to the breakthrough I had at Storyton Hall, I was charged with enough creative energy to finish my essay collection and start what might become my first novel."

"Oh, what's it about?" Jane asked, and then suddenly made an *X* with her hands. "Wait. Is that a terrible question to ask? Do writers like to keep ideas to themselves until they appear in print?"

Olivia shrugged. "I don't mind telling you because my plot isn't set in stone. I'm writing a mystery featuring a septuagenarian bookshop proprietor. She lives in an apartment above the shop, which she accesses by the freight elevator. It's difficult for her to use the stairs due to her crippling arthritis, but she still manages to kill a disreputable author by crushing him under the elevator."

Edwin said, "I like her already. Is the victim a crime writer who carries around a fake skull?"

Olivia's eyes twinkled with humor. "No, but like I said, the plot is rather fluid right now."

Their plates were cleared and coffee was served. Jane was just stirring cream into her cup when Michel marched out of the kitchen carrying a chocolate cake. The other diners watched his progress with overt envy.

Placing the cake on the table, Michel said, "For your dessert, we have a chocolate cassata cake. A cassata is a sponge cake moistened with liqueur or fruit juice and layered with ricotta. The filling may remind you of a cannoli. In this case, the sponge is flavored with rum and covered in dark chocolate ganache with a garnish of candied oranges and pistachios. Bon appétit."

Despite its complex flavors, the cake was incredibly light and airy. Jane didn't think she'd be able to eat a whole piece, but she ate every crumb and was tempted to lick her fork before reluctantly resting it on her plate.

She took a sip of coffee and said, "I wish I could bring Mrs. Hubbard a slice."

Michel and the head cook of Storyton Hall often traded recipes, and because Mrs. Hubbard baked a cake for every afternoon tea, wedding, or special event at the resort, she was forever in search of tasty new confections.

"Michel wants to send her the prototypes of his cookware line if you have room in your car. He also has a bunch of goodies from France for her." Olivia signaled for the check. "I'll be at the bookstore for a good part of the day tomorrow, but you should come over to the house in the morning. My beach is clean and private, and I can get you settled with chairs and an umbrella before I leave for work."

After agreeing to meet at ten, Jane and Edwin thanked Olivia for the lovely meal. Next, they popped into the kitchen to express their gratitude to Michel and his staff. Michel was in the middle of plating a piece of fish, so they said goodnight and headed back to the Admiral's Inn.

To Jane's relief, the bathroom had been cleaned,

and an enormous bouquet of sunflowers had been left on the counter, along with a note of apology from Francis.

Jane shared the note's contents as Edwin unzipped the back of her dress. "He's very sorry for any inconvenience and wishes us a sunny stay."

"Things are looking very sunny from where I'm standing," Edwin said as he pushed the dress off Jane's shoulders and bent to kiss the nape of her neck.

As she turned to face him, her dress pooled around her feet. She let the note fall to the floor and used both hands to pull Edwin onto the bed.

Jane's subconscious kept waiting for the alarm to go off. If not the alarm, then the barking of hungry puppies. Hundreds of miles from home, it was the high, shrill shriek of gulls that woke her.

She rolled over. Edwin was on his back, hugging a pillow to his chest and snoring softly.

Jane grabbed a pair of jeans and a T-shirt from the dresser and changed in the bathroom. She then tiptoed across the room and scooted out the door as quietly as possible.

As she walked to the main house, she rubbed her bare arms. The morning air had a little bite to it. The breeze blowing in from the Atlantic carried hints of cold winds and storms. Jane had checked the forecast a hundred times before packing her suitcase, so she expected a rainy day tomorrow, but today was supposed to be blue skies and sunshine.

Jane entered the inn and followed her nose to the coffee station in the cocktail lounge.

The room felt hushed, and the brunette behind the

bar didn't seem to notice Jane at all. Her head was bent, and she had a phone pressed to her ear.

"Of course Francis is freaking out!" Her voice had a hard edge. "He has no idea who got into the Book Lover's Loft after St. James checked out. Listen to me, Rachel, today is *not* the day to blow off your shift. You and I both know you need the money, and Francis isn't going to give you any more chances, no matter how much I beg. Just come in."

She ended the call and pulled the collar of her turtleneck up to her chin, clearly lost in thought. Then she touched her fingers to her chest and shook her head before retrieving a carton of milk from under the bar. She poured the milk into an insulated carafe and placed it on the sideboard next to a pair of coffee urns and a rectangular basket overflowing with cinnamon rolls, muffins, and croissants.

Jane got in line behind an elderly couple and waited patiently while they debated whether to have whole or skim milk in their coffee. Eventually, they went with half-and-half.

"Let's live it up. We're on vacation," the man said to his wife.

She flashed him a coy grin. "Merv, should we have muffins too? With butter *and* jam?"

Merv chuckled as he selected two muffins from a basket. "We should, sweetheart. We absolutely should."

Jane was too distracted by what the woman behind the bar had said to pay much attention to the charming older couple, and as soon as they moved out of the way, she poured coffee into takeout cups.

Francis doesn't know who entered our room. I wonder how many people can access it?

She glanced behind the bar, but the brunette was no

longer there. The only staff member in sight was Francis. He was still at the front desk, giving directions to a man in cycling gear. A map was spread out over the desk and both men were poring over it.

It's not your hotel, she reminded herself. *You're just another guest. Don't pester Francis just to satisfy your curiosity.*

Jane returned to the Book Lover's Loft to find the bed empty and the back door ajar. Edwin was sitting at a little café table in the garden, gazing out at the harbor.

"I can't remember the last time I slept this late," he said after greeting Jane with a kiss.

"For me, it was before the twins were born. They like to sleep now, but they definitely didn't when they were babies."

Over coffee, Jane told Edwin what she'd overheard in the lounge. To her chagrin, he didn't share her interest. In fact, he reminded her that they'd come to Oyster Bay to escape intrigue and drama, and then changed the subject by saying he'd googled the current water temperature.

"It's seventy-two. Warm enough to swim. You packed a suit, right?"

Jane's hand flew to her mouth. "I have my suit, but I forgot my books. I left all three on my nightstand so I wouldn't forget to pack them, and that's where they are—on my nightstand."

Edwin gestured at their little cottage. "Good thing our room has a built-in lending library."

While Edwin showered and shaved, Jane perused the bookshelves. She started with the books on the top shelf near the window, reading titles as she slowly sidestepped to the right. When she reached the end of the wall, she walked back to the window and started again.

She'd never seen such an eclectic collection of books.

Old fiction, contemporary fiction, biographies, children's classics, classic literature, coffee table books, and memoirs were shelved higgledy-piggledy with nonfiction books. If she wanted to, Jane could read about military history, travel, architecture, home repair, philosophy, natural history, self-help, and finance.

"Ready?" Edwin asked.

Jane started. She'd been so absorbed by the books that she hadn't realized he was dressed and impatient to get going.

"Almost." She handed him an illustrated guide to identifying shellfish and birds that reminded her of *Where the Crawdads Sing* and a battered hardcover on the mythical sea creatures of Iceland.

Edwin turned to a random page and grimaced. "You might not want to look at this *before* you swim."

The last book she selected was a dog-eared Mary Stewart paperback.

"I haven't read her in years. When I was in high school, I used to fantasize that I was related to Mary. I wanted to be a heroine in one of her novels."

Unlike the other books, which had been tightly wedged into place, the paperback came away easily. Someone must have removed another book from the shelf and forgotten to return it, but Jane knew how to remedy the problem.

I'll buy a copy of Olivia's first book to fill this space.

It was the least she could do to repay Olivia for booking this room, treating them to an incredible dinner, and opening up her home to them.

When Jane added the third book to the beach bag, Edwin pretended to stagger under its weight.

"We forgot to have breakfast," he said as they walked to the car.

"I'm still full from last night. Are you hungry?"

Edwin shook his head. "All I needed was coffee. It's probably better if we don't smell like bacon or sausage before we get in the water. Otherwise, one of your Icelandic sea monsters might come looking for us."

"I'm not going far enough out to tempt any carnivores. I've only been in the ocean a few times. It makes me nervous because you never know what's right under you. I think you should stick close to shore too. Olivia's beach is private, which means there are no lifeguards, and I'm not going to punch a shark in the nose because you decided to swim into its territory."

Olivia lived on a narrow spit of land that jutted out into the ocean like a finger. The few waterfront lots on the Point were very expensive, and because every lot was at least two acres, Olivia didn't have many neighbors. The structure closest to her beachfront home wasn't a sleek, modern mansion but an old lighthouse.

"I grew up in the lighthouse keeper's cottage," Olivia told Jane and Edwin as she gave them a tour of her home. Her black poodle, Captain Haviland, accompanied them through the spacious white kitchen into an elegantly comfortable living room with a breathtaking ocean view. Instead of following them outside to the deck, however, he flopped down on his dog bed and closed his eyes.

Olivia gave him an indulgent smile. "We both got up early this morning, so we went hunting. I had my metal detector and Haviland went after shorebirds."

Edwin was intrigued. "Do you find good stuff or is it mostly trash?"

"It's mostly trash, but there have been exceptions. Jewelry, coins, bullets—we've dug up our fair share of all three. I keep everything in pickle jars in the storage closet downstairs. I'll show you on our way down to the beach."

Like the rest of Olivia's house, the storage closet was neat and tidy. Beach chairs hung from hooks on the walls, oversize towels were stacked on the shelves of a metal cupboard, and there were several plastic laundry baskets filled with beach toys.

Pointing at the toys, Olivia said, "Michel and his family come here most Sundays. They have a key. Take anything you want, and don't worry about locking up when you're done. I leave the house open all the time. It used to drive Sawyer crazy."

She turned away, but not before Jane caught the flash of sorrow in her eyes.

Edwin removed two beach chairs from their hooks and then surveyed the jumbo pickle jars lined up on a high shelf. Each jar was labeled with the year.

"You've been a detectorist for a long time," he said.

Olivia tapped the lid of her current jar. "This hasn't been the best year. Too much trash and too little treasure." She gestured at the metal detector, which was propped up in the corner of the closet. "Want to give it a whirl?"

Jane said, "I do. I don't plan on spending much time in the water. Reading and beachcombing is my idea of excitement. I'll wade in, but I won't go far enough to get my hair wet. I've never seen a shark up close, and I don't want to see one now."

With chairs, towels, and an umbrella in hand, Jane and Edwin followed Olivia down a sandy path that cut through the dunes. On either side of the path, sea oats bobbed in the breeze. A lone gull wheeled overhead, and the sound of waves rushing into the shore dominated all other sounds.

Olivia showed them a good place to set up their umbrella and chairs. As Edwin anchored the umbrella, Jane positioned the chairs, covered them with towels, and dropped a book in each towel.

Picking up one of the books, Olivia let out a laugh. "Sea creatures, eh? I've been swimming in these waters since I was knee-high and have seen only two sharks. One was a sandbar shark and the other was a bonnethead. Neither species is dangerous to humans. Is it possible for bull sharks, sharpnoses, or blacktips to be out there? Yes. That's why I stay out of the water at dusk or dawn, I don't go in if I have a cut, and I don't swim too far from shore. Keep on this side of the sandbar and you'll have nothing to worry about."

Edwin kicked off his shoes and curled his toes. "I'm ready! Are you coming, Jane, or are you treasure hunting?"

"Treasure hunting."

Pulling off his T-shirt, Edwin tossed it on a chair and raced toward the water. He splashed through the shallows, giddy as a young boy. He waded in until the water reached his chest and then dove forward. A second later, his head broke the surface, and he whooped in delight. He waved at Jane and Olivia before floating on his back and stretching out his arms. His toes poked above the waterline.

"He looks like an otter," Jane said.

Olivia turned on her metal detector and fiddled with the controls. "The ocean is good for the soul."

"Could you imagine living anywhere else?"

"Not permanently. But I could see myself spending a few months a year in Storyton."

Jane was dying to ask Olivia about her relationship

with Butterworth, but before she had the chance, Olivia handed her the metal detector and showed her how to sweep it over the sand as she walked.

"Haviland and I went past the lighthouse this morning, so you and I can search this way."

Olivia turned to the right, and Jane fell into step beside her. The metal detector remained mute for what felt like a long time, and when it finally piped up with a series of beeps and chirps, Olivia said there was likely tin nearby.

"Not worth stopping for. You'll hear a lower, throatier beep when it passes over a precious metal. Want to keep going?"

"Yes, but I don't want to make you late. I know you need to get to the bookstore."

Olivia checked her watch. "I can spare another ten minutes. I want you to find something interesting before I leave."

As they continued walking, Olivia asked after Jane's great-aunt and -uncle.

"Uncle Aloysius is working with a memory loss therapist, and it's going well so far. Aunt Octavia is less stressed too."

"And how's the puppy training coming along?"

Jane laughed. "They're training *us* quite well."

The metal detector issued a different sound than the high beeps Jane had heard up until then.

"Is that a promising sound?"

Olivia nodded. "It is. I wish I'd brought my trench shovel. It looks like we'll have to dig for our mystery object. We can use our hands, but it'd be easier if we had a big shell or a piece of driftwood. I'll look by the waterline."

Jane laid down the metal detector and meandered into the dunes in search of a stick. She climbed to the top of the nearest dune and froze.

There, in the trough between the dune she was standing on and the next dune, was a body. Jane saw a flash of sun-reddened cheek, but the rest of the person's face was turned toward the sand.

Not a person. A corpse.

Moving a little closer, Jane suddenly recognized the dead man.

Jane opened her mouth to alert Olivia when she heard her own name carried by the wind. Edwin was shouting—calling to her in a strangled voice. She'd never heard anything like it from him before—a piercing cry of fear and pain.

"Jane! Help!"

She turned away from the body and began to run.

Chapter 5

Jane had always been a slow and awkward runner. There were just some things she couldn't do well, and running was one of them. She'd never lost sleep over the fact. She did plenty of other things to stay active. She hiked, cycled, and had martial arts training twice a week.

At this moment, she would've traded all her other abilities in exchange for speed. As her bare feet sank into the wet sand, she felt like she was lumbering when she needed to sprint. Her lungs burned and her heart thudded against her rib cage. She pumped her arms and tried to move faster, but her body wasn't built to race lightly over the sand.

Up ahead, she saw Edwin's head disappear under the surface of the water.

"Edwin!"

The wind stole her cry and carried it away. It also dried the tears beading in her eyes before they had the chance to slip down her cheeks, which meant she could see the waves swirling over the place where Edwin had gone under. There no was no sign of him. No splashing or flailing.

The ocean had carelessly erased the man she loved.

Suddenly, Edwin's head broke through the water. He was much closer to shore than he'd been before. He was alive and breathing.

Jane let out a sob of relief.

As she hurtled toward Edwin, she saw the curve of his shoulders rise above the surface like the shells of two sea turtles. Then his broad back rose out of the water as he began to frog kick to the shore.

Jane kept running as Edwin swam through the shallows. She didn't understand why he kept swimming. He was in the shallows and could easily stand, so why didn't he?

When he reached the water's edge, he pushed himself up on all fours and crawled over an expanse of broken shells until he reached dry sand.

Then he flopped onto his back, his face turned to the blue sky, and went still.

OhGodohGod.

Jane forgot about the body in the sand. She forgot about Olivia. There was only one person in this place of sea and sand and sky. There was only Edwin.

Please be okay. Oh God, please be okay.

Her mind tried to make sense of Edwin's pained cry. Of his reason for crawling on the sand. Had he been bitten by a shark? Stung by a jellyfish?

She couldn't risk glancing at the water because she couldn't take her eyes off Edwin. As long as her gaze was fixed on him, there was hope that everything would be okay.

Jane had almost closed the distance between them when Edwin suddenly moved. He rolled to his side, shifting his weight to his elbow, and groaned. His free hand went to his neck and his mouth opened wide.

Dropping to her knees beside him, Jane scanned Edwin's body. She saw no blood. No lacerations. No teeth marks. But when she looked at the trail he'd made in the sand, she saw damp, ruddy shadows caused by blood and water.

"What happened?" she asked, pushing his hair out of his face.

He sucked in a breath, and when he exhaled, he made a sound like a grunting pig. Fighting for another breath, he pushed out the word, "Feet."

Jane scrambled to the other end of his body and gasped. Two barbs were impaled in the bottoms of Edwin's feet. They looked like black arrows without their fletching. Jane couldn't tell how deeply the barbs had penetrated Edwin's flesh, but the skin around the objects had turned an angry purple.

"Stingrays," Edwin muttered. His hand was still at his throat, and his breath sounds were shallow.

"I'll get help." Jane kissed his brow and hurried over to their beach chairs. Her phone was in the outer pocket of the tote bag, and she dialed 911 and shouted that she needed an ambulance immediately.

"Should I pull the barbs out?" she asked after providing the address and explaining to the woman who'd answered the call that while Edwin was conscious, he was clearly in pain and his breathing was labored.

The emergency response officer told her to leave the barbs alone and to focus on keeping Edwin calm and hydrated until the paramedics arrived.

Jane threw the tote bag on her shoulder and grabbed a towel before hurrying back to Edwin. She held up his head and encouraged him to drink some water.

He waved away the bottle, pointing at his throat and trying to inhale through his nose.

"Help is coming, sweetheart. Everything's going to be okay. I promise you."

She rolled up the towel and placed it under his head. She sat so that her body cast shade on his face and tried to keep him cool by splashing water on the towel and pressing it to his forehead.

She was alarmed to see that his feet had swollen to nearly twice their usual size. His ankles looked red and puffy. But his labored breathing scared her the most.

Squeezing Edwin's hand, she told him to relax his muscles. "I know it hurts, but let your body go limp. It'll be easier to breathe."

She wiped granules of sand from his cheek and willed the EMTs to hurry. She glanced back down the beach but saw no sign of Olivia.

She must be waiting for help too. Who'll get here the fastest? The police? The EMTs? Please, please, be the EMTs.

"Least . . . no . . . sharks," Edwin wheezed.

"Shh. You can tell me all about how you stepped on a stingray when we're off this beach. I'm guessing that's what happened. Either that, or you were attacked by two baby narwhals."

Jane heard a sound in between the rush of waves hitting the shore. Sirens. They were close.

"I'm going to flag them down. Focus on breathing. I love you."

Jane raced toward the dunes.

Cresting the rise, she saw an ambulance and two police cruisers in the parking area behind the lighthouse. A pickup truck was approaching her from the beach, the words Ocean Rescue printed on its side.

She frantically pointed at the water, and the truck headed to where Edwin was lying on the sand.

By the time she returned to his side, the EMTs had moved him onto a stretcher and placed an oxygen mask over his face. Jane was so relieved to see the mask fog up that she almost hugged the first responders.

"How is he?" she asked the two men as they lifted Edwin up.

"His feet are swelling like ticks and he's having trouble breathing, which means he's having a severe allergic reaction to the stingray poison," the first man said. "We gave him an epinephrine injection and we'll keep him on oxygen. Once we transfer him to the other rig, we'll get him to the hospital quicker than a cat on a hot tin roof."

Jane stared at Edwin's face, willing the mask to fog up again. When it did, she smiled at him.

"You're doing great. Gold star for breathing."

He reached for her hand, and she grabbed his and planted a kiss on the sandy skin. The sand in her mouth didn't bother her. As long as Edwin could breathe, nothing bothered her.

The men loaded Edwin into the truck and told Jane to hop into the cab. As they drove to the parking lot, Jane said, "My friend is farther down the beach. She . . . we found a body. Are the police here to help her?"

The second man nodded. "Ms. Olivia's call came in a few minutes before yours, but don't worry about her, ma'am. She's got lots of friends in the department. They'll treat her right. You ladies have had some morning, haven't you?"

"That's one way to put it," Jane said, craning her neck to see Edwin.

Once she was buckled into the passenger seat of the ambulance, with Edwin riding in back with the other EMT, Jane was finally calm enough to wonder how Olivia was doing. Not only had she found the body of a famous author on the beach behind her house but that same author was supposed to headline an event at her bookstore that afternoon. Would she cancel the event, or was it too late? If things went ahead as planned, how would Olivia explain St. James's absence to her customers?

These were the questions Jane's resort manager side focused on. The other part of her—the part that had been involved in multiple murder investigations in her own backyard—mulled over the question of how St. James's body had ended up on the beach behind Olivia's house.

As the ambulance raced toward CarolinaEast Medical Center, Jane tried to recall every detail of the scene. She'd had only a few seconds to take it in before she'd heard Edwin's cry of distress, but Sinclair had taught her how to recall details by reviewing a memory in slow motion.

Jane placed herself back on the beach. The metal detector was in her hands. She felt the arm support hugging the skin under her right elbow and felt the weight of the arm shift as she moved the search coil over the ground. She saw the readings on the control box and heard the low-pitched beep. Next, she remembered putting the detector down on the ground so she could dig in the sand.

She'd been searching for a stick or piece of driftwood when she'd spotted the author's body.

Concentrating hard, Jane recounted what she'd seen first.

His shoes. White slip-on sneakers. Barely scuffed.

Next, there'd been the wrinkled hems of the dead man's stone-colored chinos above a pair of tan ankles. The pants were sand dusted, as was St. James's black leather belt. His blue linen shirt had come untucked, allowing Jane to see more tanned skin. His arms were bent into *L*s. The gold watch on his left wrist winked in the sunlight. His fingernails were neatly trimmed.

Jane remembered that his head was turned toward the sea, his glassy gaze fixed on his left hand. His lips were parted, and sand peppered his cheek and jaw. Sand clung to his eyebrow, to the curve of his ear, and to the strands of his wavy hair.

But the sand around his body was smooth. There were no footprints.

Either Justin St. James had traipsed through the sea oats or he'd walked close to the water's edge. The tide had been coming in all morning, which meant his tracks could have been washed away.

But the water doesn't rise all the way to the dunes. He must have left prints somewhere.

Once again, Jane pictured St. James's body. There'd been no obvious injuries. No bruises. No blood. He looked like he'd fallen flat on his face after drinking too much. What could mimic a drunken collapse? A heart attack?

Jane supposed it was possible. People in their forties did suffer heart attacks, but Jane didn't believe that someone who looked as fit and energetic as Justin St. James had just keeled over in the sand.

Did someone put him there?

There was no sense trying to contact Olivia now.

She'd be tied up with the police for a while, and as soon as she finished giving her statement, she'd have to deal with the bookstore event.

The ambulance passed by a sign for CarolinaEast Medical Center, and Jane jerked upright in her seat, all thoughts of Olivia and St. James instantly banished. Once again, her attention was fixed entirely on Edwin.

Catching sight of her fearful expression, the ambulance driver said, "The docs here are great. They know we're coming in hot, and they'll be ready and waiting."

A team of health-care workers in blue scrubs waited for them outside the ambulance bay. They loaded Edwin onto a wheeled gurney and pushed him through the halls into a treatment room. Jane ran right alongside the gurney but was forced to step back when Edwin was moved to an exam table.

There was a flurry of activity as people surrounded Edwin. They took his temperature and blood pressure. While a nurse placed an IV line in his arm, a physician asked him several questions. When she was satisfied with his answers, the doctor sat down on a stool to examine Edwin's feet.

Someone handed Jane a clipboard and asked her to fill out the necessary paperwork. Though she accepted the clipboard, she didn't even glance at the papers. Instead, she tried to edge closer to Edwin—to let him know that she hadn't left his side.

Finally, the doctor turned to meet Jane's anxious gaze. She gave Jane a reassuring smile and introduced herself as Dr. Lewis.

"Is he allergic to anything? Are there medicines he can't tolerate?"

"None that I know of."

After Dr. Lewis jotted down a few notes on a chart,

she explained that she'd numb Edwin's feet and remove the barbs. Once they were out, she'd clean and
dress the wounds. Edwin would receive intravenous an-
tibiotics and hydrating fluids.

"We'll be keeping a close eye on his oxygen levels
too."

A nurse wheeled over a tray of instruments and
parked it near Edwin's feet. Jane took one look at the
preloaded syringe on the tray and immediately glanced
away. Spying another stool tucked in the far corner of
the room, she pushed it to the head of Edwin's bed. She
then laced her fingers through his and tried to distract
him with stories of her childhood injuries.

As she talked, Edwin winced a time or two. Other
than that, he gave no indication of discomfort.

After Dr. Lewis removed the barbs and cleaned the
wounds, she told Jane that Edwin required stitches on
both feet. As she sutured, she and the nurses compared
notes on the most unusual beach-related injuries they'd
seen.

"Umbrellas can be surprisingly dangerous," Dr. Lewis
said. "If a strong wind picks up and they come unan-
chored, they turn into projectiles. We've all seen lacerations from shells, fishing hooks in every part of the
body, and some nasty jellyfish stings. I guess everyone
has regional hazards, don't they?"

Jane was grateful for the doctor's prattle. It made her
feel like Edwin was out of danger. He was in the capable
hands of these health-care workers. His wounds had
been treated and he was getting medicine. He'd had a
close call, but because of the EMTs and the people in
this room, he was going to be okay.

"Vacations never seem to live up to our expectations," the doctor said. "Where are you folks from?"

"Storyton, Virginia. It's a small town in the mountains."

Dr. Lewis beamed. "My colleague stayed at a resort there. He raved about it. Said it was the best rest he's had since medical school. He talked about this falcon-training class so much that we started calling him Lord Patel instead of Doctor Patel."

"Storyton Hall has an aviary with falcons, hawks, and owls. All of the birds have had injuries that make it impossible for them to survive in the wild, so we use them for educational purposes. The falconry classes are one of our most popular activities."

"Do you work there?"

"I sure do."

Dr. Lewis tied the last suture and stood up. She peeled off her gloves, tossed them on the tray of instruments and looked at Edwin.

"Because of the severity of your reaction to the stingray toxins, we're going to admit you. Your feet should heal nicely, but I want to make sure your breathing is completely normal before we let you go. I know you weren't planning on a twenty-four stay at Hotel Carolina-East, but hey, at least you'll be putting your feet up."

Edwin pushed his oxygen mask away from his mouth. "Thank you, Doctor."

She smiled. "Glad to be of service, but it was the EMTs and that epinephrine injection that saved the day."

"That'll be the last time I touch the ocean floor without checking to see what's down there first."

Dr. Lewis held up the stingray barbs. "Would you like to take these home? They're pretty cool souvenirs."

Edwin turned to Jane. "The boys would kill me if I didn't."

The man who'd asked Jane to complete the paperwork returned. Seeing the blank clipboard, he asked her to accompany him to the admissions area. She grabbed her tote bag, told Edwin she'd be right back, and followed the man down the hall.

She'd filled out the necessary forms and was waiting for the man to return Edwin's insurance card when she heard her phone buzz from inside the tote bag.

The notifications filling her screen were all from Olivia. The most recent was a plea for Jane to update her on Edwin's status.

Jane wrote, **Stingray barbs in each foot. Severe allergic reaction. He's going to be okay but they're keeping him overnight.**

She stared at the screen, waiting for three dots to appear, but nothing happened.

"Could you sign here, please?" the man behind the desk asked.

Jane put her phone away and reached for a pen.

By the time the admittance process was done, Edwin had been moved from the treatment room to a private room on the third floor. When Jane stepped into the room, he was lying on his back with his face turned toward the window. His oxygen mask had been replaced by a cannula.

"Hey." Jane sat on the edge of his bed. "What a story we have to tell when we get home."

Edwin opened his arms and pulled her down to him. Holding her against his chest, he whispered, "Thank you, love."

They stayed like that for a while, and Jane found comfort in the rise and fall of Edwin's chest and the feel of his hands on her back. When she sat up, she studied his face. Some of the color had returned to his cheeks, but he looked incredibly tired.

"The real heroes are the EMTs. When I get a chance, I'll send food and a thank-you note to their station."

Edwin reached for Jane's hand. "I'm sorry for ruining our vacation."

"If you'd been swallowed by a whale and I never saw you again, *that* would've ruined our vacation. This?" She waved her hand around the room. "This is an adventure."

Edwin pulled a face. "You didn't even have time to find pirate treasure, and I might have to open a second restaurant to pay the hospital bill."

"How about a chic cocktail joint? Your signature drink could be called the Stingray."

"You're laughing now, but wait until you have to push me around in a wheelchair." Edwin pushed a button on the side of his bed, which raised his upper body. "We need to buy a little bell so I can ring for you whenever I need something."

Jane glanced at the door. "Maybe I should get a nurse. You sound delusional."

Edwin planted a kiss on her palm. "I'm only crazy when it comes to you. So, did you have time to find anything interesting with the metal detector before you had to rush to my aid?"

Though Edwin was doing his best to sound alert, Jane heard an undertone of fatigue in his voice. She ran her fingertips down the side of his face and said, "I think you should rest now. I'm going to hunt down a cup of coffee and give Olivia a call. I haven't talked to her since I ran off at the beach. She's probably worried sick."

"You can't stay here all day, Jane. You should go back to the inn—check out their afternoon tea, or that bookstore event. You can ask Justin St. James why he carries around a skull named Septimius. Maybe Olivia's free for dinner. The two of you could paint the town."

"Paint the town? You sound like Aunt Octavia." Jane tried to grin, but it wouldn't stick. "I might have to leave. Not because I want to, but because the police will probably want to talk to me."

Edwin's eyes snapped open. "Why?"

"Because you weren't the only man to be carried off that stretch of beach. Seconds before you were stung, I saw a man lying on the sand between two dunes. That man was Justin St. James, and he was dead."

Edwin reached for his water glass and took a sip. Then he let his head fall back against his pillow and said, "Tell me everything."

"I had about five seconds to take in the scene before I heard you shout, so there isn't much to tell. I couldn't see any obvious injuries. It looked like he just keeled over."

"Why was he there in the first place? Olivia's beach is private, and she told us there are only a few residences on the Point. How did he end up in that spot?"

Before dashing away, Jane had caught a glimpse of Olivia's face. The surprise she'd seen there had been genuine.

Edwin said, "You should call her."

"I will, on my way to get coffee. And I won't tell you what she has to say unless you close your eyes and rest while I'm gone."

Edwin lowered his bed and mumbled something about Nurse Ratched.

Jane waited until she was on the main floor on her way to the cafeteria before calling Olivia.

Olivia answered right away. "I heard Edwin needed an EpiPen. Is he okay?"

"He is, thanks to the EMTs. He's spending the night in the hospital, just to be on the safe side. How are you?"

A dog barked in the background, and Olivia said, "I just got home. There wasn't much to tell the police, but since St. James was in front of *my* house and came to town for an event in *my* bookstore, they had lots of questions."

"I bet you do too."

"Damn right I do. Why was he there? How did he die? Why did it seem like he just dropped from the sky? The cops asked if anyone had mentioned him in the past twenty-four hours, and I had to give them names. Including yours."

For a moment, Jane was confused. She and Edwin had just met the man yesterday. Then she remembered the skull and the message on the mirror.

"I haven't looked through my missed calls or texts yet, but I'll do that as soon as I get a cup of coffee. Why is this hospital so cold?"

"It's the shock. You should sit in the sun for a few minutes—give your body a chance to warm up. Call me back once you're outside. I have something else to tell you, but I need to get changed and feed Haviland before I head to the bookstore."

"Give me ten minutes." Jane hung up and entered the cafeteria. She ordered a cappuccino and a giant chocolate chip cookie.

The cashier approved of her choice.

"I bet that cookie's still warm from the oven. They just finished baking them, and the smell has got me drooling like a dog. I can't wait to go on break so I can have one."

"Charge me for two, please. I'll treat you," Jane said.

The woman thanked her and pointed to a set of double doors leading to a small patio. "If you take the path to the right, you'll find a bench and a little fountain. It's my favorite spot."

In the small, peaceful garden, Jane took a moment to just breathe.

She could only imagine how many people had sat where she was now, their hearts constricted by fear or weighed down by grief. She was one of the lucky ones. The man she loved would heal. He would leave the hospital tomorrow and they would resume their life together.

Jane closed her eyes and sent up a silent prayer of gratitude. When she was done, she felt more centered. As she sipped her cappuccino, the sun erased the goose bumps from her arms. She broke off a piece of chocolate chip cookie and popped it in her mouth. It was warm, soft, and sweet. She ate the whole thing before calling Olivia back.

"You're on speaker," Olivia said by way of greeting. "I'm still getting ready."

"What are you going to tell his fans?"

Jane heard a clatter, followed by Olivia swearing under her breath. "Sorry, dropped the phone. The fans? I'll tell them that St. James had to pull out of the event at the last minute. The police don't want the news of his passing to be made public—not until they know the cause of death—so I don't have much choice."

"Did you notice any injuries when they moved him? Bruising or cuts or anything?"

"His face looked puffy. That was the only unusual thing I saw."

Though Jane wondered if Olivia had examined the dead man before the authorities arrived, she didn't have the nerve to ask her. Instead, she said, "Do you think he died of natural causes?"

"No, I don't. I saw the cops search his pockets. All he had on him was his wallet. No car keys. There's no way he walked here from town. My guess is he was dropped off by boat. When I get back from the bookstore, I'll see if Haviland can scent his trail. It would be easier if I had a piece of St. James's clothing."

"You'd have to get into St. James's hotel room."

After a beat of silence, Olivia said, "Or you could."

Justin St. James was a public figure, which meant the police would be very thorough in their investigations. The last thing Jane needed was to be caught doing something suspicious like riffling through St. James's hotel room.

When Jane didn't answer, Olivia said, "Death is like a black hole. You can't fight the pull of its gravity, and I have a feeling we're both going to be pulled in, like it or not."

A shiver raced up the back of Jane's neck. "Why both of us? I'm a stranger here."

"Before the cops and EMTs got to Justin St. James, I did a quick sweep with the metal detector, and I found something in the sand near his body. I don't understand why it was there, but it can't be a good thing."

"What was it?"

Olivia exhaled and said, "A brass key chain—from a hotel. Not just any hotel either. The key chain's from Storyton Hall."

Chapter 6

When Jane returned to Edwin's room, she found the door closed.

A nurse exited the room across the hall and pointed at Edwin's door. "He's asleep. You can go in if you want, or I could call you when he wakes up. You're staying in Oyster Bay, right?"

Picturing their bright, book-filled cottage, Jane said, "Yes. We're at the Admiral's Inn."

The nurse put a hand on Jane's arm. "Why don't you go back there and take a moment for yourself? We'll take good care of Mr. Alcott. Even after a nap, he'll probably go to sleep early tonight. That's what usually happens after a trauma. I'm sure you feel spent too."

"I feel like I've run a marathon—not that I've ever done that. More like stayed up all night reading." She glanced at Edwin's door again. "When he wakes up, will you tell him that I've gone back to the hotel?"

After promising to deliver the message, the nurse

tapped on the door to another patient's room and disappeared inside.

Jane headed to the ground floor in search of transportation. She'd never had cause to sign up for a car service like Uber or Lyft, but if she couldn't find a taxi or hop on a bus to Oyster Bay, she'd have no choice but to download an app to her phone and learn how to request a ride.

She was about to ask a security guard for advice when a white minivan pulled to a stop in front of the main doors. Jane saw the taxi sign affixed to the van's roof and hurried outside. A kind-faced man in overalls opened the back door and helped his elderly female passenger into a wheelchair. Then he pushed her into the hospital, reemerging again a few minutes later.

When Jane asked if he'd take her to Oyster Bay, he touched the brim of his baseball cap and said, "It'd be my pleasure, ma'am."

The man, whose name was Murphy, was a talker. Jane had barely fastened her seat belt before he peppered her with questions. When Jane told him about Edwin's injuries, his brown eyes gleamed with interest.

"Lord have mercy! That's why I don't go in the ocean. I won't even dip my big toe in. I have a nice little boat, and on my days off, I go out with my pole and my radio for hours at a time. No matter how hot it gets, my body stays in the boat. I tell my wife that no sea monster could resist me, but she says I'm only irresistible to her."

For the rest of the drive, Murphy regaled Jane with fishing stories. Each time he described how he'd reeled in a mammoth trout or flounder or tarpon, Jane pictured a shiny lure rising up through the dark water. In her mind, all the lures looked like key chains. Shiny, brass Storyton Hall key chains.

She asked Murphy to drop her at Bayside Books, and as soon as she was out of the car, she sat down on a bench in front of the store and called Butterworth.

"Miss Jane. I didn't expect to hear from you so soon."

"I didn't expect to be calling, but our trip got off to a rocky start."

Jane quickly summarized the past few hours. When she was done, Butterworth seemed at a loss for words.

Finally, he said, "I'll see if Mr. St. James has stayed with us before. If not him, then perhaps one of his fellow panelists is a former guest. Despite their size and weight, we lose a dozen key tags a year. Some are sent back to us. Others are never seen again. This will be the first found at a crime scene."

"A possible crime scene," Jane corrected.

"Can Ms. Limoges shed any light on the situation?"

Jane stepped aside to let a group of women enter the store. When the door opened, the sound of applause swept out over the sidewalk.

"I haven't had a chance to talk things over with her. She had to get to the bookstore to prepare for the author event, and I was too busy worrying about Edwin's throat swelling to the point where he could no longer breathe to think about calling her."

Butterworth made a soothing sound. "Mr. Alcott is safe. His wounds will heal, and he'll make a full recovery. You, on the other hand, could be in danger. The presence of that key chain indicates that you most likely are. Between that and the lack of footprints around the body, I don't believe this was an accident."

Murder.

The word buzzed in Jane's ear like a hornet. Butterworth hadn't spoken it aloud, but it had traveled from his brain to Jane's as if he had.

"If I'm in danger, Olivia is too," she murmured.

"I agree," Butterworth said. "You're hundreds of miles from those who've sworn to protect you, so you must rely on your training. Observe the key players. Speak with them. Try to discover motive, means, and opportunity. At the same time, you and Ms. Limoges should assist the authorities—just as you would in Storyton."

Butterworth's voice was one of calm assurance. He told her to make a plan before entering the bookstore.

Jane loved organizing. Whether it was a spice rack, a bookshelf, or her thoughts, she found peace and comfort when things were in their proper place. "I'm going to blend in with the crowd. I'll sit somewhere in the back and observe the interactions between the authors, as well as those between the authors and readers. While I'm doing that, can you find out if that Storyton key chain belonged to St. James?"

"We'll run background checks on all three authors. When we speak again, I'll have more information to share."

Jane knew the men who'd been like fathers to her—Butterworth, Sinclair, and Sterling—would go to the ends of the earth to find the answers she needed. That knowledge made her feel like she wasn't so far from home after all, and she entered the bookshop with a renewed sense of purpose.

There was only one customer at the checkout counter and a few more browsers toward the back of the store, but Jane heard a woman's amplified voice coming from the café. Crossing the threshold between the bookstore and the café, Jane saw that the tables had been removed to make room for rows of chairs. There were over a hundred, and every seat was filled. The rest of the audience stood off to the side.

For a moment, Jane forgot about Justin St. James. Seeing a room stuffed to the gills with book lovers made her heart swell with joy. Not only were they listening closely to the speaker, most of the attendees had shopping bags by their feet filled with books.

Jane's jubilation quickly evaporated when she noticed a woman hugging a St. James novel to her chest.

What did Olivia tell the audience? That St. James was ill or had been in an accident?

The man clearly had a fair share of fans in the room. His books were tucked under chairs, poking out of purses, and stacked on people's laps.

They must have been disappointed when they heard he wasn't coming, but they didn't leave. That's good news for the other authors, and for the bookstore.

Jane scanned the room for Olivia. At nearly six feet tall, with a corona of white-blond hair, she wasn't difficult to spot. She stood off to the side of the raised platform where the authors sat, looking elegant in black pants and a camel-colored silk blouse. She toyed with a necklace of amber beads as she listened to Heather O'Grady explain why she disliked a particular kind of unreliable narrator.

Heather's eyes sparked with anger, just as they had when she'd argued with Justin St. James the day before.

"All narrators are unreliable to a certain extent because all stories are told from an individual's point of view. I'm not against a character who lies. We all tell lies for one reason or another, but I'm sick and tired of the unreliable *female* narrator who suffers from alcohol or drug-induced blackouts. This self-destructive woman is plagued by regret, lack of impulse control, and a host of other *issues*. She's always the polar opposite of the smart, well-adjusted male detective who inevitably solves the case. These fictional women are always attractive. They're often addicted to booze, pills, or social media. And they all need the man with the badge to save them. In my books, the *woman* is the hero. She's flawed. She makes mistakes. But she's someone readers can respect."

A hand went up in the audience, and a man said, "I'm a big fan of your work, Ms. O'Grady. I heard you talk at a crime writer's conference in New Orleans two years ago, and I remember you saying that you wrote your first novel as a way to work through a personal trauma. You also said that none of your books mention that event. Will you ever tell your readers what happened?"

The smile Heather turned on the man when he'd first started speaking disappeared. She began shaking her head before the question was out of his mouth.

"The only people I've talked to about what happened in my past are my therapist and my boyfriend, and that's as far as I'll go. My therapist isn't going to tell a soul, and if my boyfriend does, he'll end up in my next novel."

Heather's attempt at levity elicited a few chuckles from the audience, but the man's question reminded Jane that Heather wasn't the only writer in the room to have suffered a tragedy. Olivia had as well.

She hated St. James for writing about her husband's death, Jane thought as Heather fielded a benign question about her writing schedule. *He changed many of the details, but she still recognized the story as hers. Reading it had wounded her deeply. No one would blame her for hating St. James.*

Jane didn't believe for one moment that Olivia had

murdered Justin St. James. Perhaps someone who cared about her—someone who knew just how much pain St. James's novel had caused her—decided to punish the heartless writer. After all, this was Olivia's town. She'd grown up in Oyster Bay. She'd been the proprietor of its finest restaurant for years, and now she owned its only bookstore. Her mother had worked at the public library. Her father had spent his life fishing local waters. Olivia had gone to school here. She'd married the police chief.

Who had his own friends and family, Jane thought.

Had a member of Sawyer's family killed St. James and dumped the body on Olivia's beach as a sort of tribute?

Jane negated the thought with a shake of her head. *Then where does the Storyton Hall key chain fit in?*

On the raised platform, an author named Winston Hall was responding to a question about Black crime writers.

"There aren't enough of us, that's for sure, but I'd recommend Walter Mosely, Jason Overstreet, and S. A. Cosby for starters. And don't forget Winston Hall. I hear you can pick up signed copies of both his books today."

Laughter rippled through the audience. An older woman in the back struggled to her feet and said, "I don't have a question, but I wanted to tell you how much your new book moved me. I'm a retired nurse, and I saw some of the terrible things you wrote about. When I was reading it, I almost felt like I was in the emergency room again. Either you knew somebody who worked as a nurse or you did excellent research. But I thank you for giving the folks who suffered a voice. It's about damn time somebody told their story."

Winston was clearly touched by the woman's words. He gave her a deferential nod and said, "Thank you very much. My mother was a nurse. I wrote *To Do No Harm* to honor her."

"What folks is she talking about? Who suffered?" a woman to Jane's right whispered to her friend.

The friend took a copy of *To Do No Harm* from her shopping bag. "The book jacket says that it's a medical thriller about the travesties a nurse witnessed while working in a hospital in Alabama. A doctor preys on his Black patients and she risks her life to stop him."

The first woman looked thoughtful. "Justin St. James wrote about a boy whose mom was a nurse in *Catch More Flies.* Do you think that character was based on Winston Hall?"

"Maybe. Justin said he got the idea from an old newspaper article."

As Jane looked at Winston Hall and Heather O'Grady before shifting her gaze to Olivia, her thoughts churned. Were the central plots of every Justin St. James novel based on real-life tragedies? It wasn't unheard of for authors to fictionalize sensational crimes, but why had St. James homed in on the death of Olivia's husband?

Jane hadn't read *Catch More Flies,* which was St. James's fourth novel. Though she'd read his debut novel years ago, she didn't remember the details. But if she wanted to satisfy her curiosity, she could easily peruse online summaries and reviews when she was back at the Book Lover's Loft.

You can't find the answer to every mystery in a book, whispered a niggling voice in her head.

Jane pushed the skeptical thought aside. She'd found the answer to most of life's difficult questions in books.

She'd been a young girl when her parents died, and though Aunt Octavia and Uncle Aloysius loved her with their whole hearts, there were things she hadn't felt comfortable asking them.

Luckily, she grew up surrounded by books. Thousands of them. Books of every genre. Of every subject. No one ever told her she was too young to read a certain book, so she read whatever she wanted. In the libraries and reading rooms of Storyton Hall, she'd learned what it meant to be an orphan. She made friends with the kids at school, but her truest companions existed in stories. As a teenager, she learned about her changing body and first crushes from books. Books taught her about morality, fostered her independence, and encouraged her dreams and ambitions.

Having read hundreds upon hundreds of books, Jane would never underestimate the power of the written word. If Justin St. James had deliberately immortalized another person's pain in his novels, he'd earned their enmity. Losing a loved one to a violent crime created the kind of wound that never truly healed, and reading about that crime in a popular work of fiction would be a fresh, new agony.

A burst of applause snapped Jane out of her reverie. The panel was over, and a man with silver hair and blue glasses had taken the mic. He began to explain how the book signing and checkout process would work, and Jane saw Olivia slip out of the café.

Following her friend into the bookstore, Jane joined her behind the checkout counter.

"I saw you come in," Olivia said. She reached under the register and produced a sandwich wrapped in paper and a bottle of iced tea. "Hungry? It's grilled chicken and goat cheese."

"A little. Thanks." Jane unwrapped the sandwich and took a bite.

Olivia began stacking paper bags stamped with the bookstore's name on the counter. "Obviously we need to sit down and talk. And obviously we'll have to wait until the crowd thins out."

"How can I help?"

Cracking a smile, Olivia said, "You can bag while I ring. I don't normally run the checkout part of these events, but one of our booksellers called in sick, so here I am. With the two of us back here, we'll wrap up this event in record time."

After finishing the first half of her sandwich, Jane said, "What did you say about Justin St. James?"

"Just that he wasn't able to make it. I apologized, said that I shared their disappointment, and assured them that the other two authors were here and ready to deliver plenty of thrills and chills."

Jane uncapped the bottle of iced tea but didn't take a drink. "Are you disappointed? Or are you pleased?"

Olivia went very still. Staring at Jane with those intense, ocean-blue eyes, she said, "Both. I'm disappointed because a living St. James would've meant more sales for us today, but I'm glad he's dead because he was a callous prick."

"It must be hard to sell the book he based on you."

Olivia nodded. "I hate that he made money from our story. He changed names and settings. He changed the gender of the killer and gave him a different motive, but all the locals who've read the book have asked if St. James interviewed me before writing *By the Dark Water*."

Jane turned to face the display table of Justin St. James, Winston Hall, and Heather O'Grady novels. *By the Dark*

Water was black and blue with hints of purple. The colors reminded Jane of a bruise.

"Here they come," Olivia said.

Readers drifted out of the café into the bookstore. Some browsed as they walked. Others made a beeline for the checkout counter.

Jane took up her place next to Olivia. Without being told, she greeted each customer, turned their books over to enable quicker scanning of the barcodes, and slid the books into bags while the customers swiped their credit cards or paid in cash.

"You're a natural at this, which doesn't surprise me at all. You're the kind of woman who can do anything she sets her mind to. It's one of the many reasons I like you," Olivia whispered in between customers.

Jane was blushing with pleasure when a customer placed six copies of *By the Dark Water* on the counter.

"Have you read this one?" she asked, directing the question to Olivia.

"I've read all of his novels, except the new one. I haven't gotten to that yet."

The woman tapped the top book on the stack. "My book club is going to read this next week. Someone told me that even though it's set in South Carolina, Justin St. James was *really* writing about Oyster Bay. Is that true?"

Anger flared in Jane's chest. How insensitive could a person be? Didn't this woman realize that Olivia's husband had lost his life trying to stop a ruthless killer?

Olivia touched Jane's arm and gave a little shake of her head before reaching for the pile of books. "People have asked Mr. St. James if that's the case. He always says the same thing—that he vacationed here when he

was working on the book, and that he became so enam-
ored with our town that it influenced certain scenes."

"Well, it might be the only time everyone in my book
club actually reads the book!" the woman declared.
"We're all going to be searching for things we recognize. I'm going to dive in as soon as I get home."

Jane bagged the copies of *By the Dark Water* as fast as
she could and was relieved when the next customer
placed two Winston Hall novels on the counter.

It took another thirty minutes to winnow down the
crowd from a line that snaked through the store to a
handful of customers.

"I'm going to call Edwin," Jane told Olivia. "I'm sure
he's awake by now."

"My office is in the back. Make yourself comfortable."

Admiring the various wardrobes-turned-bookcases
as she walked, Jane reached a door in the far corner of
the store. She pushed it open and stepped into a large
space filled with cardboard boxes, shelving carts, and
recycling bins.

The doors to a pair of small offices were ajar, and
Jane identified Olivia's by the prominent photograph
of Captain Haviland on the desk. Closing the door behind her, she sat in the cushy leather desk chair and
called Edwin.

He answered by saying, "I feel better."

"That nap must've worked wonders. You know, I
don't think I've ever seen you nap before."

"I'm like Batman. No one sees Batman nap, but that
doesn't mean he doesn't take them."

Jane glanced at the wall clock. The afternoon was almost gone. "I hope you aren't scheduled for a sponge
bath, because I have lots to tell you."

"I've already had a bath. A saltwater bath. In the ocean. I had a lovely foot scrub courtesy of two very large, very prickly stingrays. Now tell me everything."

Jane did. When she was done, Edwin remained silent for a long time.

"Did you fall asleep?" Jane teased.

"No, I'm just wondering who I can call to get discharged right now."

Jane bolted upright in her chair. "Don't you dare. Our hotel is forty-five minutes from the hospital. What if something happened to you? And don't tell me that you're fine. I wouldn't sleep a wink, worrying that you might stop breathing in the middle of the night."

"I can't leave you alone. I need to know you're safe."

"I'll sleep with the tire iron, and in the morning I'll pick you up. I'd drive to the hospital tonight to hang out with you, but the police want to talk to me. I need to talk to Olivia too."

Jane heard voices on the other side of the closed door, so she told Edwin that she'd call him back from the police station and got to her feet.

"Are you sure Olivia isn't involved?" Edwin asked. "She did say she wanted to dig a deep hole in the sand and drop St. James in it. And that's where he was—in the sand behind her house. Plus, she was at Storyton Hall a few months ago. She could've gotten the key chain then."

Jane told Edwin that she didn't suspect Olivia for a moment.

"She's not exactly torn up over his death, but she didn't kill him. The killer obviously knows where she lives. And where I live too." The thought scared Jane, but she couldn't let Edwin know, so she hastily added, "Butterworth and Sinclair are looking into St. James and the other authors. Can you touch base with them while I'm at the station?"

Edwin muttered about the confines of being an invalid but agreed to Jane's request.

Ending the call, she opened the office door. She heard voices again, and saw that Heather O'Grady and Winston Hall were talking quietly by the shelving carts. Seeing they were no longer alone, they smiled awkwardly at Jane.

At that moment, Olivia entered the stockroom. In a near whisper, she said, "They're waiting for you at the station. I'll drive you there." She then walked over to the two authors and stretched out her hand. "Thank you for rolling with the punches today. Mr. St. James missed a great event."

"You *still* haven't heard from him?" Heather sounded incredulous.

Olivia said, "Not a word."

The authors were parked out back, and Olivia thanked them again before unlocking the doors of her Tesla Model X.

Jane noticed the sleek, futuristic interior, and how the SUV accelerated almost soundlessly, but was too nervous about their destination to comment on Olivia's car.

"Art Henniger is the lead on this case. He came to Oyster Bay after Sawyer was killed, so I don't know him well. His partner, Lorna Locklear, was a friend of Sawyer's, and I trust her completely. She called me a few minutes ago to say that they'd found something on St. James—something she couldn't explain."

"What is it?"

"A page from a book. And because I own a bookstore, she's going to let me have a look. If I can't help, they'll bring it to the library. Everyone in town goes to them for the answers—even the cops."

An image of Sinclair scaling the ladder in the Henry James Library entered Jane's mind. How many times had he solved problems for her family, staff members, and guests?

"When Edwin and I heard Justin and Heather arguing yesterday, she called him a hack. Today, two women in the audience were wondering if *Catch More Flies* was based on Winston Hall's mom. The central storyline of *By the Dark Water* was about your husband. What if every St. James novel is a fictionalized version of a real tragedy? If so, then—"

"There are too many suspects for us to handle," Olivia said.

"Are you likely to become one? A suspect?"

Olivia shot her a curious glance. "It's possible. Everyone who knows me knows how I felt about the man. He came here to attend an event at my bookstore. His body was found in front of my house. It's only a matter of hours before I stop being a person of interest and start being something else."

"Will Sawyer's friend—Lorna—tell you how St. James died?"

"We'll see," Olivia said, pulling into a parking space in front of a coffee shop called Bayside Beans. "Lorna has a weakness for mocha frappes. I ordered the biggest size they make and asked the barista to run it out to my car. Ah, here she comes now."

Olivia put down her window, and a young woman handed her a large plastic cup. "Extra chocolate drizzle and extra whipped cream. Thanks for the tip. I didn't think I'd have enough money to hit the club tonight, but I do now."

The woman waved and jogged back inside. Olivia shoved the mocha frappe into a cup holder and tucked the straw behind her ear.

"Sounds like you gave her a generous tip," Jane said.

Olivia pulled out of the parking spot and sped toward the center of town. "Money can buy lots of things, except the thing I need most right now."

"Which is?"

Turning into the public parking lot behind the police station, Olivia's gaze lingered on the space reserved for the current chief. As grief darkened her eyes, she let out a defeated sigh and said, "An alibi."

Chapter 7

Officer Lorna Locklear was waiting for them in the lobby. She stood directly below the brass state seal affixed to the wall with her thumbs hooked in her utility belt. She smiled when she saw Olivia, but the smile didn't reach her dark eyes.

"Thanks for driving her over," she said to Olivia before offering her hand to Jane. "Lorna Locklear. My partner and I have a few questions for you. It shouldn't take too long."

"But first, coffee." Olivia held out the mocha frappe.

Officer Locklear put her hand to her heart. "My prayers to my ancestors have been answered. Are you going to hang around?"

Olivia jerked her thumb at the door. "I'm going to run home and get Haviland, but I'll be back."

The officer smoothed her dark hair, which was gathered into a fist-sized bun at the back of her head, and gestured for Jane to follow her down a hall to an interview room.

A burly, thick-necked male in his thirties was already seated in the small room. He lumbered to his feet and introduced himself as Officer Art Henniger.

Jane had been involved with enough murder investigations to know how the interview was likely to go and was unsurprised by most of the questions. After covering the basics, the officers had her review the moments leading up to her discovery of Justin St. James's body.

After hearing the story twice, Officer Locklear said, "Let me clarify something. You said you only caught a glimpse of Mr. St. James's face when you first saw him, but you were confident the body was his. What made you so sure?"

"I had time to see his clothes, how his body was positioned, and the side of his face before I heard Edwin shouting. From that moment, my attention was entirely on Edwin. He couldn't breathe, and I was scared I might lose him, but that didn't keep me from recognizing Justin St. James."

Jane's voice wobbled, and Officer Henniger slid a tissue box across the table. Jane gave him a grateful look but kept talking. "It wasn't until I was in the ambulance heading to the hospital that I thought about the body in the sand. Like I said earlier, I've seen quite a few dead bodies, and I have experience cooperating with local law enforcement. I guess I started visualizing the scene as if I were back home and had to describe it to Sheriff Evans. I didn't notice any injuries, and the profile I saw looked like Justin St. James. His face was pretty fresh in my mind because I'd just met him the day before."

"And your impression of him after that meeting was what?"

"Based on the way he was speaking to Heather

O'Grady, unfavorable." After repeating the short exchange she'd overheard between the two writers, Jane told the officers about Edwin's conversation with St. James regarding the skull and the message on the mirror.

The officers listened attentively as she described the scene in the hotel bathroom. Locklear jotted down notes while Henniger made Jane rehash the details several times.

"Let's go back to the bookstore now," Officer Locklear said when it became obvious that Jane couldn't elucidate any further. "Had you met Heather O'Grady or Winston Hall prior to the Triple Thrills event?"

"No. I'd heard of them, but I haven't read any of their books. Yet."

"What about Mr. St. James's books?"

Jane pictured the table of St. James titles in the bookstore. His body of work was hardly extensive, but his books were everywhere. They were on every online shopping site and could be found in bookstores, grocery stores, and discount warehouses across the country.

She said, "I read *Burn Down the House* when it first came out. I don't remember much about it because that was years ago now."

Henniger leaned back in his chair, adopting an open and relaxed posture. "Are you familiar with the plot of *By the Dark Water*?"

Jane wasn't fooled by Henniger's body language. He was after something, and she had no choice but to give it to him. "On Friday night, at the Boot Top, Olivia told me that its plot was similar to the murder investigation that eventually concluded with her husband's death. She said St. James set the book in South Carolina, but anyone from Oyster Bay could easily recognize certain landmarks and characters."

"During this conversation, did Ms. Limoges say how she felt about Justin St. James?"

Jane's gaze slid from Henniger's face to Locklear's. Her head was bent as she wrote something in a pocket-size notebook.

"Ms. Steward?" Henniger prompted.

There was no avoiding it. Jane was being asked a direct question. As much as she wanted to protect Olivia, she couldn't lie. The words rose in her throat like bile. "She said she hated him."

Henniger leaned forward, his body as tense as a cat preparing to spring. She saw a hint of triumph in his eyes as he said, "Did she say why?"

"Because of the way St. James portrayed her husband."

"Did she say anything else?"

An open-ended question was dangerous. If Jane repeated everything Olivia had said, her friend would probably become the prime suspect, so she focused on St. James's book.

"It hurt her very deeply to read St. James's version of her husband. It was written as fiction and the story had been changed just enough to prevent a defamation suit, but Olivia recognized the man she loved in St. James's corrupt cop. She recognized herself and her town in other scenes, and there's nothing she can do about it. The book is out there for all the world to read. She's angry about that."

A smile played on Henniger's lips. "I bet."

Jane spoke before he could ask another question. "She was very open about her feelings toward St. James.

And she was genuinely surprised when I told her I'd found a body. She had no idea why St. James was on her beach. I'm one hundred percent certain of that."

"Did Ms. Limoges say anything to you later? About Mr. St. James?" asked Locklear.

Jane had already lied by omission. She hadn't told the cops that Olivia had expressed a desire to bury St. James in the sand. Nor had she mentioned that she'd offered to help dig. How would it look if she brought up the Storyton Hall key chain?

It wouldn't look good. You're not talking to Sheriff Evans. You're a stranger in this town, so be careful.

"Later, when we spoke on the phone, Olivia told me that the dead man was Justin St. James, and that she didn't know how he ended up on her beach."

"That's all?" Henninger's brows climbed his forehead.

"That's all. I was still at the hospital and didn't have much time to talk."

The officers exchanged a glance and, after coming to a silent agreement, Officer Locklear terminated the interview. Then she slid a card across the table. "If you think of anything else, please call me. All of my numbers are on there—work, home, and mobile. You've seen how a murder investigation plays out, so you probably know that solving a murder is all about details. If a detail comes to you later, no matter how small, we'd like to hear about it. Okay?"

"What about your fiancé? Would he have anything to add?" asked Officer Henniger.

"He was too busy stepping on stingrays and going into anaphylactic shock to know a thing about St. James's body. I didn't tell him about it until later. But if you want to talk to him about our dinner at the Boot Top, you can call him at the hospital. He's in room two-twelve."

"I'll walk her out," Locklear told her partner.

Jane waited until Henniger was out of earshot before saying, "Olivia didn't murder Justin St. James."

Locklear dipped her head in a semblance of a nod, which didn't reassure Jane.

"There weren't any footprints around the body, so unless St. James fell from the sky like Icarus, someone dumped him on that beach," Jane said. "Olivia didn't do that. She didn't write that message on my mirror either. Someone took the fake skull from his car, put it in the shower, and wrote a message for him to see. Someone else was angry at Justin St. James."

Locklear paused before opening the door to the lobby. "When word gets out that he's dead, neither of us will be able to protect Olivia."

"She may have hated the man for slighting her husband in print, but she's too smart to commit murder on her own property, or to lead me right to his body. If St. James based all of his books on real stories of pain and loss, he must have dozens of potential enemies."

Jane suddenly remembered the comment she'd overheard in the bookstore. A woman had told her friend that one of St. James's books was allegedly based on Winston Hall's childhood. She shared the comment with Locklear, then added, "I'm not pointing fingers. I just thought you should know."

They returned to the lobby to find Olivia chatting with a female officer and her canine partner. Captain Haviland and the black German shepherd were taking turns sniffing each other. Their tails wagging like metronomes, the dogs touched noses. The sight made Jane homesick for the puppies and her sons.

Spotting Jane and Officer Locklear, Olivia broke off her conversation and walked over to them.

"It went that well, huh?" she said.

"I'm sorry—" Jane began.

Olivia didn't give her a chance to finish. "Don't be. Lorna already knows how I felt about St. James, so you weren't spilling any secrets." She looked at Locklear. "Henniger likes me for this, doesn't he?"

"He can like who he wants. I'm going to follow the evidence."

"The book page. Are you still going to let me see it?" When Officer Locklear didn't reply, Olivia pointed at Jane. "She's a bibliophile too. Like me, she was partially raised by a librarian, and at Storyton Hall, she's literally surrounded by books. Unlike me, Jane isn't under suspicion."

"Neither are the town librarians."

Jane didn't want to lose the opportunity to examine the book page, so she said, "I've helped our sheriff's department decode literary clues before. I'm here and willing to take a look."

"Okay," Locklear relented.

"I'll wait outside." Olivia told Haviland to heel and headed for the exit.

Officer Locklear led Jane to a room filled with cubicles. Half a dozen cops were talking on phones, reading files, or doing computer work.

Locklear's cubicle was an homage to her family and her tribe. Photos of dark-haired men and women in ceremonial dress lined the surface of her desk and were taped to her computer screen.

Seeing Jane's interest, the officer said, "I'm the unofficial photographer for the tribal council, and we've had a ton of events this year. Are you familiar with the Lumbee?"

Jane admitted she wasn't.

"Our ancestors came from the Algonquin, Sioux, and Iroquois nations. They were survivors who found their way to southeast North Carolina. Our ancestors were recognized by the government in 1885, but the Lumbee weren't recognized until 1956. Not that it mattered much. We're still fighting for the federal benefits we've been denied since there's been a government to deny us."

Officer Locklear tapped a decal that Jane guessed was a tribal seal before opening a desk drawer and removing a plastic evidence bag.

"If you need to take it out of the bag, you'll have to glove up first." Gazing at the evidence bag, Locklear added, "My ancestors didn't live in houses like the one in this drawing. Maybe yours did."

She put the bag on her desk and invited Jane to sit in her chair. Then she wheeled the chair from the next cubicle over and sat down.

"ME called. Looks like St. James's ticker gave out," Henniger called as he breezed into the room. His partner shot him a warning look, and he came over to where she was sitting and perched on the edge of the neighboring desk. "Still waiting on the tox screen. ME put a rush on it but says early next week is the best we can hope for. What's going on here?"

"Ms. Steward is a book person. Thought I'd see if this meant anything to her."

"Does it?" Henniger asked Jane.

As Jane examined the back of the page for the second time, she said, "First of all, I don't think this came from a contemporary book. The size of the paper and its thickness makes me think it's at least fifty years old. The language is very formal too. The engraving on this side appears to be of an English country house garden with a view of the folly."

"What's that?"

"A decorative building used in gardens. Big, lush gardens that require a team of gardeners. The kind with hedge mazes and gravel paths and acres of green lawn. A folly was an architectural flex. Basically, it was a very expensive decoration. See how this one looks like an antique birdcage? It's facing a lake. To the right, you can see a path lined with hedges. This folly probably existed on an English estate that may or may not exist anymore. Do you have a magnifying glass?"

Officer Locklear pointed at her top drawer. "Should be in there."

Jane opened the drawer and smiled at the rainbow of Sharpie markers inside.

"I have a bit of a Sharpie addiction," Locklear said sheepishly.

"Me too."

Jane grabbed the magnifying glass, turned over the page, and smoothed the wrinkles from the plastic evidence bag. She reread the paragraph on the page, which described the furniture and ornaments in the Tudor era drawing room in what Jane assumed was an English manor house.

The engraving, which was smaller than that of the folly, was of a fireplace. Judging by its scale, it was one of those massive stone fireplaces in which a person could stand upright. Tapestries covered the walls on either side and a coat of arms hung directly above the mantel.

Though Jane wasn't familiar with heraldry, Butterworth was an expert. She shared this fact with Officer Locklear.

"If we find out which family owned the house, we can identify it and, possibly, the name of the book."

"Can he get us an answer fast?"

Jane took out her phone. "He'll start looking right away. Can I send him some photos? A scan would be even better."

Officer Henniger glanced from his phone screen to his partner. "Heather O'Grady is here. I'll get her settled in."

"I'll be quick," Locklear promised as she pulled on a pair of nitrile gloves.

Minutes later, images of the mysterious book page flew through cyberspace to Butterworth's inbox.

Locklear pulled off her gloves. "You have my number. Please call as soon as you hear something. If I don't answer, leave a message or a text."

Jane nodded. "I can show myself out."

Eager to touch base with Edwin and to show Olivia the book page images, Jane hurried out of the station.

She spotted Olivia sitting on a bench in the small park across the street. Winston Hall sat next to her, and the pair were too engrossed in conversation to notice Jane. Captain Haviland, however, let out a series of short barks, as if trying to say, *I see you! I see you!*

The moment Olivia looked away from Winston, their connection was severed. Winston threw Jane a guarded glance and stood up. He gave Olivia a cursory wave before walking deeper into the park. In the time it took Jane to cross the street, he'd disappeared behind a bronze statue of a man and a child holding fishing poles.

"Making friends?" she asked Olivia.

"Everywhere I go." Olivia raked a hand through her short hair. "This day has been two weeks long and I'm ready for a drink. Care to join me?"

Jane was torn. She wanted to talk about St. James with both Edwin and Olivia, but Edwin was forty-five minutes away.

As if reading her mind, Olivia said, "You want to see Edwin. Of course. I'll drive you back to the inn."

However, Edwin had other plans.

"We need to talk this through together," he told Jane over the phone. "You and Olivia should absolutely have cocktails. Maybe you could sit in the little garden outside our room? I rented a laptop—that's a thing in this hospital—so we can Skype. I don't want you driving all the way here only to drive back a few hours later. You must be exhausted, and even though I had a nap, I'm pretty tired too."

Though Jane didn't believe him for a second, she played along. He was right about one thing: She *was* exhausted. When she'd rolled out of bed that morning, she'd been expecting a restful Saturday. Instead, the hand she was dealt included a medical emergency, a corpse, and a murder investigation.

"Let's get those drinks," Jane said as Olivia turned onto the road for the Admiral's Inn.

The brunette Jane had seen that morning wasn't tending bar. In her place was a man with taupe brown skin and bleached dreadlocks. He was moving around too quickly for Jane to read his name tag, but after pouring liquid into a martini glass and serving it to a woman at the end of the bar, he turned to greet his next customers.

Seeing Olivia, his face broke into a brilliant smile. "Look what the cat dragged in."

"More like the poodle. Haviland's guarding the front porch. Reggie, this is my friend, Jane. She and I are in great need of libations."

Reggie spread his hands. "You've come to the right place. Look over the menu while I get a water bowl for the Captain."

There were six craft cocktails on the menu, and they all sounded good to Jane. When Reggie returned, she ordered a lemon drop martini.

Olivia said, "I'll have my usual. Better make it a double." She pushed a folded bill into the tip jar. "Do you have an extra tray? We need to have a private conversation and would like to take our drinks to the garden behind the Book Lover's Loft."

Reggie removed a bottle of Chivas Regal from under the bar. "No problem. I'll have these brought to you as soon as they're done. I'll see if I can rustle up some snacks too."

"Do you know everyone in Oyster Bay?" Jane asked on the way back to her cottage.

"I know lots of people, but I only like a few."

Jane grabbed her laptop, and the two women settled at the café table in the garden.

After connecting with Edwin via video chat, Jane filled him in on her visit to the police station.

"They were interviewing Heather O'Grady when I left."

"I had a chance to speak with both writers," Olivia told Edwin. "Their stories are much like mine. They both lost loved ones to violent crime. The crimes were publicized in their small-town papers, but St. James somehow discovered them. Though he fictionalized the accounts, both writers recognized their families, acquaintances, and hometowns. Like me, they couldn't take legal action. They hated Justin St. James as much as I did."

Edwin frowned. "Why did they agree to participate in the Triple Thrills event?"

"Because I was going to let them confront him in a public forum."

"What?"

Olivia lifted one shoulder in a shrug. "I wanted people to see the real St. James. I wanted his readers to know that he's built a successful career on the backs of other people's tragedies. I didn't arrange for him to come to Oyster Bay. The store manager, who isn't from this area, did that. But I'm the one who decided to invite Heather and Winston."

"Do the police know this?" Jane asked.

"Lorna is a friend, and I've told her everything. I also know how bad this looks for me. I hated St. James. I let him come to my bookstore in hopes of publicly shaming him. His corpse was found behind my house. If we don't find the killer, Lorna will have to tear my life apart just to prove my innocence."

Jane heard a noise to her left and glanced over to see a staff member approaching with their cocktails. After serving their drinks, he placed a platter of cheese, crackers, dried fruit, and olives on the table.

"Here's to a less eventful Sunday," Jane said, raising her glass in a toast.

Edwin waited until the women had a chance to sip their drinks before firing another question at Olivia. "Do you suspect Heather or Winston of killing St. James?"

"I don't know what to think. Whoever dumped him on my beach came by boat. Otherwise, there'd be tire tracks in the sand. It's easy to erase footprints from the waterline to the dunes. A rake or a broom is all you'd need. The water and wind would handle the rest."

Jane pictured St. James's body. He'd been dropped in a place where the ocean couldn't reach him, but where he was likely to be found by a woman who took daily walks with her dog.

"What were you and Winston talking about in the park?"

Olivia said, "Alibis. Neither of us has one. And before you ask, Heather does. She and her boyfriend are staying at a rental condo that has security cameras. All of their comings and goings have been recorded. Last night, they had dinner at a seafood restaurant called The Wharf and returned to the condo around nine thirty. This morning, they were seen jogging in the park. After their run, they had breakfast at Grumpy's Diner. Then they went back to the condo until it was time to head out to the bookstore."

"Assuming the cops can access the camera footage and the condo doesn't have another exit that isn't monitored, it sounds like Heather's in the clear," Edwin said.

"I'm not, because no one saw me between the time I left the Boot Top and when you two showed up at my house this morning," Olivia said. "Winston's in the same boat. He had dinner out last night and then went back to his hotel room and watched a movie. This morning, he took his laptop to the coffee shop and worked on his next book."

Jane sipped her martini and gazed out at the harbor. "If either Heather or Winston had been guests at Storyton Hall, Sinclair would've told me by now. I don't see how they could've dropped a key chain by the body."

"I didn't swipe a room key. You have my word on that," Olivia said.

Edwin held up a finger. "Ladies, I need to call you back. The doctor's here."

He ended the video chat, and the two women focused on the plate of food. Jane had just popped the last olive into her mouth when the staff member who'd delivered their cocktails reappeared.

"Reggie figured you'd be ready for your next round right about now. These drinks are pretty strong, so he sent along some more substantial food. I've got a hummus and veggie plate, jerk chicken skewers, and fish taco bites for you. Enjoy."

As soon as the man left, Jane dipped a carrot in hummus and said, "Reggie is my kind of friend."

Olivia laughed. "He used to be a barback at the Boot Top, but he'd rather be behind a stove than a bar. When he told me that he really wanted to be a chef, Michel and I decided to help him realize that dream. He's taking culinary classes at ECU now but still grabs the extra bartending shift when he can."

Jane didn't have to ask Olivia if she'd loaned Reggie the money for school. She already knew the answer.

The food was delicious, and the women ate and drank as the sky turned dusky and the calm harbor water began to look like spilled ink. All around them, lights winked on. Jane stared at a pinprick of light at the end of a dock across the harbor and was reminded of *The Great Gatsby*. She thought about how F. Scott Fitzgerald had used that tiny green light to symbolize yearning. Jane wondered what he'd been yearning for when he wrote the novel. Had he been thinking of his wife? His critics? Had he craved money or fame? Or all of those things?

What motivated Justin St. James? Did he get a voyeuristi
pleasure from turning real-life tragedies into sensationalist fic
tion? And how did he choose which stories to tell?

She shared this last thought with Olivia.

"I've been wondering about that too, but not as
much as Winston. He's read St. James's body of work
multiple times, annotating as he went. All the books
have a common theme. St. James modeled his main
characters after real heroes—men and women who met
a tragic end. In his version, the heroes are parodies of
the people they were based on. They're all corrupt,
damaged, or flat-out foppish."

"He used stories from your lives, and three of you are
writers."

Olivia nodded. "Winston says the first book, *Burn
Down the House*, is based on something that happened to
romance writer Angel Sanchez. I don't know the de
tails, but Angel took her own life not long after the
book was released."

Jane's stomach lurched. "You're telling me that her
family *still* couldn't sue for libel? After *that*?"

"Angel was the only survivor of a fire that killed her
two children. Her teenage daughter dragged her out of
the burning house and then went back in to get her lit
tle sister. Neither girl survived."

Jane balled her hands into fists. Rage surged through
her like an electric charge, and she whispered, "I'm
glad he's dead. That man turned other people's pain
into a career."

Reaching down to stroke Haviland's head, Olivia
said, "And that career is all he had. He never had some
one who'd run into a burning house or jump in front of
a bullet to save him. Angel, Heather, Winston, and I
had a family. We didn't get to keep them as long as we

would've liked to, but we loved them, and they loved us. Nothing St. James wrote can change that."

Jane stared at Olivia in open admiration before turning to look at the harbor again. "If it weren't for that stupid key chain, we could forget all about the bastard."

A chime surged from Jane's laptop, and she quickly hit a button. Edwin's face appeared on the screen, and as Jane took in his grim expression, she felt a prickle of dread.

"Are you okay?" she asked.

"What? Oh, yeah, I'm fine. I can go home in the morning. But I'll call an Uber. You have more important things to do."

Jane was confused. "Like what?"

"Search the Book Lover's Loft for a book called *Manor Houses and Halls of England.*"

Olivia leaned closer to the laptop. "The page found in St. James's pocket?"

"Yep. Sinclair just sent a text. The page is from that book. An old, rare, impossible-to-find book."

After glancing over at the cottage, Jane looked a question at Olivia. The other woman smiled and said, "You don't even have to ask."

Chapter 8

Jane and Olivia searched every inch of the cottage but came up empty. The books were all standing shoulder to shoulder on the shelves. They didn't lean to the side like wind-snapped trees, nor were their covers warped from being pressed too tightly against other books. They were comfortably snug, with only one shelf offering extra room.

This had been the shelf where Jane had found one of her beach reads. She remembered how the books had slumped sideways after she'd removed the Mary Stewart novel, and how it seemed like someone had failed to return a borrowed book to that shelf.

"If that book was here, it's gone now," she told Olivia.

Olivia put her hands on her hips and scowled at the shelves. "According to Lorna, there were no books in St. James's hotel room either. When I get home, I'll see if any libraries in the area have a copy. I doubt they do, but you never know."

The two women decided they were too tired to think straight and agreed to touch base in the morning.

As Jane brushed her teeth with one hand, she used the other to jot down random thoughts and questions. She wanted to talk to Edwin once more before calling it a night, but her gaze kept returning to what she'd written on the notepad stamped with the inn's logo.

How did St. James die?

Why was the book page in his pocket?

Does his next book have something to do with a country house?

~~*What's it about?*~~ *Who is it about?*

Did he bring a laptop to Oyster Bay?

Where's his phone?

Did the killer write on our mirror? If so, how did they get inside the room?

Did St. James have company during his stay?

Other vices? Drug use? Alcoholism? Strange proclivities?

Jane remembered how Reggie had known what to serve Olivia without asking. Bartenders were observant people. As were servers, housekeepers, and front desk clerks. Someone at the Admiral's Inn probably knew how St. James took his coffee, or that he read the newspaper or looked at his phone while eating breakfast. The staff would know if he was untidy, had good manners, went for a run every morning, or smoked a pack a day. The contents of his trash would reveal receipts from area shops, restaurants, and bars. If they wanted to, the staff could learn what kind of gas he put in his car, what brand of gum he chewed, and what medications he took. They'd know if he slept alone or entertained a guest in his room.

If St. James had died at Storyton Hall, Jane's employees would've told her everything they knew about the dead man. In very little time, she'd have a clear picture of his personality and habits. Using the security cameras, Sterling would track his movements and Butterworth would analyze his facial expressions and body language. Sinclair would examine his social media profiles and make a list of next of kin.

Though Francis Belvedere didn't have former CIA or British intelligence agents working for him, he seemed like the kind of man who'd gather information before the authorities asked for it. He struck Jane as being a fellow rule follower.

How will I get him to tell me what he told the police?

The Admiral's Inn was a high-class establishment run by a man who placed great value on discretion. Jane instinctively knew Francis wouldn't gossip about a guest, even a dead one, and she didn't dare alienate him by fishing for information.

He and Olivia are friends, she thought.

Would Francis tell Olivia what he'd already told the police? Jane had a feeling Olivia Limoges was a hard person to say no to. If she asked Francis for his help, would he acquiesce?

There's only one way to find out.

After sharing her thoughts with Olivia by text, Jane called home to say hello to Fitz and Hem. The boys were having a movie night with Eloise and Landon, and Jane could tell they were distracted.

Fitz put her on speaker so she could talk to him and his brother at the same time, and over a crescendo of dramatic music in the background, he said, "We're watching *The Two Towers*. Gandalf is about to fight the Balrog."

"Eloise made white cheddar cheese popcorn and it's *so* good!" Hem exclaimed.

There was yelling in the background, and Jane asked the boys to pause the movie until they were done talking. When it was quiet, she asked, "Did you have a good day?"

"Yeah. We looked around for stuff for our Halloween costumes, but we still need a few things," said Hem.

Fitz grunted in agreement. "Aunt Octavia's going to help us so we'll be ready for the party. And we're going fishing with Uncle Aloysius tomorrow."

"After church," Hem muttered.

"Right. If we're late, Aunt Octavia is going to make us clean Muffet Cat's litter box *and* polish her silver."

Jane smiled to herself. Aunt Octavia liked to sit in the first pew near the choir and became extremely irritable when she had to wait for the rest of her family to assemble in the lobby so they could all drive to church together.

This was the only time she was ever cross with the twins. She'd rap her cane on the carpet, her face set in a fierce glower, and order them around with the irrefutable authority of a school principal or five-star general. The boys would jump to obey while Uncle Aloysius hid a smile behind his hand.

After reminding Fitz and Hem to set their alarms and to behave at youth group, Jane let her sons return to their movie.

"You need to try this popcorn when you get back, Mom," said Fitz.

Hem said, "We'll make you some."

In unison, the boys shouted "Bye!" and ended the call.

Their conversation had been brief, but just hearing her sons' voices had made Jane feel better. She could imagine them lying on their bellies with their heads propped on their hands, shoveling popcorn into their mouths as fast as possible. Merry and Pippin would be sitting close by, waiting to launch themselves on any stray kernels. The puppies would bark whenever the twins shouted out their favorite lines of dialogue, causing Eloise to laugh.

Jane grinned at the thought. She then turned off the bedside lamp, rolled onto her side, and called Edwin.

"Any news?" he asked.

"Nothing good. We didn't find the book."

Sounding as tired as Jane felt, Edwin said, "Tomorrow's a new day. We'll figure this out, love, because we'll be together tomorrow. We can do anything as long as we're together."

"If you close your eyes, you can pretend you're here right now. I left the curtains open, and I can see the moon shining on the water. I have the door cracked so I can smell the ocean. I wonder where your stingray buddies are at this moment."

Edwin snorted. "They're probably at their local hot spot, telling their friends how they defeated the pale-skinned monster who tried to attack them. My doctor told me that a group of stingrays is called a fever, and that their barbs are like our fingernails. They don't have any nerves and will eventually grow back. Remind me to wear scuba fins the next time we go to the beach. Okay?"

"Or a suit of armor. We have several in the attic."

"Maybe I'll swim in golf shoes from now on. Did you lock the front door?"

Pulling the comforter over her shoulder, Jane murmured, "Yep. I even moved the starfish to the nightstand. If anyone breaks in, I'll use it like a throwing star."

"If I thought you were in danger, I wouldn't stay here. But I honestly think Olivia dropped the key chain. It probably happened months ago, and she didn't even realize she lost it. It's the most logical explanation. St. James's death has nothing to do with you or your family. Storyton Hall is hundreds of miles away and all is well there. Now get some rest, and know that I'll be dreaming of you tonight."

"I love you," Jane whispered.

She put the phone on the nightstand and gazed out the window. Moonlight spilled over the water like milk, illuminating the boats in its path. The boats, untouched by its light, were nothing but dark smudges—a mass of shadows affixed to a black canvas.

Jane didn't believe that Olivia had dropped that key chain on the beach. Neither did Edwin. He'd said that to put her mind at ease, but it hadn't worked.

Justin St. James was connected to Olivia. Olivia and Jane met and became friends at Storyton Hall. St. James was dead. His body had been left on Olivia's beach. A Storyton Hall key chain was in the sand near his body. Storyton Hall was Jane's ancestral home. There were too many coincidences. Somehow, Olivia was connected to St. James's murder. And so was Jane.

This thought kept her from falling asleep. She tossed and turned. She kicked off her covers and pulled them back on again. She felt stuffy, so she opened the sliding glass door a few more inches and got back into bed.

As the ocean air wafted into the room, Jane burrowed deeper under the covers. She pulled the sheet up to her chin and tried to hide from the feeling that the murder of Justin St. James was not the conclusion of a chilling story but its beginning.

A high-pitched cry startled her awake. Jane slit her eyes and looked at the clock. It was six thirty-seven.

Reasoning that the noise had come from an animal, she closed her eyes again. Two breaths later, she heard muted voices followed by a whimper. The sounds flowed in through the crack in the sliding glass door.

Someone was in the garden. The cottage's *private* garden.

Jane had raised two children. She'd had two puppies living in her house for months. She knew the sound of a living creature in distress.

Adrenaline obliterated all vestiges of sleep from her body. She shot out of bed, donned the sweatshirt she'd left draped over the back of a chair, and quietly slid open the back door.

The sky was the color of dishwater and the flagstones under her bare feet were cold and slick with damp. The air was crisp, and Jane hugged herself as she hurried to the café table where she and Olivia had sat the night before.

Walking past the table, she scanned the flower beds for signs of disturbance. And as she moved deeper into the little garden, she saw a shape lying in the shadow of a dwarf palmetto.

A human-size shape.

An involuntary "Oh!" burst from Jane's mouth as she ran toward the person. When she was close enough, she saw that it was a young woman. Her lips were parted, and she stared up at the dull sky as if in awe.

"Oh no," Jane whispered as she pressed her fingers against the woman's neck in search of a pulse. Though the skin was warm, she couldn't feel the tell-tale thrum of life.

Jane leaned over until a curtain of her strawberry-blond hair dangled in front of the woman's nose. There was no breath to stir her strands.

But she's still warm.

Jane ran back to her room and grabbed her phone. She called 911 as she dropped to her knees next to the woman and began CPR. In between compressions, she shouted at the emergency operator to send an ambulance. When it was time to breathe into the woman's mouth, Jane pulled down on her bottom lip and noticed her swollen tongue. Ignoring the feeling that she was far too late to do any good, Jane blew air into the woman's mouth. She then resumed her chest compressions.

The emergency operator kept asking questions, but Jane didn't need a medical degree to know that her life-saving efforts weren't going to keep this woman alive.

Even as she continued the CPR, the woman's skin was growing cooler. Her eyes were flat. Her limbs were heavy and still. There was no moisture on her lips. Death was already drying her out—making her a husk of what she once was.

Hearing a noise from somewhere behind her, she risked a glance before filling the woman's lungs with her next rescue breath.

She saw Francis hurrying toward her.

"Oh, no. *No, no, no, no,*" he jabbered, falling to a catcher's squat next to the body. He took hold of Jane's arm and whispered, "You can stop now. She's gone."

Jane sagged in defeat. She knew the CPR was fruitless, but performing the movements had kept the terrible truth from sinking in.

The emergency operator asked what was happening. Francis scooped up the phone and said, "Francis Belvedere here. I'm the manager of the Admiral Inn. It's too late for rescue attempts. Please tell the ambulance driver not to use their lights or siren. I don't want to alarm our guests."

He hung up and passed the phone to Jane.

"Do you know her?" Jane asked.

Starting down at the woman, Francis nodded. "She's an employee." He was quiet for a full minute before adding, "Thank you for trying to help."

"I wish I'd come out sooner. I was sleeping. Until a noise woke me. I wasn't sure if it was animal or human, so I didn't get up right away. Then I heard whimpering. It sounded like something, or someone, was in pain."

Francis held out his hand and helped Jane to her feet. "You're cold. You should go back inside and warm up. I'll have someone bring you coffee. I need to tell my staff that we've had an incident, and it would be best if I handled it from here."

Jane looked down at the dead woman. Her black pants and royal-blue polo shirt embroidered with the inn's logo were rumpled but clean. A navy handbag and floral lunch tote lay in the grass near her right hand. Her auburn hair was secured in a ponytail. She wore makeup.

You look like you just keeled over on your way to work. Why were you in this garden? Jane silently questioned the dead woman.

She couldn't tell why she was here, but she knew this woman's death had not been instantaneous. The pitiful whimper she'd heard said otherwise.

Francis doesn't think she died of natural causes. Otherwise, he'd call it an accident, not an incident.

When a guest died at Storyton Hall, the staff referred to that person as a Rip van Winkle. Most hotels had a code word for a dead guest. With so many people coming and going on a daily basis, death was a part of the hospitality business. Guests had heart attacks and strokes. They overdosed on drugs or fell in the shower. Once, a guest choked on a large forkful of steak. Because they'd ordered room service, there'd been no one around to perform the Heimlich maneuver.

Most of their deaths were accidental. Some were not.

The young woman in the garden was young and fit. Like Justin St. James, she appeared to have collapsed in an unusual place.

But very close to me, Jane thought with a shiver.

"What's her name?" she asked Francis.

"Rachel Wilcox. She was scheduled to work this morning. On weekends, she put out the coffee and pastries in the lounge, but she also worked behind the desk, booking tours or excursions for our guests, and assisted with wedding planning."

Jane glanced around the garden. None of the plants looked crushed or broken. She saw no shoeprints in the damp grass.

"Do you have security cameras here?"

"We have some attached to the exterior of the main building, but none around the guest cottages or parking areas."

Francis sounded so dejected that Jane put a hand on his arm and said, "I've been in your shoes more times than I'd care to mention, which is why I know how hard this is. I'm sure you feel responsible for your staff as well as your guests, but this isn't your fault."

After casting another look at the dead woman, Francis led Jane to the patio and whispered, "I wasn't very nice to Rachel the last time I saw her. She was one of the most frustrating employees I've ever had. That girl spent money like a Kardashian and was always asking for extra shifts, but she barely worked when she was here. She'd show up late, or not at all. I had to write her up for missing a shift again last week. One more strike and I would've let her go."

"Did she have any health problems?"

"She spent her breaks vaping in her car, but other than a lack of sleep and too much partying, I don't think so. She was only twenty-four. Twenty-four," he repeated sadly. "Her whole life was in front of her."

Francis's phone buzzed, and he told Jane that the ambulance was a minute away.

"I'm going to shower and change, and then I'll meet you at the front desk. We'll get through this together."

Twenty minutes later, Jane emerged from the Book Lover's Loft wearing a long, floral dress. Her hair was in a loose chignon, and she'd put on a little makeup. Ignoring the voices in the garden, she hurried to the main building to find an ambulance parked out front.

Inside, Francis was pacing back and forth behind the reception desk, whispering urgently into his phone. When he saw Jane, he ended his call and said, "The police are coming."

"You're going to need lots of coffee—enough for the guests and the police. They'll want to speak to you, me, and the other staff members, so you'll need a private space. Do you have a conference room?"

"No, but the library will do. There's a big table we use for jigsaw puzzles. Mrs. Bingham spends every happy hour working on the puzzle, and she'll be *so* disappointed if we have to put it away."

To someone in a different line of work, it might have seemed odd that Francis was fretting over a puzzle when an employee's corpse was lying in a guest cottage garden, but Jane understood her fellow manager's desire to maintain control over his domain. Rachel's death had thrown his world off balance, and the only way he could keep his equilibrium was to hold fast to order and routine.

"I'm sure the puzzle can stay where it is. You'll need a pitcher of water and glasses for the library, and perhaps another basket of breakfast pastries. If you want to get those things organized, I'll stay here and handle any concerns or questions from the guests."

"Thank you, Ms. Steward, and forgive me for being so flustered. We lost a guest to heart failure two years ago, but that's the only time during my tenure as manager that I've had to call an ambulance."

Jane felt a stab of jealousy, but as this was not the time to reflect on her own trials and tribulations, she relayed a to-do list, ticking things off her fingers as she spoke. "Encourage the guests to go about their day. Kindly and calmly ask the staff to do the same. Keep everyone well-fed and hydrated. Don't tell the guests or staff members more than they need to know. This is your ship. You know how to steer it."

"That's right. Today, *I'm* the admiral."

Squaring his shoulders, Francis smoothed his tie and marched into the lounge. Not two minutes after he left, an elderly man approached the front desk and said, "What's that meat wagon doing here?"

"There's no cause for alarm, sir. An employee required an ambulance and is being taken care of. There's fresh coffee in the lounge."

For the next thirty minutes, Jane answered various forms of the same question. She hoped to satisfy the guests' curiosity before the police entered the inn, because once they arrived, there'd be another round of questions.

During a lull in the action, Jane took out her cell phone to text Edwin and saw he'd sent her a message ten minutes earlier.

I just got discharged and am on my way to you. Save me a coffee. XO E.

Because another guest was heading her way, Jane didn't have time to let Edwin know the reason for the police presence. Instead, she sent a quick message telling him to meet her at the front desk. Then she sent a second text, asking if the hospital had sent him home with a wheelchair.

I rented one. Will pick it up on the way. I'd rather ride a horse but hope to be on crutches by the time we go home.

A wheelchair.

For just a moment, Jane thought of all the things she and Edwin had planned to do over the next few days and felt a stab of disappointment.

Be grateful he's coming back at all, her inner voice chided. *He could've died.*

Images of the two dead bodies she'd seen in the last twenty-four hours appeared in her mind, and a chill rippled up her spine. She'd seen worse, it was true. The deaths of Justin St. James and Rachel Wilcox were clean and tidy compared to some of those she'd encountered at Storyton. And yet there was something incredibly jarring about a corpse that still looked like a living person—a living person who'd suddenly dropped to the ground and died.

A man in jeans and a sweatshirt with the police department logo strode into the inn. He gazed around the lobby, and when his eyes landed on Jane, his shoulders stiffened. Officer Henniger made a beeline for the front desk.

"Ms. Steward. You seem to have a knack for finding bodies."

"I wish I didn't," she answered glumly.

Henniger leaned an elbow on the desk and studied her. "You weren't using a metal detector this time, so what were you doing out in the garden?"

Jane repeated the story she'd told Francis.

"Do you normally get out of bed to investigate strange sounds when you're on vacation?"

Bristling, Jane said, "This hasn't been a very restful vacation so far. My fiancé is in the hospital and I found a dead man on the beach yesterday, so when I heard a cry of pain or fear or what have you, I got up. There's no way I could've gone back to sleep, especially if someone was hurt."

Henniger tapped his index finger against Francis's brass nameplate. "I need to speak to the manager, but we'll also need a statement from you, so don't go anywhere."

"I won't. And you'll find Francis in the lounge."

Jane glared at Henniger's back as he walked away. She didn't like his abrasive demeanor, nor was she accustomed to being treated like a suspect by a member of law enforcement.

You're not in Storyton, and he's not Sheriff Evans. Why wouldn't he see you as a suspect? You're a stranger who discovered both bodies. Coincidence? Henniger doesn't think so.

Jane didn't think so either. Olivia had found a Storyton Hall key chain near St. James's body and now a young woman who worked at the Admiral Inn had died forty feet from where Jane was sleeping.

She realized she wanted Officer Henniger to be dogged. She wanted him to chase down every possible lead because she had no clue what was happening. She'd come to Oyster Bay to relax, but the violence she regularly experienced at home had followed her. At least, that's what it felt like to her.

Another guest approached the front desk, clutching at a string of pearls and waving her hand wildly toward the main door.

"I saw police cars and an ambulance. What's going on?"

Jane repeated what she'd told the rest of the guests, but this woman wasn't satisfied with her answers.

"If it was an accident, why are the cops here? Was there a fight? Did this staff person get stabbed or shot? I have a right to know!"

"The source of the staff member's injury is unclear, but I believe it's routine for the police to investigate incidents of this nature. No one is in danger."

When Jane suggested that the woman help herself to coffee and pastries in the lounge, the woman scoffed and said, "Forget the coffee. A mimosa will take the edge off."

As she shuffled toward the lounge, Jane looked for a staff member to make the woman's drink. She remembered the brunette she'd seen behind the bar yesterday. She'd been talking on the phone, and at the end of the conversation, she'd urged Rachel to come in for her shift. The one-sided dialogue had stuck in Jane's mind because the bartender had seemed pretty agitated. Recalling Rachel's youthful appearance, Jane assumed that the dead woman and the bartender were about the same age.

They must've been friends. I wonder if she knows something about Rachel that no one else does. Like a connection to Justin St. James?

Jane had to find the bartender. She might be crucial to the investigation. And if she knew anything about St. James's murder, she could be in grave danger.

Whoever killed Justin St. James hadn't left Oyster Bay. They'd stuck around, waiting for a chance to attack Rachel. Jane had no proof, but she felt the truth of it in her bones. She was also positive that the murderer still hadn't left town. They were somewhere close by, waiting and watching.

Far too close for Jane's comfort.

Chapter 9

The Admiral's Inn was humming with activity by the time Officer Locklear entered the lobby.

Francis, who'd just returned from the lounge with Officer Henniger, hurried over to Locklear and said, "I've allocated the library for your use. We've set up a coffee station, and you'll find Rachel's personnel file as well as a list of our current guests on the table. May I show you the way?"

As soon as the officers were out of sight, Jane abandoned her post at the front desk and moved through the lounge into the kitchen.

Unlike the kitchens at Storyton Hall, which buzzed with frenetic energy from dawn until late at night, this room was calm and quiet. There was no one chopping vegetables, blending sauces, or kneading dough. There was no hiss of oil in sauté pans or gasps of steam escaping from beneath the lids of pots. No one shouted for ingredients or for their coworkers to get out of the way.

Plates didn't clink as they were placed under warming lights or loaded into a dishwasher.

The kitchen in the Admiral's Inn was filled with a different kind of music: the heroic strains of Symphony No. 9 in E minor from Dvořák's New World Symphony. Jane wasn't a classical music buff, but this was one of Uncle Aloysius's favorite pieces. He played it in his study whenever he was feeling nostalgic, and for a moment, Jane could see him sitting at his desk, conducting an invisible orchestra with his pen.

A man hummed along to the music as he wiped crumbs from a countertop into his cupped palm. Behind him, next to the sink, was a cardboard box brimming with cut flowers. The mums, sunflowers, snapdragons, orange roses, and dark red dahlias made a lovely autumn tableau.

The man opened a cabinet above the counter and took out eight clear vases. As he lined them up on the counter, he caught sight of Jane and smiled.

"Good morning. May I help you?"

"I'm looking for the bartender who worked yesterday morning." Jane touched a strand of her strawberry-blond hair. "The brunette."

A veil lowered over the man's features. "Are you with the police?"

"No, no. I manage a hotel in Virginia, so I know how crazy things get when there's an incident like this. I offered to lend Francis a hand until things calm down." Jane moved closer to the center island. "I'm sorry about what happened. With a staff this size, you must be a close-knit group."

The man seesawed his hand. "Those of us who've been here for years are tight, but there's no point get-

ting to know the people who come just for the high season. They're usually kids who leave after a few months.
They spend half the time on their phones and roll their
eyes behind your back whenever they're told to do their
job. Is it the same at your hotel?"

Jane's cheeks flushed with pride. "We don't have
much turnover. I know it sounds like a cliché, but we're
like a family. We have our share of arguments, and people lose their tempers every now and then, but we're always there for one another when it matters most."

"Sounds like a special place." The man selected a
chrysanthemum stem and began to strip off its leaves.
"The bartender you're looking for is Sammi. She and
Rachel were our most recent hires, and they were
friendly. Since Sammi's probably pretty rattled right
now, I'd guess she walked down to the dock. That's
where most of us go when we need a minute to ourselves."

Jane thanked the man and returned to the lounge.
The coffee urns were still relatively full, and someone
had put out a fresh supply of pastries. The early risers
among the guests had either left the inn or would soon
be on their way, which meant the next wave might not
notice the police presence at all.

After a moment's indecision, Jane left a "Back in Five
Minutes" note at the front desk and hurried to the
other end of the lobby and out through the door leading to the back porch.

The dock behind the Admiral's Inn was wider and
longer than the docks belonging to its residential
neighbors. It jutted out into the water like a wooden
ruler, with measured sections marked off as individual
boat slips. Every slip was full, and Jane guessed the expensive yachts secured to the cleats were worth more

than Storyton Hall's entire fleet of vintage Rolls-Royce sedans.

At the end of the dock was a covered seating area, and as Jane walked toward it, she noticed a transparent ceiling over her head. The network of fishing line kept the surface free of bird droppings without disturbing the view. The lines were attached to steel poles capped with nautical pennants in primary colors, which snapped like rubber bands in the breeze.

There were several people in the seating area, including three brown-haired women, but only one of them wore an Admiral's Inn name tag.

Sammi sat on a bench facing the harbor, watching a tugboat pass by the buoys marking the harbor's entrance. She was dressed in another turtleneck and, again, she had the collar pulled up to her chin as she gazed out at the harbor. Her hair was in a bun, but the wind had tugged a few strands free, and these tickled her cheeks until she pushed them away. Her expression was unreadable.

At first glance, Sammi looked like another guest taking in the view. She sat very still, her eyes fixed on the glimmering water, and if not for her shifting, restless hands, Jane might have believed she was simply relaxing for a few minutes before resuming her shift.

"Hi," Jane said, moving into Sammi's line of view. "Mind if I join you?"

Sammi made to get up. "It's all yours. I need to get back to work."

Jane sat down and turned to Sammi. "To be honest, I came out here to find you. Francis is talking to the police, so I thought I'd see if you were okay. My name's Jane."

"You're a guest."

It was a statement, not a question. It was Sammi's way of drawing a line between them. The line between guest and employee. If Jane wanted Sammi to confide in her, she needed to cross that line, and quickly.

"I work at a hotel in western Virginia," she began. "We lost a guest to an act of violence a few months ago, so I know what you're going through. It probably feels impossible to focus on your job right now—to smile at guests and serve them coffee—when your mind is a million miles away."

"Yeah." Sammi squinted as she gazed upward. "I'll just have to go on autopilot for a while."

The morning sun highlighted the unlined skin on Sammi's face and set off the natural caramel highlights in her dark brown hair. Judging by what Francis had said, Rachel was irresponsible and somewhat flighty. Was Sammi like that as well?

"Were you and Rachel close?" Jane asked, searching Sammi's face for signs of grief. Judging by the way she pulled her turtleneck over the tip of her chin, she longed for comfort and escape.

"Not really," she said, her shoulders twitching in a ghost of a shrug. "We're about the same age, but that's all we had in common. Sometimes, I felt like her mom. Rach has a mom, but she never listened to her. *Somebody* needed to keep her from going off the rails. I tried, but she just—" Sammi closed her eyes and drew in a deep breath. When she opened her eyes again, she searched for the tugboat.

Jane didn't speak but silently waited for Sammi to continue.

"Rachel lived for the moment. She spent money she didn't have. Made promises she couldn't keep. Wanted to try everything that sounded cool or exciting, even if it was bad for her. I worried about her, but I didn't really want to get involved. People like that can suck you in, you know? That's why I wouldn't let her move in with me, or lend her any money—not that she ever stopped asking."

"I don't remember if I met Rachel on Friday. I got in around three."

"She came on at four. She was in a great mood too. She sang the whole time she helped me prep the bar for happy hour." Sammi smiled wistfully. "She does that whenever she meets a new guy—sings a Beatles song. Usually, it was 'If I Fell' or 'Love Me Do,' but on Friday, she sang 'Paperback Writer' over and over again until I told her to go away."

Jane's pulse quickened at this news. Was the song a sign that Rachel had been thinking about St. James?

Letting a few seconds elapse, she watched a sailboat round a buoy in the channel before casually asking, "Do you think she was seeing the writer staying in the Book Lover's Loft?"

"Justin St. James?" Sammi chewed her lip as she considered the question. "Maybe. He flirted with every woman he saw, and Rachel would've flirted right back. She had a thing for famous people. They didn't have to be big celebrities or anything—just more famous than her—so I could see her going for him. We're not supposed to get involved with the guests, but Rachel never paid attention to the rules."

Did Rachel write the message on the mirror?

"This is going to sound strange, but do you know how many staff members have access to the guest rooms? I'm trying to find out who was in the Book Lover's Loft between the time Justin St. James left in the morning and when we arrived in the afternoon."

Sammi frowned. "Why?"

"Because of what we found in the bathroom. I'm sure you heard about it."

Sammi nodded. "I have no idea who did that. The staff thinks it was a prank—someone who wanted to mess with Mr. St. James. That person probably snuck in when housekeeping was cleaning the bathroom and hid in a closet."

Jane had never considered that possibility. "Could that person have been Rachel?"

Sammi shot her a puzzled look. "Maybe. If it was, she didn't mention it to me. I didn't ask if she spent any time in Mr. St. James's room because I didn't want to know. She was already on thin ice with Francis, and I need this job, so I didn't want to get involved." Sammi glanced at her watch and said, "Speaking of work, I need to get back."

It was now or never. Jane had to ask Sammi about the phone conversation she'd overheard. "Just one more thing. I heard you on the phone yesterday, talking to Rachel. You seemed pretty stressed on her behalf. Were you worried that she might get fired for missing her shift or for some other reason?"

Sammi didn't answer. She got to her feet and moved away from Jane, clearly eager to escape.

Doing her best to sound contrite, Jane said, "I'm sorry. I know I'm out of line, but I was just wondering if she was in trouble. The police are bound to ask the same question."

"Yeah, but it's their job to do that," was Sammi's terse reply. "I'm going now."

As Sammi walked back to the inn, Jane lingered at the end of the dock. For a few brief moments, she felt detached from violence. Out here, the sunlight danced on the water and the endless expanse of blue sky covered her like an umbrella. Out here, she was just another guest watching boats bob gently in the current or sail off toward the golden horizon.

On the end of that dock, there was peace. There was no talk of death. There was no anxiety about the future. There was no police presence, no unanswered questions, no suspicion. Out on that wooden jetty, surrounded by blue, was an endless expanse of calm.

But Jane couldn't hide from what was happening inside the inn. Not only did she have to get back to help Francis but Edwin would be arriving soon.

When she returned to the front desk, she was immediately approached by two guests who needed directions to the maritime museum as well as a restaurant recommendation. Jane found a museum brochure in the rack behind the desk and told the guests to book a table at the Boot Top Bistro.

The woman was instantly taken with the idea. "That's the place with the famous chef. The one from that TV cooking show! Let's call right now."

After thanking Jane, the guests bustled off. Because they were both looking down at their phones, they nearly collided with a tall blonde and her black poodle.

"Sorry!" the guests murmured as they skirted around Olivia and Captain Haviland.

Olivia approached the desk and said, "I just ran into Lorna. She told me about Rachel Wilcox. I don't know what's happening, but it seems like you've been caught up in a bad orbit."

"It feels more like a black hole."

"Good thing the reinforcements have arrived."

At first, Jane thought Olivia was referring to herself and Haviland, but then she stepped aside to make room for someone in a wheelchair. Though the person's face was obscured by the giant teddy bear sitting in his lap, Jane saw the bandaged feet and cried, "Edwin!"

Jane raced around the desk and came to an abrupt halt. Butterworth stood behind Edwin's wheelchair. It was strange to see him out of uniform, though his casual attire—a blazer over an Oxford shirt, pants pressed with military precision, and polished loafers—suited him perfectly.

Before she could ask what Butterworth was doing at the inn, Edwin handed the bear off to him and opened his arms to Jane. After kissing him hello, she whispered, "Now that you're here, everything will be okay."

"Let's find a place where we can all talk."

Jane waved everyone into the lounge. "This is a good spot. The food's been put away, but there should be plenty of coffee."

In the lounge, Olivia selected a table and made room for Edwin's wheelchair. After telling Haviland to lie down, she looked at Butterworth and said, "Alistair? Would you like a cup of tea?"

Alistair?

Jane hadn't heard Butterworth's first name in years. She'd called him by his surname her whole life. The other staff members called him Mr. Butterworth and strangers addressed him as "sir."

A faint blush crept up Butterworth's neck as he replied, "Please."

"How did you get here?" Jane asked him.

"By air. After speaking with Olivia last night, I felt my presence was required. She booked me on the first flight out of Charlottesville."

Butterworth and Olivia locked gazes, and though they hadn't seen each other for months, it was obvious their relationship had grown deeper since Olivia's visit to Storyton Hall.

Jane poured coffee for Edwin, stirred in a little cream, and placed the mug in front of him. Looking at Butterworth, she whispered, "Did you get up at dawn and fly here because of that key chain?"

In an equally hushed tone, Butterworth replied, "That would've been reason enough, but it's not the only reason I came."

Troubled by his grave expression, Jane said, "Go on."

"Mr. Sinclair and I were determined to learn more about the family crest from the book page found on Mr. St. James's person, and after contacting sources in the States and the UK, we came upon the answer."

Hearing voices in the other room, he paused. When the sounds faded, he eyed the doorway for a long moment before continuing. "The crest in the engraving belonged to the Stuart, S-T-U-A-R-T, family. It was carved above the mantelpiece of Edgerton House in the Middle Ages. The spelling of the family name was changed to S-T-E-W-A-R-D after King George bestowed a noble rank upon a gentleman named Edgerton Stuart. I can see that you recognize the significance of the name."

Jane nodded. "Walter Edgerton Steward built Storyton Hall."

"Lord Walter Edgerton Steward, as it happens. And like many lords before him, he improved and enlarged his home by adding to an existing structure."

"Edgerton House."

Butterworth inclined his head.

Jane passed her hands over her face. "The key chain and the book page. I can think of only one reason St. James would've had those things."

"He was writing about your family," Edwin said through clenched teeth.

Olivia waved in the direction of the lobby. "I asked Lorna if the cops found a laptop among St. James's possessions. They did, but it's password protected. His phone is nowhere to be found, which means it's probably on the bottom of the ocean. We have no proof at this stage, but I agree with you, Edwin. St. James was either writing about the Stewards or researching the family for a future book."

The room suddenly felt too warm. Jane wanted to open all the windows and let the sea air rush inside. Better still, she wanted to crawl through a window and run back to the end of the dock—to a place that seemed untouched by mystery and upheaval.

"Was St. James killed because I'm here?" she wondered aloud. Meeting Olivia's stare, she added, "Or because the two of us are together? Is the killer trying to tell us something?"

Olivia said, "St. James's body was deposited on my beach. The key chain was left in the sand. I called Alistair because I believe a murderer has set their sights on us. For what reason? I wish I knew."

Edwin looked down at his bandaged feet in disgust and then turned to Olivia. "Is there any evidence he was brought to your beach by boat?"

"The canine unit came to my place early this morning. Haviland and I went down to the beach to watch Greta, their German shepherd. She followed the scent trail from the dunes to the waterline. St. James was brought to shore by boat. Someone dumped him, erased their tracks, and hopped back on the boat."

Jane pressed her fingertips to her temples. "I wish I

had a whiteboard. I want to write down everything we know and everything we need to know. Too much has happened in the last forty-eight hours. We don't understand why St. James was killed, or why anyone would want to hurt Rachel Wilcox. But she must be connected. Twenty-four-year-olds don't just drop dead in hotel gardens at six thirty in the morning. And I know something else too. I'm going to be on the suspect list."

"As will I," Oliva said matter-of-factly. "Our best bet is to cooperate with the police while running a parallel investigation. I have no intention of undermining their efforts, but as civilians, we might learn things they can't. People are more likely to talk to us." After a pause, she added, "I have a whiteboard at the bookstore. My office can serve as our war room."

The corners of Butterworth's mouth dipped down. "If the police will permit us to leave, we should all return to Storyton. That would be the wisest course of action."

"I'm not going anywhere. Not yet." Jane looked at Olivia. "If Officer Locklear already knows that St. James wrote about you, I need to tell her it's possible he was going to write about me too. We don't have his computer, so we can't know what he was working on. She can find out. I have to tell her about the coat of arms too."

Edwin touched Jane's hand. "What about the key chain?"

"It's in a plastic bag in my purse. I can say I found it this morning, when Haviland and I were out for a walk. Is that what you want?" asked Olivia.

Jane said, "Yes. I don't want any secrets between us and the good guys."

Haviland, who'd been asleep on the rug, suddenly leaped to his feet. His back went rigid, and his black nose quivered as he faced the doorway.

Olivia put a hand on the poodle's head and murmured, "It's okay, boy."

Officer Henniger entered the room. "Ms. Steward. We'd like to speak to you in the library."

Ms. Steward in the library with a candlestick, Jane thought as she followed Henniger out of the room.

To Jane's relief, the interview was quite cordial. Henniger and Locklear took turns asking her questions, but Jane had little to say about Rachel Wilcox. She'd never heard of the young woman until that morning, and she'd been asleep in her room until the noises in the garden had startled her awake.

"I wish I could've helped her," Jane said when it was clear she had nothing else to add. "However, I do have information on the book page Justin St. James had in his pocket."

Jane told the two officers about the coat of arms, and how her ancestral home had been transported from a valley in England to a valley in western Virginia.

"I might chalk it up to coincidence, but this morning, Olivia found this in the sand, close to where we saw his body."

Jane put the plastic bag containing the key chain on the table and explained that it was from Storyton Hall.

"Did you touch this?" Henniger asked.

"No, but Olivia did."

Locklear glanced at her colleague. "Her prints are in the system."

"Funny how she found this after our team swept the area. She must have a better metal detector than we do.

Then again, she can afford to buy the best of everything," Henniger said. Lapsing into silence, he read over his notes. Finally, he gave Jane a puzzled look and said, "Why would St. James write about your family?"

"After talking to Olivia, Heather O'Grady, and Winston Hall, it looks like St. James took stories from small-town papers and used them as inspiration for his novels. I don't know why he focused on these writers, but all their stories involve a tragedy in which someone loses a life. Many years ago, I was married to a man named William. We met in college and were wed after graduation. We'd only been married a year when his rental car skidded off a bridge hundreds of miles away from home and went into a lake. His body was never recovered, and he was presumed dead."

Officer Locklear said, "I'm sorry. That must've been really hard."

"Yes. But as it turned out, William didn't die that day. He was badly injured, and though his body eventually healed, his brain never did. He didn't remember anything from before the accident and had no identification on his person, so his family and friends went on believing he was dead. Two years ago, I was reunited with him. He didn't remember me, but he got to meet his sons. He wasn't with us for long before he had another car accident. A fatal one."

"No," Locklear blurted out.

"He was in the car with someone who'd committed heinous crimes. This man was driving, and when they reached a sharp bend in the road, William grabbed the wheel. The car went over the edge and into a gully. Both men were killed. I believe William sacrificed himself to protect my family from this horrible man.

William was sick, you see. He didn't have much time left, but his death was still painful. I had to grieve his loss twice."

In a gentle tone, Henniger said, "And you think St. James planned to write about your husband's death in his next book?"

"It's just a theory. If you could get into his laptop or talk to his editor, you might be able to find out."

Locklear nodded. "One of our techs is working on the computer and we're waiting for calls from his editor, his agent, and his stepbrother. Mr. St. James wasn't married and hasn't been in a serious relationship for many years. His parents are no longer living, and the friends we've spoken with don't know what he's working on. They said he never talked about his books until after they were published."

Henniger's phone buzzed. He read the message on his screen and then showed it to his partner.

"That'll be all for now," Locklear said. "If we have more questions, we'll get in touch."

Thus dismissed, Jane returned to the lounge. Edwin, Olivia, and Butterworth were no longer there. Sammi entered the room from the kitchen and pointed to the door to the porch.

"Another guest complained about the dog, so they all left."

Jane thanked her and was about to head out to the porch when she remembered that it didn't have a wheelchair ramp. Edwin could only exit the Admiral's Inn through the front door.

She found the trio in the parking lot, staring into the dirty windows of an old, beat-up Camry.

"This is Rachel's car," Olivia explained. "It hasn't been towed to the police station yet."

"Is there anything to see?" Jane asked.

Butterworth smirked. "Other than a complete and total disregard for cleanliness, no."

"Is that a wristband on the floor mat?" Edwin waved Jane over. "Can you read the words?"

Jane peered into the car, which was just as filthy on the inside as it was on the outside. She spotted a neon-pink wristband resting on a pillow of takeout cups, crumpled napkins, and fast-food wrappers.

"It starts with a 'T.' Maybe Tap? Or Tan?"

"Tan Lines?" asked Olivia. "It's the name of a local dive bar. Reggie's cousin is the bartender. I could ask Reggie to find out if Rachel was there last night, or on Friday night, and if she was with anyone."

"While you're doing that, I wonder if you'd like to put this in your room?" Butterworth held out the giant teddy bear.

Jane flashed him a playful smile. "You should keep it. Everyone at home sees you as a big, cuddly bear."

Butterworth's expression turned steely. "I'd rather not."

"Okay, hand him over."

Walking briskly, Jane hurried back to the Book Lover's Loft. She unlocked the door, went inside, and put the bear in one of the chairs facing the water. The momentary levity she'd felt teasing Butterworth about the bear disappeared when she thought about Rachel and was compelled to return to the garden.

It felt like hours since she'd left her bed to investigate the strange noises that had yanked her from her sleep. Now the garden was cordoned off. The grass had been flattened by dozens of feet. A dozen plants had been trampled. Jane saw broken stalks and squashed flower heads.

She pictured Rachel's body from that morning. She remembered the smoothness of her skin. How warm it felt to Jane's fingertips. She remembered parting Rachel's lips and sending breath down her throat.

Staring down at the place where Rachel's body had lain, Jane thought, *I wish I could've saved you. I'm sorry.*

Jane was about to turn away and head back inside when a hand suddenly clamped down over her mouth. A ropy forearm pressed hard against her windpipe, and now she was the one who couldn't breathe.

Chapter 10

"**D**on't move and I won't hurt you," a man growled in her ear.

Jane's martial arts training kicked in, and her body reacted before her mind had time to panic. Just as Sinclair had told her to do a hundred times, she softened her knees while lowering her chin. To her attacker, it would feel like a surrender. In reality, Jane was strengthening her stance.

Knowing she had to strike before the man put her in a sleeper hold, Jane slammed her heel backward into her attacker's shin and then drove her elbow into the soft flesh of the man's flank. When he grunted in pain and surprise, she didn't ease off. Instead, she repeated the blow.

Your elbow is the hardest, sharpest part of your body. A well-placed elbow strike is more powerful than a punch or a kick.

Sinclair had drilled those words into Jane's head for decades. There were times during class when she wanted to roll her eyes at his constant repetition, but now, as she felt her assailant release his choke hold, she knew Sinclair's drills had just saved her life.

Jane turned and jumped backward, creating space between herself and a wiry man in a green hoodie. She raised her fists, preparing to defend herself should he come at her again.

Clutching his side with one hand, he held up the other in a stop gesture. "Easy! I'm not tryin' to hurt you!" He winced in pain and cursed at Jane under his breath.

"Who are you?" she demanded. Adrenaline coursed through her body and she was ready to lash out at him if he reached for her again.

Ignoring the question, the man said, "I'm looking for Rachel. You seen her?"

Jane took in every detail of his appearance, from his white sneakers to his ripped jeans and forest-green hoodie. His hands were long and bony. His fingernails were nicotine-stained. He stood in shadow, so it was hard to see the color of his eyes, but his scruffy goatee was dark blond. His narrow face and pointy nose lent him a foxlike appearance, and he shifted on his feet like an animal preparing to spring.

"Stay where you are," Jane warned. She took her phone out of her pocket and held it up. "There are cops all over this place. All I need to do is press a button and you're screwed."

There was a shift in the man's demeanor. He cast a furtive glance around and then jerked a thumb at the perimeter of yellow tape. "What happened?"

"Why were you looking for Rachel?"

He shook his head and muttered, "I'm outta here."

Pulling the hoodie over his stringy, chin-length hair, he turned to go.

Jane wanted to stop him but decided to text a single word to Butterworth instead.

Help.

As soon as she heard the whoosh of her message being sent, she shouted at the man, "I did see Rachel. She was here."

The man swiveled around. "When?"

"This morning." Jane pointed past the tape. "Right there."

His eyes flicked to the tape and back to Jane again. "What's going on?"

"I'll tell you, but only if you tell me why you grabbed me like that."

He coiled as if he meant to bolt, but then changed his mind. "I thought you were her. She owes me money."

Jane had trouble believing this. Her hair was strawberry blond. Rachel's was auburn. Even if the man had initially mistaken her for Rachel, he must have recognized his mistake once he'd wrapped his arm around her throat.

"You knew I wasn't her, but you wanted something from me. What was it?"

"Figured you was one of her friends—that she sent you to deal with me because she had some sorry-ass excuse for why she couldn't pay. It pissed me off."

"Couldn't pay for what?"

"Nah. Time for *you* to talk. What the hell happened?"

Butterworth's formidable figure appeared behind the man. He looked a question at Jane, and when she nodded, he sprang forward. Before the man knew what hit him, Butterworth had slipped his arms under the other man's armpits and locked him in a nelson hold. The man struggled, flailing around with his legs and twisting his torso, but Butterworth was as immovable as a mountain.

Jane stepped closer to the man. "Answer my questions and my friend will let you go. Why did Rachel owe you money?"

"For Dexies."

"What are those?"

The man spat, missing Jane's shoe by mere centimeters. "Addys. Study Buddies. Smart pills."

Behind him, Butterworth said, "Adderall."

"Yeah, genius, that's right. Now lemme go."

"You're her dealer," Jane said, her fingers flying over her phone's keypad. She'd asked Olivia to get Henniger and Locklear. The officers would definitely want to speak to the man pinned to Butterworth's chest like an insect in a specimen case.

Jane pointed at the café table and said, "Mr. Butterworth, perhaps our visitor would be more comfortable sitting down?"

"As you wish."

Butterworth dragged the younger man over to the café table and pushed him into a chair. He released his arms but kept two hands on his shoulders. "If you move, I'll knock you out with one blow. This is not a threat, I assure you. This is a promise."

Jane took a seat in the other chair. "Is Adderall the only thing Rachel buys from you? Or are there other items?"

The man sneered at her. "I ain't telling you a damn thing about my business. Who are you anyway? You're not a cop."

"No, but they're going to be interested in how we met, don't you think? I can say that I ran into you in the garden, or I can tell them how you assaulted me. You'd better decide quickly because they'll be here any minute."

"Whatever."

Jane jerked a thumb at the crime scene tape. "That isn't a Halloween decoration. The police are on the premises. So, you can answer my questions or spend the night behind bars. Your choice."

"Why do you care what Rachel did for fun?"

"I think she got involved with the man who stayed in this cottage. His name is Justin St. James. He's an author. Know anything about him?"

The man scoffed. "I haven't read a book since middle school. And if she messed around with this guy, so what? You his wife or something?"

The mockery in his voice grated on Jane. She'd love to wipe the jeering look off his face by telling him that he'd never see a dime from Rachel because she was dead, but she wouldn't compromise a police investigation to score a point on a drug dealer.

She was thinking of a suitable reply when she caught sight of Henniger and Locklear walking toward the garden.

"Trent Little!" Henniger called out. "Isn't this a surprise. I didn't think you ventured out in the daylight."

Trent's head whipped around. Seeing the two officers, he kicked at a tuft of grass and uttered a string of expletives.

"Mind your tongue," Butterworth warned.

"Making friends?" Henniger asked Trent.

When Trent didn't respond, Henniger's gaze moved to Butterworth. He seemed to like what he saw, for he stretched out his hand and introduced himself and his partner.

Butterworth explained that he was Jane's employee, and that he'd come to Oyster Bay out of concern for her safety.

"That sounds dramatic, but it appears that my concerns were justified. Mr. Little restrained Ms. Steward in hopes of gaining information from her."

Locklear laid a hand on Jane's shoulder. "Are you okay?"

"I'm fine. Trent was looking for Rachel. Apparently, she owes him money."

"Yeah, so what?" Trent leaned back in his chair and crossed his arms. "Rach told me to meet her. She *invited* me here. Last time I checked, it wasn't a crime to visit a friend at work."

Locklear raised a brow. "A friend, eh? We're going to have a nice, long talk about your relationship with Ms. Wilcox. We can do that inside the inn, where there's coffee and pastries, or we can do that at the station, where the coffee tastes like it came out of a gas pump. Your choice."

Trent said that he didn't have time for a chat. When he stood up and made to leave, Butterworth cleared his throat. Trent threw him a nervous glance before truculently agreeing to speak with the officers inside the inn.

Once they were gone, Jane said, "Where are Edwin and Olivia?"

"In your room."

"How did you keep Edwin from rolling himself out to the garden and launching himself at Trent?"

Butterworth said, "I didn't tell him what happened because I knew how he would react, and I'd rather not drive him back to the hospital."

"Good call." Jane smiled at Butterworth in approval.

"Besides, I really am okay. It was all over in a matter of seconds. I didn't even have time to be scared. My instincts just took over. Later, when I call Sinclair, I'll thank him for making me practice that backward elbow strike so many times. I'll also ask him to add Rachel's name to our list of research subjects."

Jane and Butterworth entered the Book Lover's Loft to find Edwin and Olivia sitting at the round table by the window, mesmerized by something on Jane's laptop. A pile of Justin St. James books was stacked near Olivia's right arm and Captain Haviland was dozing at her feet.

"Everything all right?" Edwin asked Jane.

"Just getting to know one of the locals." She looked at Olivia. "Ever heard of Trent Little?"

Olivia contemplated the name for a moment before shaking her head.

"According to Trent, Rachel bought drugs from him. He was here to collect on an overdue payment."

Edwin's eyes lit up. "Sounds like motive to me."

"To me too. He might not be the brightest bulb in the chandelier, but I doubt he'd kill Rachel and then hang around the scene of the crime. Still, I'm sure he and the cops will have a nice long talk." Jane pointed at the laptop. "What are you working on?"

Olivia said, "Creating a spreadsheet for each St. James novel. There isn't much more for us to do than take a deep dive into his books. The cops have his laptop. They'll talk to his editor. They'll find out if this Trent guy murdered Rachel. Or St. James. Or both. We don't have access to medical reports or other crucial details, which leaves us with two options; we can talk to people at Tan Lines and we can read."

"And Tan Lines isn't open on Sundays and Olivia hasn't heard back from Reggie yet, so this is the only thing left." Edwin patted the top book on the stack.

Olivia stood up. "I'm going to do my reading at home. Alistair, would you like to join me?"

"I would."

While Butterworth selected a book, Olivia murmured Haviland's name. The poodle yawned and stretched before slowly clambering to his feet.

"His joints get stiff sometimes, same as mine," Olivia said, tenderly gazing at her dog. She and Haviland left the room, but Butterworth hesitated in the doorway.

"Call me if you need anything," he said.

"I will," Jane promised.

When he was gone, Edwin said, "How much trouble could we get in? We're going to spend the whole afternoon reading."

Jane pointedly stared at his bandaged feet.

"I'm never going to hear the end of this, am I?"

"Never," Jane said, reaching for a book.

Hours later, Jane wheeled Edwin to the end of the dock to watch the sunset. She'd just finished *The Stain Remains* and didn't feel like talking yet.

Edwin had fifty pages left in *Catch More Flies* and was more than ready for a break. Francis had given Jane a bottle of wine to thank her for helping him out that morning, and Edwin had placed a delivery order with the gourmet market downtown. Between the wine, French bread, several wedges of cheese, two kinds of pâté, dried figs, grapes, peppered almonds, hummus, pickled radish, cucumbers, carrots, and tzatziki, theirs would be an elegant seaside picnic.

As the sunlight seeped from the sky, a chill stole into the air. Edwin wasn't the least bit cold, but Jane was, so she untied the cardigan from around her waist and slipped it on.

"You'll feel better after a drink," Edwin said as he put the bottle of wine between his legs and uncorked it with a flourish. After filling two glasses, he set them on the railing and began pulling out food from the brown grocery bag.

Jane watched him arrange their picnic fare on a clean towel, but her mind kept wandering back to certain scenes from *The Stain Remains*.

Edwin handed her a wineglass and said, "You have that faraway look. The one you get when you're done with a book, but it's not done with you. If it's anything like the one I'm reading, it had some tough scenes. Sad ones too."

"Very sad," Jane agreed. "Normally, I'm a fan of gritty books. The older I get, the more I like them. I feel more connected to characters who endure hardships. I want to see them come out the other side. But even the most powerful books eventually release their hold on me. Not completely, but enough that I'm able to immerse myself in new stories." She paused to sip her wine. "This was a different reading experience because I knew St. James had used Heather O'Grady's life as inspiration. If she was here right now, I'd probably hug her and burst into tears at the same time."

"Do you want to talk about it?"

Jane watched a bird wing its way across the darkening sky. It was a large bird. Its long, white wings fanned the air instead of beating it. As the bird headed toward the shoreline, she saw an elegant neck and a narrow head. An egret.

"St. James's books are famous for showing the ugliest side of humanity. In *The Stain Remains*, a female reporter is covering a charged political rally in Charlotte when her broadcast is interrupted with a breaking news story about a collision involving a high school girls' soccer team. When the school is mentioned, the female reporter is so desperate to learn more about the crash that she leaves the rally. This moment of dead air marks the end of her career."

"Was her daughter in the crash?"

The egret disappeared in the marshes to the far left of the inn. Jane pictured it making a soft landing among the cattails. Turning back to Edwin, she said, "Her daughter and husband were both in the van. The daughter dies. The husband, who was also the soccer team's coach, is injured but survives. Three teens are killed in the crash, as well as the driver of the other car. One of the girls tells the cops she saw Coach smoking a joint before he got in the van."

"Rough stuff."

"It gets much worse. The mom of one of the dead soccer players and the father of the man killed in the other car decide to avenge their loved ones by murdering the coach. Their plan goes awry and they end up killing another soccer player by mistake. The reporter guesses who the culprits are but does nothing to stop them. In the end, they kill the coach but are taken down by the hero detective while fleeing the scene."

Edwin stared at the horizon, where the last of the daylight dripped into the dark water. "Do you know the real story?"

"Heather's daughter was killed in a school bus accident. Her husband was on the bus; he was the assistant coach of their daughter's softball team. The bus went into a river, and her husband was able to get all the children out before it sank. Their daughter was unconscious, and he tried to swim with her to the shore. He didn't make it." Jane took a moment before adding, "Heather used to write puff pieces for several papers in her area. She was interviewing a local philanthropist when a colleague told her about the accident."

Edwin shook his head. "I can't imagine how horrible that must've been."

"Heather refuses to talk about that day. She became a recluse until a relative finally convinced her to seek professional help. Her therapist suggested she start a journal. She wrote a novel instead."

"I can see why she'd want to murder St. James."

Jane nodded. "The man was an antihero. If it hadn't been for the key chain and the book page, I don't think I'd spend much time being sad about his death."

"Maybe he has his own tragic story." Edwin held up his hands before Jane could speak. "I'm not excusing his behavior, but I can't think of another reason why he wrote books knowing they'd cause his fellow writers so much pain. Why do that to Heather? To Winston? Or Olivia? How did he get so warped that he deliberately created works of fiction that would make it impossible for those people to escape their grief?"

"That's one of the many things we need to find out. Unless Trent Little confesses to two murders. If he does, maybe we can forget about Justin St. James for a while."

Edwin gestured at the food. "You haven't eaten a bite. Why don't we call the boys? Talking to them will get your mind off that book."

"I never thought I'd want to scrub a book from my memory, but I wish I could unread the one I just finished." She pulled out her phone. "Let's be done with St. James for tonight. We can listen to the goings-on at home and then watch a movie. A rom-com would be nice."

"Yeah, maybe one of those meet-cute stories where a beautiful woman is walking on the beach and finds a man passed out in the sand. He's devilishly handsome, and she falls in love with him at first sight. When he finally comes to, he can't remember who he is."

Jane dunked a cucumber in tzatziki sauce and smiled. "The only clues to his identity are the round scars on the bottoms of his feet."

Edwin laughed. "Maybe I should get a stingray tattoo as a souvenir."

"I don't think you'll need a tattoo to remember *this* vacation."

The next day, Olivia asked Jane and Edwin to meet her at Bayside Books. After helping Edwin shower and dress, Jane put new bandages on his feet and pushed his wheelchair to the lounge.

After a breakfast of fresh fruit and croissants, Edwin climbed into the car while Jane struggled to fold the wheelchair.

"I don't know how people do this on their own," she said as she lifted the wheelchair into the trunk and slid into the driver's seat. "I guess Butterworth spent the night at Olivia's place."

"Good for him. It's about time he had a life beyond Storyton Hall." Edwin shot Jane a worried glance. "Would you be okay if he wanted to leave?"

Taken aback, Jane said, "Leave? You mean, *move*? Here? To be with Olivia?"

"Yes."

Jane thought about it for a moment. "It would be hard to lose him—he's been a fixture in my life for as long as I can remember—but I'd be happy for him. I think he and Olivia are well suited. His eyes light up at the mention of her name, and when they're in the same room, he can't stop looking at her."

Edwin picked up Jane's hand and brought it to his lips. "Rumi wrote, 'Whatever lifts the corners of your mouth, trust that,' and I do. I hardly ever smiled before I fell for you. You give me so many reasons to smile."

Jane leaned over the center console to kiss him.

It was a quick drive to Bayside Books. Jane parked in the lot behind the store and pushed Edwin up the ramp to the loading dock. Butterworth answered her knock on the delivery door.

"Good morning," he said, beckoning them inside as if welcoming guests to Storyton Hall. "Olivia is in the middle of a staff meeting and should be with us shortly. In the meantime, let's convene in her office. She made several phone calls last night and this morning and has learned several things of note."

"Such as?" Jane asked as she wheeled Edwin into Olivia's office.

"The cause of Mr. St. James's death."

Butterworth closed the door and pointed at the whiteboard hanging above a round table piled with books.

Two words had been written on the board in what Jane assumed was Olivia's hand.

Opioid overdose.

Jane glanced from the board to Butterworth. "How?"

"Ingestion and injection. The killer wasn't taking any chances. Opiates appeared in Mr. St. James's stomach matter as well as in his bloodstream. The ME is trying to determine which opioid is responsible, but it would appear that Ms. Wilcox was given a fatal overdose of the same drug."

Edwin inched his wheelchair closer to the board. "The killer couldn't slip something into their food and then stick them with a syringe while they were incapacitated without plenty of privacy."

"And the first dose wouldn't take effect immediately," Jane said. "I wonder what the drug was added to—coffee maybe? Not that I can picture St. James having a cappuccino with Trent Little."

"It seems unlikely," Butterworth agreed. "However, I don't think Officer Locklear would've shared this information unless she believed they had their man. Not only is Mr. Little being held on suspicion of murder but Officer Locklear told Olivia the matter might be resolved by the end of the day."

Jane wanted to share in this belief. If what Butterworth said was true, she and Edwin could spend the next two days enjoying the town. They could visit the maritime museum, do a little shopping, have lunch at Grumpy's Diner and a lovely dinner at the seafood restaurant on the waterfront. Unfortunately, she didn't share Officer Locklear's confidence.

Neither did Edwin. "I doubt Trent Little can explain the book page or the Storyton Hall key chain."

Butterworth issued a noncommittal grunt.

The three of them discussed possible scenarios in which Trent could have played a part in the two murders. Edwin was putting forth a rather wild theory when Olivia entered the office.

Her lightweight sweater and pants were Barbie pink. So were her sneakers. When Haviland loped into the room behind Olivia, Jane saw that he wore a pink collar.

"You look festive," she said.

Olivia spread her arms wide. "Today is Pink-O-Ween. The merchants in town give treats to customers who wear pink or dress in a Halloween costume. There's always a teacher workday the Monday before Halloween, so the kids get to run around town for hours on end. It started out as a small event to raise money for a local breast cancer charity, but it's grown bigger every year. We spent our staff meeting trying to decide how many pieces of candy to give to each kid, what qualifies as a Halloween costume, and whether mauve is pink or purple."

"Purple," Butterworth stated with authority.

Olivia flashed him an indulgent smile before gesturing at the whiteboard. "We can't investigate anything else until Tan Lines opens this evening, so we might as well throw ourselves into Pink-O-Ween."

"Then you don't think Trent is the killer?" asked Jane.

"He may have been involved, but there's no way he acted alone." Olivia put her hands on her hips and stared at the whiteboard. "We're not seeing the full picture, which is why I think we need to find out all we can about how Rachel spent the last three days."

Haviland sat on his haunches and gazed expectantly at Butterworth, who looked down at his clothes.

"You're right, my fine fellow, I am not wearing the correct shade."

Olivia grinned. "That can be remedied easily. Follow me, my friends. First, we'll make you all pretty in pink. After that, I'm going to put you to work." She opened a box on her desk, pulled out a pink witch hat, and placed it on her head.

"Very nice," said Edwin.

Jane wheeled Edwin to the front of the bookstore. She stopped when she reached a table covered in pink books. A Dracula with a pink-lined black cape was decorating the checkout counter with pink crepe paper streamers, and a woman dressed as Princess Aurora dumped Ring Pops into a pink candy bucket. Pink balloons were taped to every sign, and there was a pink carpet leading from the bookstore side of the building to the café side.

Olivia waved an arm around the shop and said, "Welcome to Pink-O-Ween."

Chapter 11

Olivia explained that downtown Oyster Bay would soon be teeming with people. Four blocks of Main Street had been closed to vehicle traffic, and booths of crafts and carnival games marched down the middle of the road. Children would race around, collecting candy and spending their allowance on toys, food, and games. The adults would break open their piggy banks too, as portions of every purchase would support the fight against breast cancer.

"This will be just the distraction we all need," she added. "And it'll give you and Edwin a chance to recapture your vacation vibes. You can't walk around looking normal. That's highly frowned upon."

Olivia had a whole box of pink costume items, which was why Jane was now wearing a pink tutu over her jeans, a pair of glittery pink fairy wings, and a floral headband. Edwin had been given a pink velvet coat, a black tricorner hat, and a hook to cover his right hand.

Olivia even gave him a crocodile puppet from the stand in the children's section to wear on his left hand.

"I can't be Captain Hook without a mustache," he complained to Jane.

"No worries. I'll draw one on," said the bookseller dressed as Princess Aurora.

She used mascara to brush a black mustache on Edwin's upper lip and to turn his dark eyebrows into pointy, Disney-villain arches.

Butterworth watched the bookseller's ministrations with amusement, but when Edwin's transformation was complete and Olivia turned to him, all traces of humor disappeared.

"I don't wear costumes of any sort," he announced. "Ever."

"Be that as it may, if you aren't adhering to the Pink-O-Ween rules, you might find yourself covered in Silly String."

Butterworth frowned. "Silly String?"

"It's brightly colored string shot out of an aerosol can. It's some sort of nontoxic chemical, but it can really stick to your clothes and hair," Olivia explained.

"People intentionally spend money on this item?"

Jane snorted. "Are you kidding? The twins think it's the greatest invention ever."

"Naturally."

Ignoring Butterworth's sour expression, Oliva showed him several items from the costume box. He glared at the red-and-pink devil's cape and horns, grunted at the sight of the pink clown wig and oversize bowtie, and refused to acknowledge the pink cowboy hat and gold sheriff's badge.

Finally, Olivia pulled out a clear plastic bag containing a new pink T-shirt. She glanced from the shirt to Butterworth and grinned.

"I have an idea."

Olivia handed the shirt to the bookseller dressed as Dracula and told Jane and Edwin to order drinks from the café while she and her employee transformed Butterworth into a superhero.

"She'll never get him to wear that shirt," Edwin said as Jane pushed his wheelchair into the café.

"If she does, it'll be for one reason only."

Edwin ordered two cappuccinos and glanced up at Jane. "What reason is that?"

"He's in love."

Edwin stretched out his hand, and Jane took it. They smiled at each other until the barista handed them their cappuccinos.

"I wish this thing came with a cupholder," Edwin said, glaring down at his wheelchair. "How's a villain supposed to juggle a crocodile *and* a cup of coffee?"

Haviland strode into the café as if he owned the place. He gave one of Edwin's bandaged feet a cursory sniff before approaching the counter. He then uttered a soft "whoof" that was more grunt than bark, and the barista took a doggy cookie from the bakery case and held it out for his canine customer.

The poodle stood on his hind legs and gently closed his teeth around the cookie. He didn't scarf it down right there but bobbed his head, as if in thanks, and trotted into the bookstore.

"Do you think Merry and Pippin will be that polite when they grow up?" Edwin asked Jane.

"They're being raised by two middle-school boys, so no, I don't think so."

Jane couldn't hold her cappuccino and push Edwin, so he had to remove his hook. By the time they returned to the checkout counter, Dracula was swiping a customer's credit card and Princess Aurora was helping another customer in the local authors' section.

There weren't many signed copies left from Saturday's Triple Thrills event. Jane was happy to see that most of Heather O'Grady and Winston Hall's books had sold. Having decided to buy the remaining copies for the Cover Girls, she parked Edwin in front of the pink book table, collected the books, and handed them to Dracula.

She'd just finished paying for them when Olivia and Butterworth returned from the back. Butterworth was still dressed in slacks and an Oxford shirt, but his shirt had been left unbuttoned to reveal the pink T-shirt he wore underneath. A Superman "S" had been drawn on the T-shirt, and a pair of reading glasses with black frames were perched on his nose.

"Clark Kent wishes he was this dashing," Olivia said as Jane admired Butterworth's simple costume.

"It suits you," she told him.

Edwin glanced at his crocodile puppet and said, "I'm pink with envy."

The bookstore had only been open for business for ten minutes, but customers were entering at a steady pace. All of them were wearing pink.

"Go have fun, you two." Olivia shooed Jane and Edwin out the door. "I'll put you to work when you get back. In the meantime, I've got Superman."

Jane could have sworn she saw Butterworth blush but averted her eyes before he could catch her looking.

She pushed Edwin to the end of the block and turned left onto Main Street, where the couple was immediately enveloped by the carnival atmosphere. The ever-present sea breeze was replaced by the aroma of fried food. On both sides of the street, there were banners, balloons, flags, tablecloths, and tents in every imaginable shade of pink.

"I want to send a video of this scene to the twins," Edwin said.

"When you do, ask them what costumes they'd wear if they were here."

Edwin took out his phone and panned it around. After sending the video to Fitz and Hem, he said, "They're still in their Tolkien phase, so I'm guessing a troll or an orc."

"How would the color pink fit in?"

"Dunno. The weapons, maybe? A nice pink broadsword or mace?"

Jane laughed at the thought.

"Fitz likes Gandalf the most, so he'd be a wizard with a pink beard. And Hem likes Gimli, so he'd be a dwarf with a pink beard."

"That's a fellow with fine taste," said someone to Jane's left.

She turned to see a middle-aged little person wearing roller skates, a pink poodle skirt, and a black blouse. Her blond hair was in a high ponytail and her nails, lipstick, and eyeshadow were all the same shade of bright, shimmery pink.

"My husband loves dwarfs too." She jerked her thumb at the building behind her, which was Grumpy's Diner. "Grumpy's my man, and I'm Dixie. I'd bet a buttered biscuit you're Olivia's friends from Virginia."

"We are." After she and Edwin introduced themselves, Jane said, "It's a good thing we saw Olivia this morning. I've heard it's a no-no not to wear pink today."

"You probably heard that folks who don't support the cause get doused with Silly String, but that's only for kids. The adults get pushed off the end of the pier."

Jane couldn't tell if the woman was serious, and when she looked to Edwin to check his expression, Dixie barked out a laugh.

"I'm just pullin' your chain! Are y'all hungry? We've got all kinds of fun specials today. Raspberry milkshakes, pink pancakes, Save the Tatas cheesy tots, lobster stew—you name it."

"We need to build up an appetite, but after I push this guy around town, I'll be ready to eat everything on your menu."

Dixie chuckled. "It's a big menu, but you won't need to read it." Turning to Edwin, she said, "Grumpy's got a special just for you. Shanghai barbeque stingray."

Edwin shook his head in amazement. "Small towns. They're the same the world over."

"Ain't that the truth," Dixie agreed cheerfully.

Someone called her name from inside the diner, so she told Jane and Edwin to come back later and skated away.

"I like her," Jane said as she pushed Edwin toward the craft booths.

"Me too. She could be the Mrs. Hubbard of Oyster Bay, though. We'd better not tell her any secrets."

They spent the next hour perusing jewelry, paintings, garden sculptures, wood carvings, homemade food, artisan soaps, candles, potted succulents, quilts, tea towels, and a vast array of pink-ribbon items from T-shirts to painted pumpkins.

Jane bought bars of handmade soap embedded with seashells for all the Cover Girls, a pumpkin-scented pink candle for Aunt Octavia, and a ship in a bottle for

Uncle Aloysius. Edwin bought a pair of whiskey glasses engraved with krakens for Sam.

"He's going to love these. He always shouts, 'Release the kraken!' whenever he releases Wildfire into the field. That horse can run. It's like watching the wind in animal form."

By the time they reached the carnival games, bags dangled from both wheelchair handles. Even after tossing their empty coffee cups, Edwin told Jane that she'd better not play any games because they had nowhere to put a prize.

However, when they reached the Whac-A-Mole game, Jane insisted on giving it a try.

"It's cheaper than therapy," Jane said as she handed money to the game operator.

The man waited until four other players paid, then pressed a button to start the game. A plastic mole popped out of the hole in front of Jane, and she gave it a good wallop with her soft, black mallet.

The faster the moles popped out, the more she smiled. Edwin yelled his encouragement, and when the bell rang signaling the end of the round, Jane was laughing.

"You came so close to winning," Edwin said. "Too bad that blindfolded old lady with the broken arm beat you."

Jane punched him in the shoulder. "Very funny. I was just warming up. I'll win this time."

She ended up coming in second by ten points. The boy who beat her gave her a self-effacing shrug before accepting the prize Jane wanted to win.

"You could probably buy that online for half the money," Edwin said.

"Would you like to push yourself back to the book-store?" Jane retorted with a glare.

Edwin wisely remained silent as Jane passed another bill to the game operator. She then relaxed her grip on the mallet, took a deep breath, and waited for the buzzer to sound.

When she won, she pumped her fist in the air and pointed at the pink-and-purple Superman doll hanging over the game operator's head. "That one, please."

"What are you going to do with that?" asked Edwin.

Jane grinned. "Give it to Butterworth for Christmas, of course."

When they returned to Grumpy's Diner, there were no tables available. The wait was thirty to forty-five minutes, but Dixie had a suggestion.

"You can order lunch to go. One of my kids will run it to the bookstore for you. And if you want to take the kid back to Virginia, you've got my blessing. I have more where that one came from."

"I've felt that way about my boys before," Jane admitted with a smile. "Could we order some extra sandwiches for the bookstore staff? And Olivia too? Do you know what she likes?"

Dixie was already scribbling on her order pad. "I sure do."

After paying for the food, Jane and Edwin continued on their way.

As soon as they returned to the bookstore, Olivia put them to work.

"Jane, you can bag books at checkout. Edwin, how do you feel about reading a story to the kids in the children's section? Their parents are losing steam and could use a break."

"As long as it's a book about Captain Hook, I'm game."

Olivia began wheeling him toward the back. "I have at least *three* books about him. Just don't scare the little ones. We want to entertain the tiny trolls, not traumatize them."

Butterworth kindly collected the bags hanging from the wheelchair handles and carried them to Olivia's office. When he reemerged, Olivia asked him to take Haviland for a walk in the park. Butterworth seemed relieved to escape the chaos for a few minutes and soon departed.

Pink-O-Ween officially ended at five o'clock, but all the booksellers who came in to work the evening shift were in costume. There was a pink-haired Nancy Drew, a Willy Wonka with a pink waistcoat, and a Mrs. Frizzle in a pink dinosaur dress.

Olivia said good night to her employees and waved for Butterworth, Jane, and Edwin to follow her to the back.

"Thanks for your help today. I know it wasn't exactly vacation-worthy, but you got to experience a local tradition from the trenches."

Jane sank down in one of the chairs in Olivia's office and let out a contented sigh. "I loved it. For a few hours, I forgot about murder. All the noise and color—and the energy—it was just what I needed."

"Especially the Whac-A-Mole," added Edwin.

Poking him in the arm, Jane said, "And how many times did you throw darts at water balloons? Ten?"

"That's a gross exaggeration. It was more like seven. And in my defense, it was the only game I could do in a wheelchair with a load of shopping bags on my lap."

Butterworth's left eyebrow twitched. "It took you seven times to hit the number of balloons necessary to claim a prize? Maybe you should practice your aim at the archery fields when we get back home."

Edwin glowered at him. "There's nothing wrong with my aim. The game is rigged so you have to win multiple times. You have to trade in several small prizes for a larger one. *I* didn't want a bouncing ball. *I* wanted the retro-looking gumball machine, so I had to keep playing."

"A gift for the twins?" asked Olivia.

"Yes. I thought they could fill it with dog treats and use it as a training tool."

Olivia glanced at Haviland. "You heard the magic word, didn't you? Well, after letting all those children pet you today, you've earned one."

She walked behind her desk, opened a drawer, and offered Haviland a jerky treat. As she shut the drawer, her gaze landed on her phone, and she leaned over to read the message on her screen.

"Lorna called a few minutes ago. Stay where you are while I call her back. Whatever she tells me—or decides not to tell me—might influence tonight's plans."

Butterworth closed the door and stood at parade rest in front of it. Jane didn't think the booksellers were likely to come crashing through the door in an effort to eavesdrop on Olivia's conversation but kept her thoughts to herself. It was in Butterworth's nature to be on guard. He was a protector, and his two favorite women were in the same room.

"I'm going to put the phone on Speaker for now. If Lorna asks, I'll tell her she has an audience. Otherwise, try not to make any noise."

Officer Locklear sounded too tired to notice that Olivia's voice sounded a little distant.

"I only have a minute, but I wanted to tell you that Jane Steward is in the clear. You too. We're charging Trent Little with two counts of homicide."

"He confessed?"

They heard the telltale pop and hiss of a soda can being opened and the sound of the officer swallowing. "Sorry. My throat is as dry as my mother-in-law's chicken. Little didn't confess, but he'll probably come around. We now know that ketamine killed both our vics."

"And Trent deals ketamine?"

"He has a previous conviction for possession and intent to sell. Served twenty months. Had a minipharmacy in his backpack at the time of his arrest that included ketamine and other Schedule III controlled substances. Word on the street is that he's known for having a steady supply of Special K in all its forms. Powder, pills, and liquid. I can't tell you anything else because the investigation is still ongoing, but I'll get in touch with Ms. Steward tonight to let her know she's free to go home after we get her statement. I doubt I'll get to that until tomorrow."

Jane held up her car keys and pointed at the fob. Olivia nodded and said, "Thanks for letting me know, Lorna. I know Jane will be relieved. Neither of us could figure out how a key chain from her hotel or a book page referring to her family ended up near St. James's body. Do you know how they tie in to the murders?"

"Not yet. Trent claims it was unusual for Rachel to buy ketamine. She prefers other drugs like Adderall and coke. We'll conduct a thorough search of her home and vehicle, but I doubt she shot herself up in the garden. She wasn't alone out there, and we think Trent returned to the scene in hopes of finding money or recovering any leftover product from her car or person. Either way, your friend can rest easy. This mess won't follow her back to Virginia. I'm afraid it's all ours."

Olivia hung up and Jane wrote KETAMINE OVERDOSE on the whiteboard.

"We might know the method, and money appears to be the motive, but there are still way too many holes in this case for me to believe it's over."

"There are too many 'whys' left," agreed Edwin. "Why St. James? Why Olivia's beach? What's the connection to Storyton Hall? Does Trent have access to a boat?"

Jane looked at Butterworth. "What do you think?"

"That this investigation is far from over."

Olivia splayed her hands. "It sounds like we should go out for drinks tonight. Some of the locals are sure to talk about Trent's arrest, and if we want to learn more about him, and Rachel, we need to cozy up to the folks at Tan Lines. We'll have to make friends fast, so we should pretend to be celebrating. That way, we can buy several rounds of whiskey."

"How about an engagement?" Edwin suggested.

"Perfect." Olivia plucked the sleeve of her pink blouse. "We can't go there looking like this either. Tan Lines is a jeans-and-T-shirt kind of place. Worn jeans and faded tees. Baseball caps. Stained. Frayed. Worked in. Slept in. This bar smells like smoke, stale beer, and fish. People are loud and unfiltered. To blend in, we need to look totally unexceptional."

"We both have jeans and T-shirts," Jane said.

"Not the right T-shirts. You can't look like tourists.

I'll borrow a shirt and a cap from Grumpy for you, Edwin. Dixie will lend me some of her daughter's tees for us gals. I'm sorry, Alistair, you'll have to stay behind with Haviland. You could walk in there wearing a garbage bag and everyone would still think you were a cop, a spy, or an assassin."

Butterworth crossed his arms over his chest. "The establishment has an outdoor seating area, does it not?"

"Yes, but it's the end of October. No one will be out there."

"Then I'll keep watch from the car. Haviland can keep me company."

Seeing there was no point in arguing, Olivia, Butterworth, and Haviland returned to her house, while Jane and Edwin shed their borrowed costumes and drove to a seafood restaurant overlooking the harbor. The décor was on the kitschy side and the service was slow, but the food was delicious.

Jane wasn't that hungry when they sat down, but by the time their food was served, she was ready to pounce on her lemon pepper scallops.

"These are *so* good," she moaned.

Edwin picked up a leg of his Alaska snow crab and cracked the knuckles at either end. "Mine's delicious *and* fun to eat. I bet the twins would love to attack a crab. I'll make this for them when we get home. I packed a cooler, so we should hit the seafood market before we leave."

"It's weird to think that this is our last night of vacation. We'll have plenty of stories to tell, but I don't feel very relaxed."

"Of course you don't, which is why I called the Walt Whitman Spa and asked them to pamper you for a few hours on Wednesday. And I don't want to hear how you're too busy to go. After pushing me around for two days, you'll need that massage."

Jane smiled at him. "That was very thoughtful, but we have a masquerade ball on Saturday. There's *so* much to do. You'll be lucky if you're on crutches by then. Do you want me to call Mabel to see if she can modify your costume?"

"Into what? Tiny Tim? No, thanks. I'll pad my shoes with sponges if I have to, but I'm not changing my costume."

The more they talked about the party, the more Jane began looking forward to being back in Storyton.

After they paid the check and headed back to their car, they paused for a moment to watch a yacht strung with purple and orange lights leisurely motor across the harbor.

"It's beautiful here," Jane said as she and Edwin held hands. "But Dorothy was in a magical place too, and she still knew that there's no place like home."

Edwin squeezed her hand. "No matter where we are, you're home to me."

Jane had never heard of the band on her T-shirt, but Olivia explained that Wicked Sandman was well-loved by the regulars at Tan Lines. Her T-shirt featured a map of North Carolina breweries, and Edwin's was a trout-shaped state flag. All the shirts had been made soft by wear. They were clean but marked by the occasional pen or grease stain.

Olivia cast a critical eye at their outfits. "Your jeans are too nice, Jane. The lighting isn't great in there, so you can probably get away with them, but those sneakers won't work. Do you have anything else?"

"Flip-flops."

"Perfect." Olivia turned to Edwin. "I'll carry in the flowers and tell the bartender what's about to happen. Give me a few minutes to chat with my neighbors and then signal me. I'll make sure you have an audience. After that, we'll let the whiskey do its thing, and start dropping Rachel and St. James into our conversations. What are we hoping to learn?"

"We want to know if St. James visited the bar Friday night," Jane said, ticking things off her fingers as she spoke. "If anyone saw him with Rachel. Was Trent here Friday night, Saturday night, or both? What did people think of Rachel? What about Trent?"

She'd slipped a copy of *Catch More Flies* into the pouch of Edwin's wheelchair. There was a huge photo of St. James on the back cover, and Jane hoped it would trigger a reaction from someone at the bar.

"I'll be right outside if you need me," Butterworth reminded Jane as they piled into Olivia's SUV.

Tan Lines was a glorified shack located between a stretch of swampland and a bait and tackle shop. Christmas lights lined the roof, and giant LED flamingos flanked the front door. The neon sign showed a woman covering her breasts with her hands while a smiling crab snipped the strings of her itsy-bitsy bikini top.

Despite it being a Monday night, the unpaved parking lot was nearly full. Olivia backed into a spot between two commercial pickup trucks and handed Butterworth the keys. "See you soon."

Jane got a good leg workout pushing Edwin over the uneven parking lot, and when Olivia opened the front door, a cacophony of shouts, shrieks, laughter, and music burst out from inside.

Olivia made a beeline for the bar, while Jane did her best to steer the wheelchair through the crowded room without bumping into anyone. By the time she found an empty table, Olivia had procured bottles of beer for all of them.

"I'll be at the bar," she said, placing two bottles on the scarred surface of the table.

"I guess we need a story about why you'd propose to me in this fine establishment," Jane said.

Edwin glanced at the fishing nets, buoys, and license plates nailed to the walls. "Who wouldn't want to make a major life decision in a place where SpongeBob would hang out?"

Jane raised her bottle. "To SpongeBob."

After taking a pull of beer, Edwin withdrew a small box from his pocket and waved at Olivia. She hurried over and placed the bouquet of grocery store flowers on the table. She then returned to the bar, whispering to the other customers before sitting back down.

Half of the patrons watched as Edwin took Jane's hand. The boisterous chatter dropped by several decibels, as did the music.

Though Edwin had suddenly become the center of attention, he didn't seem to notice. His focus was entirely on Jane.

Gazing into her eyes, he said, "There was a time when I couldn't imagine sharing my life with another person. I did everything I could to avoid letting anyone get too close. I traveled the world. I met all kinds of people and had some wild adventures. I've seen so many wonders. Palaces and waterfalls and the northern lights. But I didn't start living until I fell in love with

you, Jane Steward. You taught me that the greatest wonder isn't out there." He pointed at the door, then laid
his hand over his heart. "It's in here."

Behind him, a woman began to sniffle.

Edwin opened the ring box and held it out to Jane.
"Will you marry me?"

Inside the box was a square-shaped, art deco style
rose gold ring. Made of dozens of small diamonds that
sparkled despite the dim light, it was elegant and sophis-
ticated. It was a ring for a particular kind a woman—one
who'd lived long enough to know what mattered most in
life.

"A square represents balance," Edwin said. "That's
what we have together, my love. Balance, respect, peace,
and happiness. This ring also represents our family.
You, me, Fitz, and Hem. I'm asking you to be my wife,
but I'm also asking to become the twins' legal father.
What do you say to my dual proposal?"

There was no need for Jane to fake surprise. Her face
glowed with joy as she threw her arms around Edwin
and kissed him with gusto.

The bar erupted in applause.

Chapter 12

The bartender poured shots of whiskey as fast as she could. Olivia and Jane distributed them, while Edwin told the story of how he'd nearly run Jane over with a horse.

"It might not be the best way to get a woman's attention, but it worked! She gave me what for right there in the middle of Main Street, and I was a goner." He raised his beer bottle and cried, "To feisty women!"

His toast was met with a roar of approval. More shots were poured. Everywhere Jane looked, people were tilting their heads back and tossing whiskey down their throats.

"If you're from Virginia, why'd you propose here?" asked a sour-faced woman.

"My girl loves to read, so we drove here to meet one of her favorite authors. Anyone heard of Justin St. James?"

His question was met by head shakes or blank stares until a man sitting at the bar said, "I've read a couple of his books, but I had no idea he was in town."

Jane handed him a shot glass and said, "Bayside Books had an event called Triple Thrills. There were three authors: Justin St. James, Heather O'Grady, and Winston Hall. I heard one of them came to *this bar* to do research for a future book."

Such a remark would've elicited a strong reaction from Jane's friends. At Tan Lines, visiting authors were interesting to only a small handful of people.

"I was here Friday and Saturday," said a man with weather-beaten skin and an easy smile. "What do these folks look like?"

Jane took out her phone and showed him an image of the event poster. He didn't recognize any of the authors, nor did his wife. Others asked to see the photo, but no one remembered seeing the writers.

"Their loss. I could tell them a story or too that would make their toes curl," boasted a powerfully built man in a paint-splattered tee. "Twenty-six years as a corrections officer. Somebody should write a book about *my* job."

"Why don't *you* write it, Hank? It would give you something to do besides fantasy football and putting a dent in my barstool," quipped the bartender.

Laughter rippled through the room, and the subject turned to the *Monday Night Football* game.

"I don't think we can compete with the NFL," Jane whispered to Edwin.

"The whiskey's hitting their bloodstream, which means the noise level is about to go up. There'll be some heated debates about teams, but other people will want to hang on to the feeling of revelry our announcement gave them. They'll wander over to us, and we'll tell them that we're staying at the Admiral's Inn."

Jane smiled. "A subtle way of finding out if they know Rachel?"

"Exactly. We should let Trent's name slip at some point too."

Just as Edwin had predicted, the patrons began discussing football, which led to a boisterous argument over the decisions made by the Carolina Panthers coaching staff in yesterday's game.

After listening to ten minutes on the topic, a middle-aged couple in matching Harley-Davidson tees abandoned their seats at the bar and meandered over to where Jane and Edwin were sitting.

"Where you from in Virginia?" the woman asked.

At Jane's reply, the man beamed at his wife. "The Blue Ridge Parkway is one of our favorite places to ride. We were just there in September."

"It was gorgeous," his wife agreed. "We went apple picking and visited a few breweries. I didn't want to come home, but we had to clock back in on Friday morning. We both work for the US Postal Service, and Uncle Sam only gives us so many days off. Right, babe?"

Her husband slid his arm around his wife's waist and reeled her in for a quick kiss.

"I know how you feel," Jane told the woman. "We're hitting the road tomorrow, and I'm going to miss being spoiled by the folks at the Admiral's Inn."

The woman's face fell. "That's where Rachel worked. We knew her—the girl who died. She made lots of mistakes, but she wasn't a bad person. Know what I mean?"

Jane nodded. "She was very young."

"And pretty. Thought she could charm every man she met, but she didn't have the sense God gave a goose. Trent, the guy they arrested, didn't take IOUs. Rachel was always trying to get other folks to pay for her good time, but she never returned the favor. Then she'd show up here in a new dress or wearing new shoes and want us all to admire her, even though we knew she'd bought the stuff using money she'd gotten by begging, borrowing, or stealing."

"Did she have family? A boyfriend?"

The man shrugged. "I know her old lady. She did what she could to raise her right, but there comes a time when we can't control our kids anymore. As for boyfriends, Rachel had plenty. She went through 'em quick. As soon as they didn't give her what she wanted, she'd toss 'em away."

Having shared this much, the couple seemed to have nothing left to say and wandered back to the bar.

Jane and Edwin spent the next forty minutes hearing similar comments about Rachel and Trent. No one seemed surprised that Rachel had come to harm, or that Trent was the responsible party.

"Sounds like she owed half the town money," Edwin said when he and Jane were alone again.

"If not the town, nine out of ten people in this bar."

Olivia, who'd been settling up with the bartender, rejoined Jane and Edwin. "Ready to go?"

Just then, a man shouted, "I love this song! Turn it up, Latrice!"

The music boomed through the space, so loud that Jane felt the bass thunder off the walls and into her bones. She pointed at the door and shouted, "Let's go!"

A dozen patrons waved or hollered "Congratulations!" as they headed for the exit. Jane smiled back but didn't stop pushing Edwin's wheelchair at a robust clip until they were outside.

After moving through a haze of cigarette smoke produced by the small crowd congregating on either side of the front door, Jane inhaled deeply and said, "I don't know how Betty does it. Night after night. I know the Cheshire Cat is a little pub in a little village, but still."

"She doesn't have to shout over the music either," Edwin pointed out. "The only time the pub gets rowdy is when someone's accused of cheating at trivia."

Olivia laughed. "I remember Betty. I liked her. In fact, I liked all your friends, which surprised me. It usually takes me a few years to warm up to people, but the women in your book club are, well, for lack of a better word, special."

"They are. Did one of those special ladies help you pick out this incredible ring?" Jane asked Edwin.

"Nope. It was Fred Yoder, the guy who owns Circa. While you were looking at the books, I was looking at rings. Fred and I had a few minutes to talk, and when he showed me that art deco ring, I knew it was meant for you. I slipped him my credit card and he ran it through while he was ringing up the compasses for the boys. He dropped my card, the receipt, and the ring box in my pocket on our way out the door."

"I love you, you sneaky devil," Jane whispered in Edwin's ear.

When they reached the car, Butterworth was standing at the back bumper.

Jane said, "You didn't sit down for a second, did you?"

Butterworth flicked a speck of sand from the cuff of his jacket. "I deemed it prudent to have a clear line of sight to the door."

"I'm sure you won't want your room to smell like smoke, cheap whiskey, and beer, so we can compare notes on the way back to the inn," Olivia said.

After settling Edwin in the passenger seat and stowing the wheelchair in the trunk, Butterworth took the keys from Olivia and drove out of the parking lot.

Jane waited until they were back on a paved surface before saying, "I don't think St. James visited Tan Lines. It's true that not many people know who he is, but we talked to a few regulars and none of them saw him on Friday night."

"Rachel was there both nights," Edwin added.

Olivia said, "Correct. She left earlier than usual on Friday and stayed late on Saturday. The bartender—Latrice—is Reggie's cousin. She's usually very tight-lipped about what goes on during her shifts, but Reggie put in a good word for me, which is how I learned that Trent was skulking around the parking lot both nights. Rachel left with a group of women her age on Friday. They weren't friends, but they knew her well enough to give her a ride."

"Where'd they drop her off? Do you know?" asked Jane.

"At the Admiral's Inn."

They'd stopped at a red light. Butterworth turned to Olivia and said, "She must have been followed. Rachel was in debt to a drug dealer and either sought refuge with a hotel guest or hid somewhere on the property. If the police find her DNA on Mr. St. James's body or vice versa, they'll conclude she spent Friday night with him. They may also assume she was gone by the time Trent Little came calling, leaving Mr. St. James to face a hostile drug dealer."

Olivia nodded. "It sounds plausible. The police have enough evidence against Trent to make a double homicide charge stick, but there's more to this story."

"Trent was either working for someone else or he was set up," Edwin said. "Unless someone made it worth his while, he wouldn't risk murdering St. James, or dumping his body on Olivia's beach."

Jane glanced at the dark storefronts on Main Street. It was a Monday night in October, and the town had seen an eventful day. It was resting now and wouldn't wake again until tomorrow. She and Edwin would drive through it once more in the morning. After that, she didn't know when they'd return. If ever.

As they drove by Circa, Jane brushed her ring with her fingertips. She wished the beautiful piece of jewelry had the power to banish her maudlin thoughts, but it didn't.

At the next red light, she saw the reflection of the car in the hardware store window. "The killer wrote the message on the bathroom mirror. They didn't leave that skull as a warning, but as a promise."

"Maybe the key chain was a warning to us," said Olivia.

"The answer has to be in one of St. James's books. He wrote about the killer or someone they loved. If this was an act of revenge, they've accomplished what they set out to do. Rachel either saw something she shouldn't have or was killed by Trent." Edwin put his hand over Jane's. "Either way, it's time for us to go home."

Butterworth found Jane's eyes in the rearview mirror. "We'll keep looking into this after we return to Storyton."

"Edwin and I will leave after I talk to the police, but I think you should stay here, Butterworth. You should stay with Olivia."

Olivia pivoted in her seat. "You think I'm in danger?"

"I don't know. But by this time tomorrow, I'll be surrounded by people. You'll be alone in your beautiful house on the Point. Yes, you have Haviland. Yes, you

can take care of yourself. Even so, I think Butterworth
should stay with you for a few days."

"What do you think, Alistair?"

"That there's another alternative," said Butterworth.

Olivia smiled at him. "I could come to Storyton."

He smiled back. "Precisely."

"The bookstore manager will be back on Thursday,
which means I could be in Storyton by Friday afternoon. Until then, I'd very much enjoy your company,
Alistair."

Butterworth practically hummed with pleasure.

Back at the inn, he insisted on doing a sweep of Jane
and Edwin's room.

"I might be injured, but I'm not entirely incapable of
protecting Jane," Edwin groused.

Ignoring him, Butterworth said, "Avoid unnecessary
stops tomorrow. It's a long drive, and I won't rest easy
until you're back in Storyton."

"I'll pack our lunch and limit myself to one bathroom break. Maybe two." Jane put her arms around
Butterworth's barrel-like chest and whispered, "Take
care of Olivia."

"I shall," he promised.

Jane wanted to spend a few minutes staring at the
twinkling lights of the harbor, but she was too tired. She
helped Edwin into bed and then got under the covers
and snuggled up against him.

His lamp was still on, so she pivoted her left hand,
admiring the way her ring glinted in the light.

"Do you really like it?" Edwin murmured sleepily.

"I really love it. And I really love you, barbs and all."

Edwin laughed. "Which makes me a happy man." He
drew her in closer and then began moving his fingers
through her hair. "I'm sorry our vacation wasn't much

of a vacation. Maybe next time, we should go to a remote island—a place where the only authors are on the covers of the books we pack."

"Tell me more about this island," Jane mumbled. She was only half awake now. The sensation of Edwin's fingers slowly stroking her hair coaxed her to a deep state of relaxation. Her mind stilled and her breathing slowed. By the time Edwin finished describing tidal pools and gentle waterfalls, she'd already drifted away.

They checked out early the next morning. The employee manning the front desk told Jane that Francis was in bed with a head cold, so she wrote a note, telling him to get well soon and to bring his partner to Storyton Hall for a complimentary weekend stay when they were ready for their next mini-getaway.

"Do you mind if I grab some coffee to go?" she asked the employee.

"Not at all. Sammi can get you some from the kitchen if the urns aren't out yet."

Jane didn't see the bartender in the lounge, and because she still had to stop by the police station, she decided to poke her head in the kitchen.

Sammi sat on one of the stools facing the center island. Her upper body was hunched over and her head rested on her folded arms.

Jane hesitated. Was the bartender asleep or merely resting?

"Excuse me," she whispered.

Sammi's eyes flew open and she jerked upright.

"I'm sorry. I didn't mean to startle you." Jane took in the younger woman's swollen eyes and the wad of balled-up tissues near her elbow. Perhaps she had a cold too. "Are you okay?"

"Yeah." Embarrassed, the bartender turned away. She grabbed a tissue from the box on the counter, blew her nose, and collected the other tissues from the island. After throwing them in the trash, she began scrubbing her hands at the sink. "Breakfast doesn't start until seven."

Sheepishly, Jane said, "I was just hunting for coffee, but I can grab some in town. Sorry to bother you."

Sammi dried her hands on a dishrag and then pressed it to her face. Jane realized she'd been crying.

Moving closer to Sammi, Jane said, "You look like you could use a friend right now. And a nice hot cup of tea. If you show me where it is, I'll make you some."

"That's okay, thanks. I need to get to work."

Edwin was waiting in the car and Officer Locklear was waiting at the station, but Jane couldn't leave. She couldn't walk away from such an unhappy woman.

"Is it Rachel?" she asked softly.

Sammi's red-rimmed eyes met Jane's. "I'm *so* mad at her. She was always pushing people to their limit. Always trying to get one over on them. Pocket a few bucks or score free drinks. She wanted people to cover for her when she was late. Lie for her when she screwed up. If she wasn't so self-absorbed, she'd probably still be alive."

Jane nodded in understanding. "She died before she had a chance to learn from her mistakes. Who knows what kind of person she might have become if she'd lived for another ten, or fifty, or seventy years? I've changed so much since my twenties. Most people do."

"I told her so many times to ease up on the partying,"

Sammi whispered. "She swore she didn't do any of the hard stuff, but she'd try anything once. I think she wanted to impress that writer guy—show him that she wasn't just a small-town girl. She probably told Trent that St. James would pay for the drugs, but I bet the writer was interested in more than a night of fun. If he wouldn't fork up cash for the drugs, Rachel would've freaked out. She had a master key. She probably tried to scare him with that skull and the message on the mirror. There's no way Trent did that."

"Did you share this with the cops? Or do you feel like you'd be betraying Rachel?"

Sammi let out a long, slow exhale and picked at a loose thread on her sweater. Once again, she was wearing a turtleneck. "I told them. I felt bad about it, but I didn't want anyone else to be blamed for Rachel's actions. I like my coworkers, and Francis is a great boss."

Jane touched Sammi briefly on the hand. "You have nothing to feel bad about. You've done your best in a terrible situation. You tried to be a friend to Rachel, but sometimes people don't want the kind of friendship we have to offer. I'm sorry things turned out the way they did."

"Me too." Sammi managed a small smile. "Thanks for listening That's usually my job."

"Take care of yourself," Jane said.

She turned to leave, but Sammi asked her to wait. She filled two takeout cups with coffee and placed a carton of half-and-half and a sugar bowl on the island. Jane doctored the coffees, pushed the lids on tight, and said goodbye.

"Stay safe out there," Sammi said as Jane left the kitchen.

The coffee was so hot, she was unable to drink it

until she and Officer Locklear were seated across from each other in a small conference room. Jane walked Locklear through her movements Saturday morning from the moment she heard noises in the cottage garden until Trent snuck up behind her.

Locklear asked dozens of questions and made Jane repeat herself many times before she seemed satisfied.

"If this case goes to trial, you may be called as a witness."

Jane said, "I hope it doesn't. I can't forget what happened, but I'd like to go home and try to put it behind me."

To Jane's surprise, Locklear placed the evidence bag with the book page from *Manor Houses and Halls of England* on the table. "I don't like loose ends, but this feels like one to me. Any fresh insight as to why Mr. St. James was carrying it around?"

"No idea. What about his editor?"

"She refused to tell me anything about his next book without a court order. I won't waste my time asking a judge to grant me one—not with the direction the case has taken. I guess we'll find out when the book comes out."

Jane's eyes widened. "There's going to be another book? That's certain?"

"It's the only thing his editor *would* tell me. It's supposed to come out around this time next year. On Halloween."

With the interview completed, Locklear walked Jane back to the lobby and thanked her for her time.

And that was it. Jane's trip to Oyster Bay was officially over. She tossed her empty coffee cup in the trash can by the door and exited the building. Edwin was waiting for her in the park across the street. Winston Hall's latest release was splayed open on his lap, but his gaze was wandering. It swept the park and the sidewalks. It moved up and down the street. Anywhere but at the book.

"Distracted?" Jane asked when she reached him.

He closed the book. "I'm ready to go home, but it's unsettling to leave like this. Everything feels unfinished."

Joining him on the bench, Jane watched a woman pushing a stroller come to an abrupt stop. Her toddler had dropped his toy cat and seemed both confused and bereft over its loss. When his mom returned the toy, her little boy hugged it to his chest. But the moment his mother started walking again, he dropped it for a second time. A jogger paused to retrieve the cat, and he smiled at the little boy as he handed it to him. The boy stared at him with apprehension.

Jane wondered why the jogger had made the child uneasy. Was it because he was a stranger? Or was the child upset because the man had touched his beloved toy?

The jogger wasn't part of the game. The boy didn't expect anyone but his mother to play.

Edwin touched Jane's temple. "What's going on in there?"

"I was thinking of how random interactions can change the course of someone's life. Trent isn't exactly a pillar of the community, but his arrest feels awfully convenient." She waved her hand toward the police station. "I'm not accusing them of laziness or of cutting corners. They've gathered enough evidence to file charges against him, but when they ask him about the book page or the key chain, he won't have an answer."

Edwin nodded. "Loose ends."

"That's why I wanted Butterworth to stay. I don't expect him to find out what really happened, but nothing's going to slip past him either."

"It's weird, picturing him at the bookstore. If he stands by the door and glares at everyone who comes in, Olivia's going to lose a ton of sales."

Jane chuckled. "He could be in charge of storytime. He could read *The BFG* or *The Smartest Giant in Town*. He has the perfect voice for those characters."

"Could you imagine him reading *Jack and the Beanstalk*? One *fee-fi-fo-fum* and the kids would start bawling."

The thought of Butterworth sitting, arrow straight, on one of the small, painted chairs in the children's section made Jane smile. "Olivia brings out his tender side, so if she asks him to step out of his comfort zone, he probably will."

"He wore a pink Superman T-shirt for her. That man's in love."

"All the more reason to leave him behind." Jane stood up and grabbed the handles of Edwin's wheelchair. "Let's go swap this for your crutches and head home."

Edwin raised his face toward the cloudless sky. "I hope this sunshine follows us all the way back to Storyton."

I hope it's the only thing that follows us, Jane thought.

Chapter 13

By the time Jane pulled the car into the garages at Storyton Hall, she was stiff and sore. She hadn't spent six hours behind the wheel for years, and her lower back protested when she finally stood upright.

She was retrieving Edwin's crutches from the back seat when she heard an explosion of zealous barking. Seconds later, Merry and Pippin raced into the garages in a blur of black coats and white paws, mouths parted and tongues lolling. The puppies hopped around Jane and Edwin, covering their hands with doggy kisses.

When Jane bent down to embrace the dogs, their enthusiastic welcome knocked her over, and she found herself lying flat on the floor, trying to fend off an assault of wet noses and tongues.

Edwin propped his crutches against the car and offered her a hand. "I think they missed you."

"I might not get up. This hard floor feels pretty good on my back."

"Why don't you take a nice long, hot bath? I'll rustle

up something for dinner, and later, I'll give you a back rub."

Jane clambered to her feet. "And *you* need to take it easy for the next few days. Have the boys help you in the kitchen tonight."

Edwin gave Pippin a scratch on the back of his neck. "Where are Fitz and Hem, eh? Can you go tell them we have a full car that needs unpacking?"

As if they understood Edwin's request, the puppies trotted out of the garages. When they cleared the building, they began barking loudly.

"If they actually come back with the boys, I'm going to think they're related to Haviland."

Jane opened the cargo area and pulled out their suitcases.

"Mom!"

"Edwin!"

Fitz and Hem stood in the doorway, their gazes darting from their mother's face to Edwin's bandaged feet.

"What happened?" they asked in unison.

"You can guess at dinner. Whoever figures it out, wins a prize." Edwin tucked his crutches under one arm and beckoned the boys over with the other one. "Come here and let me see if you got taller since I last saw you."

This was how Edwin always wrangled hugs out of the boys. Now that they were in middle school, they were less demonstrative when it came to hugs and kisses, but they willingly accepted Edwin's one-armed squeezes.

Jane said, "My turn."

Hugging her, Fitz said, "I thought you were coming home tomorrow."

"Things didn't go exactly as planned. Can you guys grab some bags?"

The twins did as she asked, and before long, the car

had been emptied. Jane didn't want to sit down again until dinner, so she unpacked, called Eloise to tell her that she was home, and went through the mail. As she opened bills and made a pile of junk mail for the recycling bin, Edwin and the boys worked on dinner.

Jane paused to listen to the rise and fall of their voices, the rush of water filling a pot, the clank of a saucepan being placed down on a stove burner, and the click, click, click of Merry and Pippin's paws, and felt lighter than she had in days. These sounds were the music of her family. She heard them all the time, but tonight, there was a special beauty in these mundane noises.

Putting her hand on the doorframe leading into the kitchen, Jane thought of all the sounds that had soaked into their house over the years. It had seen and heard so many things. Their memories lived in its rooms. Their pictures hung from its walls. Their laughter and dreams floated up to its rafters, while its floorboards soaked up their worries and tears.

Jane flashed back to the sight of Rachel's body in the garden and felt a stab of sorrow. Had the young woman grown up in a home like this? With a bright, warm kitchen and beds with clean sheets and soft blankets? Was her photograph smiling out from its place on a bookshelf or on top of a chest of drawers? Would a house be waiting for her to walk through the front door? Was someone inside grieving her loss tonight?

"Five minutes 'til chow time," Edwin announced.

Jane set the table and opened a bottle of wine. She rarely let the twins drink soda, but their homecoming had taken on a celebratory air, so she told them they could have root beer with dinner.

"I have something for you too," she told the puppies. "Auntie Olivia sent you turkey and apple chew treats."

Hem intercepted Jane before she could hand over the treats. "Can we do it? We're trying to get them to lie down on command and they need more practice."

Jane handed over the treats and moved closer to Edwin. "What's for dinner?"

"Edwin's Tuscan chicken pasta with a slight change. We're out of sun-dried tomatoes, so I snuck in some extra spinach and even more cheese."

"I'll carry the bowl to the table. Sit down before you pop your stitches."

The twins had been patiently waiting to guess what had happened to Edwin. In between bites of pasta and sips of root beer, they tossed out every idea that popped into their heads.

"You stepped on a broken bottle," said Hem.

"Nope."

"Shells," said Fitz.

"Nope."

"You got stung by a jellyfish."

Edwin wanted to eat, so he started shaking his head instead of answering. The twins named every sharp object they could think of before deciding the accident hadn't occurred at the beach.

"Someone ran over your feet with a motorcycle," said Fitz.

Hem didn't even wait for Edwin to respond before saying, "No way. That would've broken bones. He just has bandages. Did you step on one of those things the cops use to pop car tires?"

"A spike strip?" Edwin gave a little shudder. "Man, that would *hurt*."

Jane said, "Can you give them a hint so we can talk about something else?"

Acquiescing, Edwin told the twins that his injury had occurred at the beach.

"Was it a horseshoe crab?"

"A shark?"

Edwin grinned. "No, but I *was* in the water when it happened."

Hem finally guessed correctly, and Fitz was too interested in hearing the whole story to feel disappointed over losing out on the prize.

Edwin waited until they'd finished eating before producing the stingray barbs for the boys to examine.

"Whoa," Fitz whispered as he handled a barb. "I'm glad you didn't die."

"Me too," added Hem.

The men at the table exchanged shy smiles—the male equivalent of saying, "I love you." Jane wished she could take a photo of the moment so that whenever anything went wrong in her world, she could look at their precious faces and remember all that was right.

Later, after a hot bath and the promised shoulder rub, Jane popped into the boys' room to give them their compasses.

"Bilbo could've used this when he was lost in Mirkwood Forest," said Fitz. "Thanks, Mom."

Hem said, "I'm sorry your vacation was so crazy, but I'm glad you're back. Ms. Eloise is great and all, and we love hanging out with Uncle Aloysius and Aunt Octavia, but—" He looked to his brother for help.

"But we like it when it's just us—the four of us—plus Merry and Pippin."

"Me too," said Jane.

*   *   *

The next morning, Jane woke up early. She got ready as quietly as she could and crossed the mist-shrouded Great Lawn to enter Storyton Hall through the terrace door. She took the staff stairs to her great-aunt and -uncle's apartments and rang their buzzer.

"Jane! What on earth?" Aunt Octavia exclaimed.

"I thought you'd probably be pouring your second cup of tea right about now and wanted to join you."

Aunt Octavia tut-tutted. "I hope you didn't drive all night to have tea with an old woman."

Jane followed her into the kitchen and watched her aunt pour her a cup of her favorite breakfast blend.

"Aloysius went for a walk. He loves these crisp, still October mornings. Muffet Cat and I prefer to start our day with tea and a roaring fire. Let's go to the sitting room, and you can tell me everything."

Years ago, Muffet Cat had showed up at Storyton Hall in the middle of a storm. He'd been a malnourished, dirty, lost kitten, and though Jane had never owned a cat before, she did her best to nurse the tiny cat back to health. The tuxedo now weighed twenty pounds and spent most of his time on Aunt Octavia's lap.

"Where's our mighty mouser?" Jane asked when she saw the sofa was unoccupied.

"Drinking water from my bathroom glass, the little tyrant. I bought him a fancy electric water bowl and he won't go near it. If I put a regular cereal bowl down on the floor, he'll turn up his nose and walk away. And don't get me started on his food! I must've tried forty different brands by now. He takes two licks of whatever I give him and then tries to bury it."

Jane laughed. "I guess he doesn't remember he was once a starving, shivering stray."

"I think our brains protect us from the hardships of

our youth. Maybe it's the same for cats." Aunt Octavia lowered herself onto the sofa with a sigh. She fanned out the skirt of the pumpkin-orange housedress Mabel had made for her and fixed Jane with a benign stare. "Let's hear the real reason you came home early."

In between sips of tea, Jane told her the whole story.

Aunt Octavia listened closely without interrupting. Jane could practically see her opening filing cabinets in her mind as she stored and retrieved information. When Jane finished speaking, Aunt Octavia reached for her cane and tapped its tip lightly on the carpet.

"In my eight decades on this earth, I've learned to recognize the difference between a coincidence and a pattern, and I believe the key to this puzzle lies in the book St. James was writing. If the publisher still plans on releasing it, it's either already written or they'll hire a ghostwriter to finish it. You need to find out if this book is about our family."

"How?"

Before Aunt Octavia could reply, Muffet Cat waddled into the room and let out a meow of complaint. He glared at Jane until Aunt Octavia reached into one of the many pockets of the housedress and withdrew a bag of treats.

Patting the sofa cushion beside her, she cooed, "Don't be cross, darling. Jane isn't here to steal your supply of tuna fish."

Muffet Cat shot Jane a disapproving look before performing a nimble leap onto the sofa. For such a large cat, he could still move with the liquid grace that separated felines from the rest of the animal kingdom.

Aunt Octavia gave Muffet Cat a handful of treats and then turned her attention back to Jane. "You must know someone who has a reason to inquire after the book's plot. When I think of all the authors who've stayed with us, all the publishers, editors, copywriters—there must be one person you can ask."

Jane wracked her brain but couldn't think of a single person she could call on for help. She watched Muffet Cat devour his treats. When he finished, he spun around three times and settled down for a good long grooming session.

"I might not know anyone in New York, but I *do* know a bookstore owner. Maybe Eloise can think of something."

Aunt Octavia bobbed her head in agreement. "If there's no truer friend than a book, there's no better person than a book-loving friend."

Later, after the twins rushed off to catch the school bus and Edwin poured a giant cup of coffee and carried his laptop to the kitchen table, Jane asked if he wanted a ride to the Daily Bread.

"I'm working from home today, so I can do some serious healing before tomorrow's lunch service," he said. "If I can come up with the November menu, I can place orders with my suppliers and be ahead of the game for the rest of the week."

Jane left him to it and headed to the garages to fetch her bike. After sitting in the car for so long the day before, she needed some exercise.

The mists still clung to the low mountains surrounding Storyton, and the sky was the color of a dull knife. It was a day for soft sweaters, quiet voices, and extra cups of coffee.

A perfect reading day, Jane thought as she pedaled toward Broken Arm Bend.

The famous curve in the road had sent dozens of patients to the local doctor. The elementary students sang songs about the treacherous bend. Once, Jane had found the stories and songs amusing. But that was before the car William had been riding in had gone over the edge. Before he'd died for a second time.

The twins had met William, but they didn't know he was their father. Jane planned to tell them when they were older—in high school, maybe. By then, he'd be a shadowy figure in their memory. He'd stayed at Storyton Hall for only a few days, and in that time, he and the boys had bonded over their shared love of animals. They remembered him as the nice man who'd died in a car accident at Broken Arm Bend, and that was all.

They didn't know he'd been drugged and tortured for years—molded into the perfect spy. His mission was to insert himself back into Jane's life in order to discover the location of Storyton Hall's secret library.

Despite the indefatigable efforts of his handlers, William was his own man at the end. Everyone believed he'd forced that car off the road, ensuring that the person who'd been responsible for all his pain and torment died alongside him.

Jane didn't want her sons to learn their father had been imprisoned and tormented. Not yet. She wanted to guard their childhood against these horrors for a few more years, which was why she hated the thought of Justin St. James twisting a story already replete with pain and sorrow.

Why us? she wondered as she crossed the bridge over Storyton River. *Why Olivia? Or Heather? Why Winston? Or Angel Sanchez? How did he pick which small-town stories to use in his books?*

Butterworth had told her that Sinclair had compiled every article on the original events that had later become the subjects of St. James's novels. Storyton Hall's head librarian was searching for a common denominator, but so far, all he'd found was that St. James seemed interested in tragedies occurring to other writers.

"And we don't have any of those in my family," Jane muttered to herself as she turned onto Main Street. "Readers and book collectors, yes. Authors? No."

The shops lining the road were stone cottages with tidy front gardens and narrow alleyways. Most of the cottages were two-story structures, and the majority of the shopkeepers lived in the apartments upstairs. Others rented the space to employees or vacationers.

Eloise used to live above the bookshop, but she and her husband, Landon Lachlan, now lived in the renovated carriage house around the corner from Jane's house. A kindergarten teacher had rented her shabby chic apartment, and though both women were pleased with the arrangement, the teacher joked that she was going to have to ask for a raise to pay for all the books she kept buying.

Jane slipped her bike into the rack in front of Run for Cover, then paused to take in the charming window display. Eloise had turned dozens of pool noodles into pumpkins, creating a pumpkin patch right there in her window. In the center of the pumpkin patch stood a friendly scarecrow, who was reading to an audience of smiling blackbirds.

"I see you're running low on *The Hallo-Wiener*," Jane said as she entered the shop.

Eloise, who'd been unpacking a box of books, dropped an armload of paperbacks on the floor and rushed over to hug Jane.

"I talked to Edwin this morning. He told me—whoa." Eloise held on to Jane's left hand. "He told me about the bad stuff, but he did *not* tell me about this. It's gorgeous. Do you love it?"

"I do. I didn't think I'd be one of those women who'd glance at the ring on their finger a hundred times a day, but I definitely did that while I was driving yesterday. The sun kept hitting it just right."

Eloise rolled her eyes. "I know you love my brother, but the guy can be a moron sometimes. There you are, finding dead bodies left and right, and he's in a wheelchair because he stepped on not one but two stingrays. I know it was an accident, but I *really* wanted you to get some rest and have a little fun."

"We had fun. Just not as much as I'd hoped."

Gesturing toward the tiny kitchen in the back of the shop, Eloise said, "Let's have a chat before I have to open."

Jane sat at a table crowded with catalogs from publishers. She picked up the thin booklet on top. It was from one of the big publishing houses and featured a list of books with release dates four months away. There was a short description of each book, as well as an image of its cover.

"How far ahead of the pub date do they send you these?" she asked, pointing at the booklet.

"Anywhere from three to six months. They're mostly online now, but some of the publishers still send out booklets. I love flipping through them during my lunch break."

Jane put the booklet back in the pile. "I need to find out what St. James's next book is about. The police said it's scheduled for publication sometime next year. His editor wouldn't tell them anything without a court order. In the meantime, they've arrested a known drug dealer for the crimes, so that court order isn't going to happen."

Eloise plunked two coffee cups on the table and slid into the chair across from Jane. "Is it possible the drug dealer *did* kill the two people?"

"Even if he was involved, he's never heard of Storyton Hall. My home is a loose end, which is why I need to know if St. James was writing about my family when he died."

Eloise threw Jane a sympathetic look. "Would you try to stop the book from coming out?"

"I'd hire the best lawyer in the country!" Jane cried. "A whole team of lawyers! I'd throw lawsuit after lawsuit at those publishers."

"You'd only create more buzz for the book," Eloise argued.

Jane's shoulders sagged. "Probably. But I couldn't just sit back and let it happen."

The two friends sipped their coffee in silence for a moment. Jane waited for the peace of the bookstore to settle around her like a blanket fresh from the dryer. Here in the kitchen, the scent of paper was obscured by coffee, and though Eloise didn't show the slightest inkling of impatience, Jane had seen the stack of cardboard boxes scattered around the bookstore. She had books to shelve. To rearrange. To admire and recommend and sell.

"Do lots of people buy his books from you?"

"An average amount. Of all the thriller writers, I sell Lisa Jewell the most. Harlan Coban, Tana French, Jeffery Deaver, and Karin Slaughter are popular too." Eloise put her hand over Jane's. "If it would make you feel better, I won't stock his books anymore."

Jane shook her head. "I'd never ask you to do that. People should have access to the books they want to read."

"I figured you'd say that," Eloise said. "And ever since I talked to Edwin, I've been thinking about the book page found in St. James's pocket. If he was doing research on your family because he planned to write about William's accident, why go so far back in time? I mean, he was reading about relatives living hundreds of years ago in a different country. Why?"

This question hadn't occurred to Jane, and she felt like an idiot. How many deaths had occurred at Storyton Hall? How many people had checked in as guests, wheeling suitcases or carrying duffel bags, only to be wheeled out on a gurney?

So much violence. So much loss. Because of greed. Because they wanted to steal from the secret library.

Eloise knew about the library. In fact, she'd spent the past year helping Jane sell or donate a number of its most valuable books, maps, and documents.

"In the stories I heard growing up, Walter Edgerton Steward was the relative credited with creating a secret library and hiring men called the Fins to guard it. After too many threats to himself and his family, Walter dismantled the house and rebuilt it as an even bigger and grander place in a valley where he knew of all comings and goings. Everyone in the village depended on Storyton Hall for their livelihood. Strangers were viewed with suspicion. Visitors were closely observed. To this date, no one has discovered the library's location, and none of its treasures have been stolen."

"Okay, but what does any of this have to do with St. James?"

Jane held out a finger. "What if St. James planned to make a deal? He wouldn't write about my family if I gave him access to the library?"

"You'd never take that deal."

"He didn't know that. He must've found something in that manor house book to hold over my head. I need to get my hands on a copy."

Eloise's hand flew to her mouth. "I should check my email. I put out a request on this indie bookseller discussion board I belong to and forgot to see if anyone replied. It's been two days since I posted."

Jane followed Eloise behind the checkout counter and stood close enough to see her computer screen.

"There," Eloise pointed to an email notification. "Someone replied."

She clicked on a link, and a new window opened. Before Jane could read the name of the website, Eloise had already scrolled past a thread on the scariest books ever written until she came to another thread, "Urgent: Can You Help Me Find This Book?"

"He did it!" she exclaimed, thumping Jane on the arm several times in her excitement. "He found a copy! It's in the UK, and the quickest he can get it to us is Friday. Are you okay with the price?"

The book cost three hundred dollars, with an additional fifty-dollar shipping fee.

"Yes! Tell him to get it in the mail right away. *Please*."

Eloise had Jane's credit card on file, so she quickly completed the transaction and closed her laptop lid with a satisfied grin.

"Booksellers. We might not wear capes, but we can still save the day."

Jane slung an arm around Eloise's shoulder and squeezed. "My best friend, the hero."

"This hero is going to be late opening her store."

Eloise bounded away to unlock the door. An elderly woman stepped in, holding the hand of a little boy wearing an orange sweater and a knit hat.

"I hope I didn't rush you," the woman said. "Georgie was so excited for storytime that I had to bring him early. He can't wait to hear you read a spooky book. If it's too spooky, I'll have to cover my eyes."

Georgie looked up at her and said, "Don't worry, Grandma. I'll protect you."

"Thank you, sweetheart."

Eloise mouthed *So cute!* to Jane, who put her hands over her heart and nodded in agreement.

Run for Cover had worked its magic again. Jane had entered feeling anxious and stressed and left feeling energized and hopeful. That was mostly due to Eloise, but the exchange between the woman and her grandson reminded Jane of how lucky she was to have family and friends who were willing to protect her should life get too scary.

As she cycled home from the bookstore, she decided to spend the rest of the day going over details for the Boos and Booze book club meeting she was hosting on Friday. Tomorrow, she'd get together with Mrs. Hubbard to discuss the All Hallows' Ball.

Maybe there's nothing to fear, she told herself as she huffed and puffed up the hill. *Maybe we left it all behind us in Oyster Bay.*

She didn't believe that, or course, but there was nothing more she could do at present, so she decided to focus on more pleasant things. On food, family, and friends. Book clubs and Halloween parties. Costumes and candy.

And she decided, having gotten her exercise, that she would just pop into the kitchens in search of something made of chocolate.

Chapter 14

The Cover Girls were just some of the locals attending the All Hallows' Ball. Even though most of the attendees were current guests of Storyton Hall, tickets had also been purchased by locals, residents of neighboring towns, and, in a few instances, from other states.

After grabbing a quick lunch, Jane called a meeting with Sinclair, Sterling, and Lachlan to review the guest list. They met in the surveillance room, which also doubled as the office supply closet and Sterling's favorite place to drink his coffee in peace.

Lachlan glanced at Butterworth's empty chair. "Is he on his way back?"

"Yes. He and Olivia should be here in about four hours," Jane said. Looking at the chair, which was bathed in light from the television screens on the wall behind the table, she wondered what it would be like if Butterworth's seat remained empty.

I'd miss him, she thought. *But it's time for him to pursue his own happiness.*

As if sensing her train of thought, Sinclair said, "I'm glad to hear that Ms. Limoges is staying in his cottage. I can't think of a safer place."

Jane smiled. "You'll have to get used to calling her Olivia. I think Butterworth has lost his heart to her."

"Good for the old codger." Sterling saluted Butterworth's chair with his mug.

Sinclair directed Jane's attention to the papers spread out in front of him. "We divided the guests into three categories. If they've stayed with us before, we're assuming our regular background checks will be sufficient. All the locals are known to us, so our unknown factors are new guests and those who are attending the party but aren't staying at Storyton Hall. We have about fifty people to examine more closely."

"Do any of them have ties to Justin St. James?"

Pushing his coffee cup off the edge of his spreadsheet, Lachlan said, "We've been cross-referencing the party attendees with all the people connected to the real-life stories that inspired St. James's fictional ones but haven't had any hits yet."

"We're talking a boatload of names here," Sterling added. "First, you've got the family involved in the tragedy. Whether that was a fatal house fire or a gunshot wound, a core group of people was devastated by the incident. From there, we searched for the names of close friends, distant relatives, police officers, healthcare workers, lawyers, reporters, etcetera. We've had five days to read his novels and research the key players, but even if we had a hundred, we might overlook someone."

Jane put a hand on Sterling's arm. "I always ask so much from all of you. Every time there's a crisis, you have to perform your regular department duties while also keeping everyone safe *and* doing everything in your power to forestall any new threats." Pointing at the wall calendar over Sterling's desk, she said, "I went over the vacation schedule and saw that none of you have picked dates for next year. January will be here in two months, gentlemen, and I want you to block off your weeks and get away from Storyton Hall. That's an order."

Lachlan twirled his wedding ring around his finger. "I'll have to check with Eloise first."

"Naturally," agreed Jane. "Did she have any luck finding out the plot of St. James's final book?"

"She called everyone she knows in the publishing business but came up empty-handed."

Though it was the answer Jane had expected, she was still disappointed. She thanked Lachlan and went on. "I spoke with Olivia last night. Trent has confessed to possession charges. He insists he had nothing to do with the murders, that he never laid eyes on St. James, and that killing Rachel would be bad for business."

Sinclair removed the handkerchief from his breast pocket and began polishing his spectacles. "It sounds like we have every reason to be on our guard. If the killer is coming to Storyton Hall today or tomorrow, they won't go unnoticed. One of us will be in this room watching at all times. If there's nothing else for us to cover now, I'll return to the library and continue researching guests with criminal records."

"Before you go, did you find out who benefits from St. James's death?" Jane asked.

Lachlan said, "His attorney was tight-lipped. He told me to wait for the will to become public record, which will take at least sixty days. The executor of the will has been notified of St. James's death but has yet to submit an application to the clerk of court."

"Sounds like the executor is in no hurry to start the process. Either this person isn't getting anything from St. James, or the attorney is the executor and filing the application isn't on the top of his list."

Jane frowned. "I know that St. James wasn't married and that his parents are no longer living. But he has a stepbrother, right? Remind me why we're not hyper-focused on this man."

"His stepbrother is Alexander Hoyt," Sterling explained. "Justin's mom married Alex's dad. Alex is ten years older than Justin. Their parents' marriage didn't last long, and when it ended, the two boys rarely saw each other. As adults, they don't appear together in any social media posts. St. James lived in Charleston and Alex lives in a farmhouse in a small town outside Greensboro, North Carolina. He's a metalwork sculptor and a bunny breeder."

"A rabbit-loving artist? Interesting."

Sterling smiled at Jane. "Guess he's a gentle giant type. In the few photos I could find, Alex was posing with his rabbits. They're a special breed called Harlequin rabbits. On his website, Alex says that his dad, a welder, taught him about metalworking and rabbits. Alex looks compact and strong and has a bushy beard and brows."

"Sounds like a dwarf from *The Hobbit*," said Lachlan.

Jane's hands flew to her temples. "I need to pick up the twins' costumes!"

Sinclair got to his feet. "Go. We'll text you if anything comes up."

The village was surrounded by fiery colors. It looked like a sunset had melted over the trees marching along the hills. High above the hunched backs of the mountains, the sky was ocean blue.

It had been days since she'd left Oyster Bay, and Jane's feelings about the coastal town were confused. Before she'd found St. James's body on the beach, she'd been falling in love with the place. Now, it seemed like all the beauty she'd seen, from the lights reflecting on the water to the egrets soaring to their nests in the marshes, were marred by murder.

That didn't make sense to her. After all, she'd encountered plenty of violence in Storyton. That violence didn't always revolve around strangers either. Ever since she'd become the manager of Storyton Hall, it seemed like half the town had been pulled into one dark narrative or another.

Despite the chaos these types of events created, Jane still loved Storyton. This was her home. She knew every shop, street, and woodland trail. She knew how the valley changed its look with every season. She was unsurprised when snow and ice storms shut it down in the winter or when flash floods made certain streets impassable in the spring.

Storms. Violence. Loss. No matter what hardship was thrown her way, she never had to face it alone. Her people were in Storyton. They were her anchors. As long as she was in this place, she would never go adrift.

As she searched for a parking spot, she saw a dozen familiar faces. People smiled and waved, and she waved back. When she finally parked at the post office, she got out of the car to the sound of church bells ringing out the hour.

This tiny town, which she loved so dearly, could be a peaceful haven if not for Storyton Hall and its centuries-old secret. Without the library and its priceless holdings, the types of crimes committed would be small ones. Shoplifting and trespassing, instead of murder.

Until the secret library was empty, Jane would forever be bracing for the next threat. She'd been taking things slowly to avoid media attention, and to keep the sales and donations anonymous. Some of the most extraordinary titles in the collection were already gone, but she needed to pick up the pace. Until that attic turret was filled with dust and cobwebs, neither Jane nor any of the Fins could relax.

After this weekend, I'll do what I should've done years ago. Just let us get through it unscathed.

Having uttered this plea to a higher power, Jane entered Geppetto's with a lighter step.

The toy shop was filled to capacity with local parents and visitors from "over the mountain," a term the villagers used to describe places beyond their isolated valley. Locals went over the mountain to patronize big box stores, see medical specialists, or catch a plane. Then they happily returned home, where life was slower and quieter.

There was nothing quiet about Geppetto's today. During the last two weeks of October, Barnaby Nicholas moved half of his inventory into storage to make room for a gallery of Halloween costumes. Every year, he put together an array of spectacular outfits, from the cute and comic to the spectacularly spooky. Anyone who wanted to stand out in the trick-or-treat crowd got their costume from Geppetto's.

What he didn't offer were sexy costumes. If a little girl wanted to be a mermaid, Geppetto had a costume that was both magical and modest, and parents were grateful to find alternatives to the offerings they saw online.

Weaving her way around a man examining a werewolf costume and a woman carrying a robot costume in one hand and a flower fairy costume in the other, Jane got in line to pay.

Barnaby was flitting between the register and the closet behind the checkout counter, which was where he stored custom orders. His cheeks were flushed with exertion, but his smile said that he was having the time of his life.

When Barnaby had first come to Storyton, he'd been a slender, clean-shaven forty-year-old. Now, with his round belly, white beard, and red cheeks, he looked like Santa Claus. It was an appropriate comparison. He was patient, jolly, and kind, and all the children in town saw him as a surrogate grandfather.

As Jane waited in line, she was entertained by the other shoppers.

"Mia wants to be Belle, but all he's got left is Rapunzel," one woman squawked into her phone. "He's got a Jane costume—from *Tarzan*. It's *yellow* and comes with an umbrella. There's one Alice in Wonderland left, but the cat costs extra. No, she *can't* carry Fluffy around instead."

The woman ended the conversation and went over to the rack of storybook characters to grab the Alice in Wonderland costume. After picking out a blond wig, she selected the Cheshire cat puppet from the accessories area. By the time she took her place in line behind a man with three vampire costumes draped over his arm, it was Jane's turn to check out.

Barnaby popped in a pair of plastic fangs and cried, "'Tis the season to be ghoulie!" He pointed at the closet. "It's stuffed to the gills with costumes for tomorrow's ball. And I did not rob Mabel of any sales. She had so many requests and—"

"Only so many hours in the day," Jane finished for him.

He laughed. "That's right. She and I have entered our busiest seasons. Between now and the first of January, we'll be working hard and sleeping even harder. Hold on a minute while I find your order."

As soon as Barnaby vanished into the closet, a man and woman got into a heated debate over a *Star Wars* costume.

"I saw it first," said the woman.

"My hand was already on it," argued the man.

The woman refused to let go. "I promised my son that I'd find him the best *Star Wars* costume in the store. This is it. Do you want me to break my promise?"

"I promised my daughter the same thing!"

"Your daughter? This is a *boy*'s costume."

The man glared at her. "Says who?"

Barnaby emerged from inside the closet, and Jane jerked her thumb toward the warring shoppers. "You should put on a referee costume."

"Last-minute shoppers are stressed-out shoppers. Let's see what a little chocolate and kindness will do. Do you mind waiting while I sort this out?"

"Not at all," Jane said.

Barnaby hurried over to the adults. "Friends, friends. There is a solution to every problem. This is the last costume and you both want it, so the best way to sort this out is to let an unbiased party decide who gets it. That unbiased party is my Magic Eight Ball. Do you both agree to abide by its answer?"

Though neither of the adults looked pleased by Barnaby's suggestion, they reluctantly agreed.

"The first person to get a positive answer gets the costume. The person who doesn't will receive a discount on a different costume. Fair enough?"

The adults nodded, and Barnaby handed the Magic Eight Ball to the woman. She shook it, frowned, and showed him the reply.

"One of the wishy-washy responses, I'm afraid. Now you give it a shake, sir."

The man beamed when his reply surfaced in the toy's window.

"That's pretty definitive," Barnaby said as he showed the message to the woman.

She passed the costume to the man, and Barnaby rewarded her with the promised coupon and a candy bar. "For being a good sport."

"You could solve the world's biggest problems with a Magic Eight Ball and a chocolate bar," Jane said when Barnaby returned to the checkout counter.

He gave her a very Santalike wink. "Adults are just tall children. Here's your order. A gray robe and wizard's hat for Hem and a black robe and skeleton gloves for Fitz. I suspect they're responsible for the number of *Lord of the Rings* orders I had this year. I've never unpacked so many elf ears or goblin masks."

Jane said, "One of the kids is having a pizza party tomorrow. The whole class is invited. After they eat, they're all going trick-or-treating together. Hem and Fitz thought it would be a wonderful idea to pretend that Storyton was Middle Earth for the night."

"As long as no one ends up at Mount Doom, it's a fine idea."

Barnaby punched numbers into his register and Jane handed him her credit card. While she waited for the machine to print the receipt she needed to sign, she saw that the shop had become even more crowded. When a man held the door open for a woman with a baby stroller, Jane heard whistling coming from outside.

It took a second for the tune to sink in. When it did, Jane went rigid.

That song. It's "Paperback Writer."

Barnaby placed the receipt on the counter and then patted his shirt pocket. "I had three pens an hour ago. Where do they go?"

"I'll be right back," Jane said before rushing toward the door.

The woman with the stroller was struggling. One of the wheels was stuck on the metal transition strip and there wasn't enough room for her to reach around the wide stroller and free the wheel.

"I got it!" Jane called. As she reached for the wheel, she craned her neck to see beyond the Halloween decorations in the window to the sidewalk beyond.

The moment the stroller was free, Jane squeezed past the woman and burst outside.

She looked to the left and saw a couple walking a white terrier. Behind them was a woman carrying a reusable shopping bag, and behind her was a woman with her phone pressed to her ear.

Glancing to the right, Jane saw the owner of Spokes, the bike shop, talking to a man in cycling gear. There were more pedestrians farther up the block. People in barn jackets and down vests. People in flannel shirts and sweaters. People wearing knit hats or baseball caps. She saw dogs on leashes. Baby strollers. A deliveryman pushing a hand truck stacked with boxes.

The garden gate in front of Tresses Salon opened,

and Mrs. Pratt stepped onto the sidewalk. Seeing Jane, she bustled over.

"What do you think?" She pivoted her head this way and that, drawing Jane's attention to the subtle pink and purple highlights in her gray hair.

"Beautiful. It really suits you." Jane jerked her thumb at the toy store. "I have to go back in and sign my credit card receipt. I came outside because I thought I heard someone whistling 'Paperback Writer.' "

Mrs. Pratt grinned at her reflection in the window. "The Beatles song?"

"Yes. I'll tell you why it spooked me when I come back out. In the meantime, keep your ears open."

Barnaby had Jane's receipt and a pen sitting to the side of the register. She didn't want to interrupt his current transaction, so she signed the paper, grabbed her purchases, and rejoined Mrs. Pratt.

"Do you have time for a coffee?"

"Always," said Mrs. Pratt.

They found a table at the Canvas Creamery, and Phoebe brought them two cinnamon spice lattes.

"Is this a private convo, or can I sit with you until a customer comes?"

Jane patted the chair beside her. "I was just going to tell Eugenia how Rachel, the young woman who was killed outside my hotel room, was singing a particular Beatles song two days before her murder. I heard someone whistling that same song in Oyster Bay during a street fair. I was surrounded by people, so I couldn't identify the whistler. And I heard it *just* now, outside of Geppetto's."

"Pretty weird coincidence," said Phoebe.

Mrs. Pratt studied Jane's face. "You're worried. Even

though a man was arrested for the murders, you don't think what happened at the beach is staying at the beach."

Jane took a fortifying sip of her latte and nodded. "You know me too well."

"I'm going to text the other Cover Girls," said Phoebe. "Eugenia can tell Roger and you can ask Edwin to listen for someone whistling that tune. Half the merchants in town will be on alert. That should be enough."

As Phoebe's fingers flew over her phone's keypad, Jane said, "If they do hear it, tell them to take a pic of the whistler. No one should engage this person. They could be dangerous."

Mrs. Pratt looked disappointed. "That's too bad. Roger has a whole display of antique weapons in his shop, and I'd love to try out the spiked club. He said I could hit a pumpkin with it, but that doesn't sound like very much fun."

"Just a photo," Jane repeated.

Phoebe waved her phone in the air. "Eloise wants you to stop by the bookstore. She said something about a special delivery from England. Does that ring any bells?"

Jane bolted out of her chair. "It's a book, and it could be the answer to all my troubles."

"Books can't solve all our problems, but they can always help us escape from them for a little while," Mrs. Pratt said.

Phoebe put a hand on Jane's arm. "Before *you* escape, Eloise wants a decaf cappuccino. I'll make it as fast as I can."

She hurried around the counter and took up her position behind the espresso machine. Over the hiss of the milk frother, Mrs. Pratt said, "I'm going to take a walk around the village. I want everyone to check out my gorgeous hair and *I* want to see if I bump into any whistling strangers. Until tonight!"

When Mrs. Pratt opened the door to leave, some of the parents who'd been shopping at Geppetto's entered the shop. Jane paid for Eloise's cappuccino and told Phoebe that she'd see her in a few hours.

"Stay safe!" Phoebe called out.

This earned Jane curious stares from the group of parents. Averting her eyes, she darted outside and trotted down the street.

She entered Run for Cover to find a line of customers at the checkout counter. Eloise caught her eye and jerked her head toward the back. "Your special order is in the kitchen."

Jane held up the coffee cup. "Here's yours."

After setting the cup down next to the register, she hustled through the swing door tucked between the biography and cookbook sections.

The parcel on Eloise's table was still cocooned in bubble wrap. Jane couldn't believe Eloise hadn't opened it.

"My curiosity would've gotten the better of me," she murmured to herself.

But Eloise was the most loyal person Jane had ever known. She wouldn't have unwrapped that book in a million years. She'd leave it sitting on the table until Jane arrived. And then she'd continue giving her customers her undivided attention, even though she knew her best friend was about to examine a rare and unusual book.

Jane used Eloise's kitchen scissors to sever the tape holding the bubble wrap in place and used her fingers to rip off the final layer of protection. Once she'd removed the white tissue paper, the book in her hands seemed so small. So inconsequential.

Compared to contemporary book covers, the cover of *Manor Houses and Halls of England* was very plain. There was no dust jacket and the cloth was tobacco brown. The title was stamped on the spine in faded gilt letters. The book felt old and tired. Its covers were bent. It had age spots. Whole chunks of pages were loose, like vertebrae separating from a spine.

Jane ignored the title page and turned directly to the table of contents. She spotted the listing for Edgerton House and carefully turned pages until she reached fifty-two.

The muted chatter from the bookstore all but disappeared as Jane read the opening paragraph.

"One of the oldest manor homes in England, Edgerton House is set in the tranquil countryside. The former castle was remodeled in 1768 to include a new entrance, a gallery, an expanded library, and attic bedrooms. The grounds include five hundred acres of sweeping lawns, ancient woodlands, and ornamental gardens. The interior is lavish, featuring paintings and sculptures by Renaissance masters, Flemish tapestries, and elegant carvings."

The author went on to describe the windows, the aspect from the front of the house, the staircase in the Great Hall, notable portraits, and so on.

Jane turned the page and let out a small gasp.

The entire page was taken up by an engraving of the new and improved library. Jane looked at the massive fireplace. She looked at the floor-to-ceiling bookshelves lining the western wall. She looked at the large windows and the paintings hung from the wood paneling on the eastern wall. Everything about the room, from its proportions to the rows upon rows of book spines, was as familiar to Jane as her own face.

"You okay? You look like you've seen a ghost."

Jane hadn't heard Eloise crack the door just wide enough to see into the kitchen. Pointing at the book, she said, "The ghost of a room."

Eloise couldn't resist coming all the way into the kitchen to take a closer look. As she bent over the engraving, her eyes flew open wide. "That's the Henry James Library! I mean, the furniture is different, but I'd know that room anywhere. What does the caption say?"

"That there appeared to be a hidden door in the paneled wall—one that Lord Stewart was unwilling to talk about."

A tiny frown appeared on Eloise's brow. "I guess there's a room behind that hidden door. Do you think it was the same size as Sinclair's office?"

Jane flipped forward two pages and shook her head. "I don't know. The author goes on to talk about the folly and the views of the lake. This page shows the folly as well as the engraving with the coat of arms. It's the same page found on St. James's body."

"If your ancestor had a collection of priceless books squirreled away in his house, he wouldn't want attention drawn to that hidden door." Eloise's voice sounded dreamy. "When people hear about a hidden door, they automatically imagine a secret passageway. Or a secret room."

Returning to the engraving of the library, Jane said, "If the killer has this book, there's a chance they think the door to Sinclair's office *is* the entrance to the secret library. If that's true, I'll be happy to let them in."

Eloise stared at Jane as if she'd lost her mind. "Why

would you ever be happy to have a murderer creeping around Storyton Hall?"

"Because I won't have to guess what costume they're wearing or how to track them inside Storyton Hall. I know they'll wind up in the Henry James Library. And when they do, the Fins and I will be waiting."

Chapter 15

That night, the Cover Girls rolled into Jane's kitchen wearing their favorite Halloween-themed book shirts.

Anna and Violet put their covered dishes on the center island and then had a good laugh at the fact that they'd worn the same shirt. It featured a ghost with reading glasses and the text READ MORE BOOOOOOKS! Anna's was black and Violet's was purple.

Betsy's shirt had the Macbeth quote, "something wicked this way comes," floating above a bubbling cauldron. Mabel's just said I LOVE SPOOKY READS. Eloise wore an orange sweatshirt of a skeleton stretched out on the sofa with a book in its lap and the words JUST ONE MORE CHAPTER.

"This brings me back to my teacher days," Mrs. Pratt said as she smoothed down the front of her *Cat in the Hat* shirt. She read the titles of the bookstack on Jane's sweatshirt and nodded. "You don't get much spookier than *The Shining* and *Salem's Lot*.

Phoebe pointed at her GHOULS JUST WANNA READ shirt and said, "And eat. And drink."

Jane had made pomegranate champagne punch and poured it into glasses moments before the doorbell rang. She now picked up a glass and said, "Here's to the only meeting I always look forward to!"

The women drank their punch and chatted. They drifted around the kitchen, removing plastic wrap and Tupperware lids from bowls and platters, warming up dishes in the oven, and rooting around Jane's drawers for serving utensils.

A few of Jane's friends had already seen her ring, but the rest paused to admire it between sips of punch or the organization of food.

"The whole village will want to see you get married." Mrs. Pratt draped her arm around Phoebe. "And *you* need to catch Jane's bouquet."

Phoebe blushed. "Gil and I just started dating over the summer. And he lives in Chicago, remember?"

Mrs. Pratt waved this off. "He runs a greeting card company. Why couldn't he do that from here?"

"Why don't you ask him? He's coming to see me next weekend."

Mrs. Pratt beamed. "He's crazy about you, Phoebe. One day, he'll come for a visit that'll end up lasting the rest of your lives."

Betsy finished arranging tortilla chips around a bowl of her seven-layer taco dip. She'd piped a sour cream spiderweb on top and told her friends her dip was called Ectoplasm, in honor of their book pick, a ghost story by Darcy Coates.

Violet balled up the empty chip bag and tossed it at Mrs. Pratt. "If you want another wedding so badly, you and Roger should tie the knot."

"We're happy just as we are. Roger likes his apartment above the shop, and I like things in my house just so. Roger is the love of my golden years, and I thank my stars for him every day, but I will *never* share a bathroom with a man again!"

The Cover Girls hooted with laughter.

After filling their plates with monster meatballs, mashed potato ghosts, witch finger cheese straws, and roasted root vegetables, the women sat down at Jane's dining room table and shared what they liked and didn't like about *The Haunting of Ashburn House.*

As Mabel reached for the pepper shaker, she said, "I thought it was the perfect mixture of creepy without being hide-under-the-covers terrifying. Thank you for picking a book that didn't give me nightmares, like *Dracula* did."

When they'd all shared their favorite scenes or memorable quotes, the talk turned to the All Hallows' Ball.

"I can't wait to see everyone in their costumes," said Anna. "Mabel, your fingers must be sore from all that sewing."

Mabel splayed her hands on the table. "My fingers, hands, eyeballs, shoulders, and back."

Jane smiled at her. "Good thing you have an appointment at the Walt Whitman Spa on Monday afternoon."

"I do?" Mabel looked baffled, and then delighted. "I do? Oh, that's wonderful!"

Eloise turned to Jane. "Edwin said he booked you a massage to help you recover from your unvacation. Did it help?"

"A little. I tried to relax, but I couldn't hit the Off switch in my brain. I kept asking myself why I thought it was a good idea to have a masquerade ball. *Masks!* At

Storyton Hall! After all I've seen, I should've known better."

Betty poked two holes in her napkin and held it over her face. "Kids love masks because for one night, they get to be someone else. A superhero or a princess. A monster or an animal." She lowered the napkin and frowned. "They give adults a sense of freedom too. Either we can pretend to be something we're not or that mask lets us be our truer selves."

"It also allows potential murderers to blend in with a crowd," Jane muttered.

Eloise pushed away her plate. "Ladies, let's tell Jane about our *other* reading while we eat dessert."

While the other Cover Girls cleaned up after dinner, Phoebe and Violet carried platters of chocolate-dipped strawberry ghosts, caramel apple bites, pumpkin truffles, and red velvet cookies into the dining room. Jane brewed a pot of decaf and heated water for tea.

When they'd all reconvened and were passing the desserts around, Jane said, "Okay, tell me about this mysterious reading."

Eloise made a sweeping gesture, incorporating everyone at the table. "When Edwin called me from the hospital, he told me about his injury, and about you finding St. James's body. As soon as I got off the phone, I went to see Sinclair. He explained that he, my husband, and Sterling would be devoting all their spare time reading the newly deceased author's books. I sent a group text to the rest of the Cover Girls, and *we* decided to read everything Winston Hall and Heather O'Grady had written. I also made calls to their hometown bookstores. I figured the booksellers might know something about the two authors that wasn't common knowledge. Booksellers are very observant people."

Seeing the glint in Eloise's eyes, Jane knew her friends had made a discovery.

"You found something."

"We did, but we didn't realize it until today. Landon and I were talking about the investigation over breakfast. When I asked him what ketamine was used for, he told me that it's one of the most widely used sedatives in veterinary practices. Not just in the States either. All over the world."

Jane picked up a truffle but didn't bite into it. Instead, she put the treat back on her plate and said, "Is the something you found a veterinarian?"

Her friends nodded.

"Heather O'Grady's boyfriend? He's a vet," Betty said. "And that's not all. Winston Hall's son works at a compound pharmacy. One of the services the pharmacy offers is ketamine therapy. The drug can be used as an antidepressant and to treat other mental health issues."

"We don't know where either of these people are right now, but we know where Winston and Heather are. Winston has a signing at the Fountain Bookstore in Richmond tonight. Heather's even closer. She has a talk and signing at noon in Charlottesville tomorrow. Neither writer has another event until next weekend. They'll both be in Pittsburgh for a crime lover's conference."

"Which means that they—or their family members—have plenty of time to drive to Storyton."

"To attend a costume party," added Mrs. Pratt.

Jane ate the truffle so fast that she barely tasted it. Then she leaned back and crossed her arms over her chest. "Okay, ladies. Let's figure out how we're going to identify our masked guests. It's not in my nature to stalk my partygoers, but I'll do whatever it takes to keep Storyton Hall from turning into the Haunted Mansion."

The next morning, Jane woke up early and couldn't go back to sleep. Edwin had gotten home after midnight, and she didn't want to wake him by tossing and turning while she obsessed over all the things that could go wrong at the masquerade ball.

Slipping out of bed, she dressed quietly in the dark and tiptoed downstairs to let Merry and Pippin out of their crates. She fed them a light breakfast and decided to take them for a walk on Tennyson's Trail.

The dogs were thrilled to be outside, but Jane was shocked by the cold. The air had a bite to it, and the frost-covered ground crunched under her feet as she headed for Storyton Lake.

She didn't expect to encounter any guests. They'd all be nestled under downy white comforters in their quiet rooms while the staff prepared for the day.

Storyton Hall employees would be cleaning streaks from windows and mirrors, polishing brass kickplates and silver serving pieces, running vacuums, and dusting. They'd be freshening the floral arrangements, laying out newspapers in the lobby, or fluffing pillows on reading sofas and chairs.

In the kitchens, the day would've started long before Jane got out of bed. The first person to arrive would be the baker, and he'd have the whole space smelling of homemade bread and breakfast biscuits before the next round of staff arrived.

This group would organize the kitchens for the breakfast and lunch services by washing and chopping fruits and vegetables, making salad dressings, and preparing soups and sauces. They'd accept deliveries from local farms and stow fresh produce, cheese, milk, cream, butter, and hundreds of eggs in the walk-in refrigerator. And they'd brew coffee. Giant urns of rich, aromatic coffee.

Outside the manor house, however, nothing stirred. Jane heard an occasional bird chirp or the rustling of a squirrel, but overall, the world felt somnolent and muted.

Even the lake was silent. Unlike summer, when the constant croaking of frogs competed with the whirr of dragonfly wings and the persistent drone of cicadas, this last day of October held the hush of winter.

Merry and Pippin seemed determined to make up for the lack of noise. They wanted to investigate every scent. Their noses quivered with interest and their heads darted back and forth, as if they were afraid of missing something.

Suddenly, both dogs stiffened. Their ears perked and they stared off to the right, to where another path curved around the lake.

Jane tensed too.

She told the dogs to sit, but they were too focused on whatever had caught their attention to obey her command.

When Pippin began to growl, Merry got agitated and shifted on his feet.

Jane heard the crack of a stick and saw two shapes emerge onto the other path. When she realized that one of those shapes was a black dog, she instantly relaxed.

Captain Haviland let out a solitary bark of greeting.

The puppies pulled on their leads, their tails whipping back and forth as they whined and snorted in excitement.

"Go on, then," Jane said, releasing them.

Within seconds, the three poodles were saying hello in the universal manner of all friendly dogs. While they sniffed and circled each other, Jane walked toward Olivia until the two women were standing at the edge of a short dock.

"Couldn't sleep?" Olivia asked.

"Too much on my mind. What about you?"

Oliva's gaze traveled over to Haviland. "Someone was unsettled by his new surroundings. To my surprise, he's fond of Alistair, so I'm not sure what was troubling him. I've learned to follow his lead, so when he wanted to get up and get outside, I put on my coat and trailed after him."

There was something ominous in the way Olivia described her dog's behavior. It was as if Haviland wanted to scout the area for potential threats. If only she could allow him to roam freely during the party. She was certain he'd sniff out an enemy before they had a chance to do any harm.

When Jane voiced this thought aloud, Olivia laughed. "Funny you should say that, because I brought along a pair of wolf ears on the off chance you'd be okay with Haviland coming to the party as a wolf. Of the big, bad variety, of course."

"Are you coming as a pig?"

Narrowing her eyes in rebuke, Olivia said, "Red Riding Hood. Fairy-tale characters aren't exactly my style, but it was the best I could do on such short notice."

"And what will you be carrying in your basket? Treats for Grandma or a bottle of pepper spray?"

"Actually, Alistair wants to turn my prop into a live-stream camera. He gave it to Mr. Sterling last night. It should be ready to go later this morning."

Jane grinned. "We can always use another pair of eyes. The Cover Girls are helping too. There are fifty people coming to tonight's ball who we need to watch more closely than the other guests. Each of my friends will track five of those people, but it'll be tricky because we have to match names with costumes as soon as our guests arrive."

"How many people are attending this event?"

"Three hundred. Add my staff to that number, and Storyton Hall is going to be packed to the gills."

Looking pensive, Olivia said, "If you wanted to go unnoticed at a masquerade ball, what costume would you wear?"

Jane mulled over the question for several seconds. "Nothing flashy or unique. I'd pick a traditional look, like a vampire or a mummy—something other people might wear. If there were six Draculas at one party, it would be hard to track a particular Dracula's movements. Unless . . ."

Olivia let out a low chuckle. "I could practically see a cartoon light bulb pop up over your head. You've had an idea?"

"I need to talk to the twins, but there might just be a way to know where every Dracula is at any given time. Which is great if a Dracula is up to no good, but not very helpful if the real villain is one of ten Batmans or Jokers."

"Speaking of superheroes, Superman has probably cooked me a full English breakfast by now, so I should be heading back."

Jane liked the thought of Butterworth bustling around

his kitchen, making tea and frying sausages. She knew his toast would be cut into precise triangles and he'd serve marmalade instead of jam. His table would be set with cloth napkins and the flatware would be placed exactly two inches away from the edge of the table.

Does he wear an apron over his clothes?

She was tempted to ask Olivia but decided against it.

The two women separated the three dogs, and Jane carried on with her walk. Running into Olivia had lifted the solitary feel of the morning, and though Jane was glad of it, she knew she needed time alone to store up energy for the hours to come.

She returned to her house to find Edwin in the kitchen with a mixing bowl in his hand. He wore a pair of thick socks and his fuzzy slippers, but Jane noticed that he tried not to move around too much.

Merry and Pippin raced across the floor to say hello to Jane, and then Edwin crooked a finger at her. "Do you have a kiss for the chef?"

"Always," she said.

She slipped her arms around Edwin's body. He was toasty warm and smelled like coffee. She put a hand on his unshaved cheek, and he feigned a shiver.

"You're cold," he whispered, rubbing her back vigorously before kissing each cheek, the tip of her nose, and, finally, her lips. Jane worried that she was hurting him and tried to pull away. As if reading her mind, Edwin said, "I'm okay. I gave my feet the mummy treatment this morning, so I'm perfectly capable of holding you."

She leaned her head against his shoulder and said, "What are you making?"

"Chocolate chip pumpkin pancakes with a side of Maplewood bacon. Though if the twins had their way, there'd be a platter of bacon and a side of pancakes." Edwin kissed her forehead and then pressed a mug into her hands. "Fill that up and go read for a bit. The twins won't be up for a while, so relax while you can."

"I don't think I can read right now. I had an idea I want to run past you. After that, I'll make a to-do list for today and run into the village to pick up our costumes and see the sheriff."

Edwin slipped on a pair of oven mitts and and raised a hand to either side of his head. "Go on. I'm all ears."

Jane laughed. "If someone came along five years ago and told me that you'd be in my kitchen, making pancakes and cracking Dad jokes, I would've thought they had a screw loose. But here we are."

"Here we are," he repeated. "In my favorite place. In this house. With the boys, the dogs, and you. It's my favorite moment too. Until our next favorite moment."

"I love you." Jane gave him a tender smile before pointing at the oven. "And I think your bacon's burning."

Chapter 16

After breakfast, Jane walked up the driveway and entered Storyton Hall's kitchens.

She put in an order for a sausage, egg, and cheese biscuit and then strolled through the lobby. She smiled at the guests helping themselves to coffee from the large silver urns. Other guests sat on sofas or chairs near the fireplace, looking snug and content as they read their books or perused one of the daily newspapers.

When Jane paused to say hello to the front desk staff, they all told her how much they were looking forward to the All Hallows' Ball.

"Could you print me a list of the guests slated to check in today?" Jane asked. "I'm heading into town and won't be able to look at it until I get back, so there's no rush."

Proceeding to the surveillance room, Jane found Sterling and Lachlan standing in front of the bank of TV screens.

"Anything to see?" she asked, closing the door behind her.

Lachlan shook his head. "It's pretty quiet. Most people seem to be sleeping in. The breakfast orders are just starting to trickle in now."

"Yeah, the kitchen was surprisingly calm. It won't be like that tonight. Thank goodness we opted for a buffet. A sit-down dinner might've killed Mrs. Hubbard."

Sterling grunted. "She'd be fine. Her sous chefs on the other hand . . ."

"I had an idea. I don't know if it'll work, but we might be able to track suspicious partygoers in real time. From this room—even when they're not on camera."

Turning to face Jane, Sterling said, "Go on."

"The twins borrowed my credit card because they wanted to buy two nano GPS chip trackers and register for a monthly subscription. The chips are supposed to hang from the dogs' collars. That way, if they run off for whatever reason, the boys can find them. The thing is, one of my wunderkinder pushed the wrong button on the online order page, so we now have two *hundred* nano trackers instead of two."

Sterling's eyes flashed with delight. "I'll have to give those boys a pat on the back next time I see them."

"Or tell Mrs. Hubbard to add extra treats to their Halloween bags," Lachlan suggested.

"You won't do either of those things," Jane said firmly. "They need to learn to be careful with online ordering. Not every mistake turns into a happy accident. I'm on my way to see the sheriff, but I wanted to tell you what I learned in book club last night."

"Doesn't what happens at book club stay at book club?" Sterling teased.

Jane didn't have time for levity, so she told the two men about the people connected to Heather O'Grady and Winston Hall who had access to ketamine.

The light in Sterling's eyes vanished, and he glanced at Lachlan. "Call the others. We need to meet."

Jane moved to leave, but Lachlan put a hand on her arm. "Can I run over to your place and pick up the trackers? I need to see if they're thin enough to slip into people's pockets or stick onto their clothes."

"We won't have to work that hard. I know how we can get every person at the party to voluntarily carry a tracker."

"How?" asked Sterling.

A tiny smile tugged at the corners of Jane's mouth. "Barnaby said that adults are just kids in bigger bodies. I think he's right, which means all I have to do is offer a prize that all the partygoers will want to win."

Sterling and Lachlan exchanged puzzled glances.

"Okay, I'll bite," said Sterling. "What's the prize? What's something everyone wants?"

"A free spa day. Meals included."

Lachlan made a check mark in the air. "That should do it."

"She's a clever one, our boss," Sterling said affectionately.

Jane left them to their cameras and television screens and, after filling up a takeout cup in the lobby and swinging by the kitchens to collect the breakfast biscuit she'd ordered, drove to the sheriff's station.

The duty officer was on the phone when Jane approached the desk, but he smiled and signaled for her to continue down the hall to the sheriff's office.

Sheriff Evans was seated behind his desk, squinting

at something on his computer screen. There was a full cup of coffee on his desk blotter, and the arm of his glasses poked out from beneath a pile of papers behind the phone.

Jane knocked on the open door. "Good morning. Do you have a few minutes?"

"For you? Always. In fact, I was about to call you." His gaze traveled to the cup in her hand. "Is that for me?"

In answer, Jane placed the cup and brown bag containing the breakfast biscuit on his desk. He invited her to sit down and, after taking a sip of coffee, gestured at his computer screen. "I was just reading about our John Doe from the woods. We were able to confirm his identity this morning, and I'm currently searching for his next of kin."

Dread seeped through Jane's body. If Sheriff Evans wanted to speak to her about the dead man Sam had found the day before she'd left for the beach, the death was probably connected to Storyton Hall.

"Was he one of our guests?"

"No. He was renting the Shaws' cabin, just as Sam believed. However, he gave them a false name. He paid them by Venmo in advance, and because the funds came through without a hitch and he said he'd be the only person staying on the property, the Shaws didn't dig any deeper."

Why would they? Jane thought ruefully. *They don't have to run background checks on their guests because they have an attic filled with priceless books.*

"What's his real name?"

Sheriff Evans swiveled his computer screen so Jane could see the photo of a bearded man in overalls cradling a bunny.

"Alex Hoyt?"

The sheriff's brows twitched in surprise. "You recognize him?"

"He's Justin St. James's stepbrother. Sterling found him online while he was running a search for St. James's next of kin."

"It seems our paths have converged." Sheriff Evans unwrapped the breakfast biscuit and took a healthy bite. He chewed, swallowed, and jerked his chin at the computer screen. "I just finished reading an email from the Shaws when you came in. Apparently, Mr. Hoyt has rented their cabin several times over the past year. They gave me the dates, but they don't strike me as being especially significant. I'll forward them to you so you can look them over."

Jane couldn't stop staring at Alex Hoyt's face. His eyes seemed kind, and the fluffy, black-and-white rabbit was clearly content to be held in his large, work-worn hands. Was this the photo of a man who'd rent a cabin in the woods in order to snoop around Storyton Hall? Or had he really come to this quiet town for a well-deserved vacation?

Vacationers don't book rental cabins under false names.

"What killed him?"

The sheriff closed all the windows on his screen, leaving only a blank, blue field. "Ketamine overdose. There was bruising under the hairline, and the ME found a puncture wound consistent with a syringe needle. I asked her to check for ketamine after you and I talked, and there it was. Deputy Phelps has already reached out to the investigating officers in Oyster Bay."

Jane ran her hands over her face. Why would someone kill St. James's stepbrother? And why was Alex at

Storyton Hall? Was there a chance the murders had nothing to do with the secret library?

Suddenly struck by an idea, she said, "Was he at the Shaws' cabin on September twenty-seventh?"

The sheriff didn't need to consult his email. He lowered his sandwich to its waxed paper and nodded. "Is there something special about that date?"

"We had a family birthday party, and Uncle Aloysius showed up a little late because he had to walk back from the folly. He was meeting with a man about a sculpture. He wanted to commission a memorial to mark the place where the young poet died over the summer. He'd already met with several sculptors by then, and he didn't mention Alex by name. That was probably because Uncle Aloysius preferred another artist."

The sheriff balled up the waxed paper and tossed it in the bin next to his file cabinet. Then he opened the file in front of him and made a note on the inside cover. "Would you ask your uncle about the date as soon as you get home? I'd go myself, but I need to talk to Officers Henniger and Locklear."

"I will," she assured him. "There's something else you should know—about the other two authors I met in Oyster Bay. They both hated St. James. And even though the police cleared them of his murder, they might have overlooked other family members. My book club friends have spent the past week reading everything they could about Heather O'Grady and Winston Hall."

Sheriff Evans leaned over until his belly hit the edge of his desk and said, "What did they find?"

Involuntarily, Jane mirrored his movement. "They're

both close to people with access to ketamine. One is a veterinarian. The other manages a compound pharmacy."

"What are their names and their relationship to the authors?"

Jane told him, and he added the information to his notes. When he was done, he drummed his fingers on the arms of his chair. "If the killer is hoping to gain access to a particular room in Storyton Hall, it would be a good idea for your aunt and uncle to have some company. Deputy Emory has volunteered to spend the night in their apartment. My other deputies will be attending the party as characters from *The Three Musketeers*. Except for Phelps. He's going to be Robin Hood. I'm the Sheriff of Nottingham."

"You'll be as dashing as Alan Rickman, I'm sure."

"Hardly, but the costume allows me to carry weapons. I'll have a shoulder holster under my cape and a baton in my sword scabbard. My deputies will also be armed. We plan to arrive an hour early. Can we get together for a briefing before the party starts?"

Jane was about to reply when Deputy Phelps darkened the doorway. "I'm on with the officers in Oyster Bay. They want me to patch you in on the call."

"Talk soon," Jane said, getting to her feet.

Sheriff Evans moved to touch the brim of his hat. When he realized he wasn't wearing it, he nodded instead. "Thanks again for the breakfast. Call me after you speak with your uncle."

It was a short walk from the sheriff's station to La Grande Dame, and Mabel had Jane's order bagged and ready to go. There was a line of customers waiting to collect their costumes, so Jane waved at her friend, grabbed her costumes from the rack next to the register, and called out, "See you tonight!"

At least six people in addition to Mabel responded, "I can't wait!"

The drive back to Storyton Hall was too short for Jane to look at Alexander Hoyt's death from multiple angles. After parking the truck and dropping the costumes off at home, she sent a text to the Fins.

Body near Hilltop Stables is Alex Hoyt. Another ketamine overdose. Rented cabin under false name. I'm going to see if Uncle Aloysius met with Hoyt before he died. Meet me in surveillance room at 11.

Jane had to question her great-uncle with care. Over the summer, he'd begun exhibiting signs of dementia and, after a thorough evaluation, was diagnosed with vascular dementia. Since then, he'd been taking medication and working with a therapist to exercise his memory. In an effort to keep his brain stimulated, he and Aunt Octavia were taking an online painting class, and he was also learning how to bake bread.

When he opened the door and ushered Jane into their apartment, she saw his apron and knew she'd interrupted one of his baking sessions. She also knew it was important not to distract him while he was following the directions of a recipe.

"What are you baking today?"

"Herbed Parmesan. We're having a dinner guest, so I wanted to make something tasty to go with the pasta."

Deputy Amelia Emory and Aunt Octavia had become thick as thieves over the summer, bonding over their love of Pre-Raphaelite art and Victorian novels.

"Is it in the oven?"

He flashed her an impish grin. "The dough's proofing in the dryer! It's a handy little trick I learned. I throw my bath towels in on high, and once it's nice and hot inside, the towels come out and the dough goes in." He pointed at the digital timer on the counter. "Fourteen minutes to go."

"Can I ask you about the sculpture for the folly?"

"Of course. Would you like some cider?"

Jane was antsy to talk and be on her way, but her uncle looked so cute in his checked apron that she could only smile and say, "I'd love some."

She accepted the cold cider and waited while her uncle fetched something from her office.

"Here's the sketch of the final design," he said, handing her a folder.

Jane had already seen the sketch but didn't want to make her uncle feel bad by reminding him of it, so she carried the folder to the table and sat down.

"I know you interviewed a few artists. Did they all supply sketches?"

Uncle Aloysius gestured at the folder. "They're in there."

Jane flipped through pages of brochures, cost estimates, and drawings of a boy with a fishing pole, a tidal wave, a bench inside a circle, and an abstract spiral.

"Do you remember a man called Alexander Hoyt? From North Carolina?"

"Yes. He breeds bunnies." Her uncle sat down across from her and reached for the sketches. "This is his sketch."

Hoyt had made the bench inside the circle.

"He made a few of these for his local library, I think. He said they were really comfortable, and he thought people would like to sit in the folly and look at the lake. I like the idea of benches there, but I wanted the memorial to be something special. The spiral is my favorite. Not only does it have a lovely shape, but it's actually a small fountain. Did I tell you that?"

"I think it's the perfect choice," Jane said. "How did you pick these artists?"

"Deputy Emory helped me find them. Except for Mr. Hoyt. *He* reached out to *me*. I liked his online gallery, even though he hasn't made many pieces in the last five years, but I decided to let him throw his hat in the ring."

Jane studied the printouts taken from Alex Hoyt's website. "How many times did you meet with him?"

"Just the once. I don't remember the exact date, but it was in September. Why the sudden interest in Mr. Hoyt?"

"He was in Storyton last week, staying at a rental cabin. I was wondering if he might've come back to see you."

Uncle Aloysius shook his head. "I know I have memory issues, but I would've remembered if he was here more than once. He has a distinctive look. Short and strong, with lots of hair and a full beard. Like a dwarf from the books the boys love. What's the author's name? Tolkien! That's him!"

He was so pleased that Jane couldn't help but smile. "Do you remember anything else about Mr. Hoyt? Other than his art? And his bunnies?"

"Only that he was very interested in the history of Storyton Hall. He wanted the full tour, but I had plans with you and the boys. I told him that I'd be happy to show him around whenever he was back in the area. He looked so crestfallen—like the boys do whenever I tell them we can't go fishing. I think . . . I might have given him something. A token. But I can't remember what it was."

Jane gave her uncle a chance to revisit the memory, but when he clearly couldn't recall what he'd given Alex Hoyt, she said, "Was it a key chain, by chance?"

"Yes!" He snapped his fingers. "That was it! I only had the key to the canoe hut on it, so I took the key off and gave it to him. He was tickled and said he had every intention of coming back. He mentioned something about having to get someone to look after his bunnies first, as he lived alone, but that was the extent of our conversation."

His timer went off, and he rubbed his hands together with glee. "I need to fetch my dough. Is there anything else I can do for you, my dear?"

"You've been very helpful, as always. I'll show myself out. Good luck with your bread."

As Jane walked back through the living room, Muffet Cat glared at her from his cushion on the sofa. Jane didn't even notice. Her attention was entirely focused on a different animal.

Rabbits.

Chapter 17

Jane called Sheriff Evans from her office.

"Have you informed anyone about Alexander Hoyt's death? A family member or friend?" she asked as soon as he answered her call.

"I spoke with his father, but only briefly. He's in an assisted living community, and one of the nurses told me I'd have to call back later. Mr. Hoyt has a serious heart condition, and they didn't want him getting more upset than he already was. The nursing supervisor told me that Alex visited his father quite regularly. He paid for his care and was respectful to the staff. She described Alex as quiet. His dad often napped during his visits, so Alex would write in a notebook or type on a laptop, seemingly in his own world."

Though Jane felt terrible for Alex's father, she didn't have the headspace to think about him for long. "When will you call back?"

"I'll give it another hour. Was there something you wanted me to ask him?"

"Other than if his son talked about Storyton Hall? Yes. See if he knows who looked after Alex's rabbits when he traveled. Even if he was a very private person, whoever took care of his bunnies must've known him fairly well. Maybe this person knows the real reason he came to Storyton. The fake reason is that he wanted to make a sculpture for the folly."

Sheriff Evans said, "Go on."

"Uncle Aloysius interviewed some regional artists for the project, and I just learned that Alex Hoyt was one of those artists. Alex sent my uncle a note about his work, and my uncle set up an interview. He said Alex was fascinated by Storyton Hall. He asked all sorts of questions about its history and requested a tour of the manor house. My uncle had a family commitment and couldn't fulfill Alex's request."

Jane went on to tell the sheriff about the key chain.

"And you think it's the same key chain found on Justin St. James's body?"

"Yes. Not that I can explain how it got there."

Over the sound of rustling papers, the sheriff said, "I'll call his place—see if anyone picks up. I tried before but will let it ring and ring this time. If that doesn't work, I'll reach out to the Guilford County police chief to see if he can send an officer to Hoyt's house. Bill Donahue and I go way back."

"Any news from Oyster Bay?"

The sheriff sighed. "A red paint marker was found in Rachel Wilcox's glove box. It's probably the same marker used on the hotel mirror. The cops are tightening up their case against Trent Little. They think he and Rachel cooked up a scheme to get money out of St. James, and when it didn't work, they killed him."

"What about Winston's son or Heather's boyfriend? They both had motive and means."

"We can cross Winston Hall's son off the suspect list," the sheriff said. "He's at work, on the other end of the country. He was at his pharmacy last week too. Monday to Friday."

Another phone rang in the sheriff's office. He told Jane that he needed to take the call and hung up.

Jane headed into the surveillance room. She found Lachlan nursing a cup of coffee while he watched the monitors. He sat up straighter in his chair and said, "We're vetting every guest as soon as they walk in. Mr. Butterworth takes their names as he serves them champagne. He then sends them on to the reception desk. We're comparing names and driver's license photos in real time. No one gets a room key until we confirm their identity. It's been smooth sailing so far. We had one hiccup when a follicly challenged gentleman didn't match his driver's license photo."

"Follicly challenged?"

Embarrassed, Lachlan said, "Bald. It took a minute for Mr. Sinclair to go online and figure out that the man had recently ditched his toupee. We had to stall for time, so the front desk staff pretended they were having computer issues. We pacified the guests for the inconvenience by handing out drink vouchers for the Ian Fleming Lounge."

Jane walked over to the whiteboard and put a finger next to Winston Hall's name. "His son didn't do it. He might have sent his dad the ketamine, but he didn't do it. That's one less suspect for us to look for."

"Eloise knows the owners of the bookstore where Heather and Winston are signing today. She's going to call as soon as their events are over and find out when the authors left and where they're headed. That way, we'll know when to expect them in Storyton—*if* this is their destination."

Staring at the board, Jane thought, *What if we're wrong? What if the cops in Oyster Bay have the killer in custody and I'm putting everyone on edge for nothing?*

"I keep coming back to the Justin St. James books," she murmured, half to herself and half to Lachlan. "He wrote four novels based on the lives of four writers—Angel Sanchez, Olivia Limoges, Winston Hall, and Heather O'Grady. Why make the fifth one about Storyton Hall? About William? About me?"

Lachlan kept watching the monitors but nodded to show that he was listening.

"St. James was given an overdose of ketamine and dumped on Olivia's beach," Jane continued. "Soon after, Rachel Wilcox was found dead outside my hotel room. The same hotel room where someone had written, 'Your story is over' on the bathroom mirror. Olivia, Winston, and Heather were in Oyster Bay. As was I. The only person who wasn't there was Angel Sanchez. I know she committed suicide. I know we verified the coroner's report. But is there someone *else* connected to Angel we might've missed? Like Rachel, for example? Could she have been Angel's relative? A cousin? A niece?"

"Rachel wasn't connected to her by birth or marriage. Angel's living relatives are all in Florida. We talked to her uncle and to one of her cousins. Neither of them recognized the names related to this investigation. We sent them a list to share with the rest of their relations but got no leads."

Dropping into the chair next to Lachlan, Jane studied the monitors. She loved seeing the wonder on her guests' faces. Every time they pointed at the grandfather clock or paused to admire a floral arrangement, she smiled. They moved toward the reception desk with such anticipatory steps that they were practically dancing. Jane sensed the thrum of excitement in their wide-eyed gazes and whispered exchanges and hoped their visit to Storyton Hall would exceed all their expectations.

I won't let you down, she silently promised them.

Lachlan's phone buzzed. "It's Eloise."

She heard the animated tone of Eloise's voice but couldn't make out any words. After Lachlan said goodbye, he gestured at the whiteboard. "Winston Hall told the owner of the Fountain Bookstore that he's staying in Richmond tonight. He's having dinner with friends at the Jefferson Hotel, and one of those friends happens to be the mayor. He and Winston were college roommates."

It was with genuine pleasure that Jane put a line through Winston Hall's name. "I didn't want him to be involved. I really like him. Heather too. But if they're both innocent, one of the guests at tonight's masked ball is a murderer."

"Everything's going to be okay," said Lachlan, turning from the screens to look her directly in the eye.

In that instant, Jane believed him.

She was back in her office, digging around online for any information on Angel Sanchez that might have been overlooked, when Sheriff Evans called.

"I hope you're sitting down," he said.

Jane groaned. "Nothing good comes from conversations that start like that."

"I don't know if it's good or bad, but it's definitely surprising. I called Alexander Hoyt's business line and let it ring and ring. I got so used to the noise that I nearly spilled my coffee when someone finally answered. It was a woman, and when I told her who I was, she explained that she was Alex's animal caretaker."

Opening her top desk drawer, Jane pulled out a stress ball with a goofy face and squeezed it until the eyes popped out. "And?"

"The woman—Kay—lives next door and has known Alex for years. She helped with the rabbits whenever he went out of town or planned to spend the day with his dad. She said Alex was very close with his dad but never talked about any other family. Not his mother or his famous stepbrother. However, there's a bookshelf full of Justin St. James books in his office. He had advanced reader copies, large print copies, and the international copies with covers done in German, Japanese, and Greek—you name it."

"I wonder if Justin sent them to Alex. If so, were they a gift, or was Justin rubbing his success in his brother's face?" Jane mused aloud.

The sheriff said, "There's another reason why Mr. Hoyt might have a collection of St. James novels."

"Which is?"

"He wrote them."

Jane nearly flattened her stress ball. "*What?*"

"I had a video call with Kay. She showed me Alex's office. The room is a shrine to Justin St. James novels. There's a big desk with a top-of-the-line computer and laser printer. Kay showed me Alex's desk calendar, and his trip to Storyton was marked off with arrows through the dates and the initials VA, which I assume is for Virginia."

Jane barely gave him time to finish before asking, "What else was on the calendar?"

"Several entries were marked DAD—these were probably the days he visited his father—and there was a dental appointment and car maintenance at a local dealership. There were several names I didn't recognize, but Kay explained that these were people coming to see rabbits. That's all for October. November had more of the same. However, there was something special about December first. The date was circled in red and said, **MS DUE** in bold letters."

Jane repeated the initials to herself. "'MS' for manuscript. The next book is due to the publisher on December first. No wonder St. James's editor wasn't worried about it being finished after his death. If Alex was actually writing the books, there was no reason to worry."

"Especially if they don't know Alex is dead."

The news that Alex was the central figure behind the Justin St. James novels was definitely a shock, but Jane couldn't tell if it changed their current situation. "Can Kay get on his computer?"

"It's an open investigation, so I can't have her riffling through drawers or computer files. Chief Donahue is en route to the house as we speak and will handle the search."

"These murders took careful planning. The killer must've been tracking Alex and Justin for months. This person was able to drive between Oyster Bay and Storyton, which means their job allows them a certain amount of freedom."

The sheriff said, "Or they had help. If Heather

O'Grady and her boyfriend were in it together, for example."

"I still don't see how they could have gotten into the Book Lover's Loft, or why they'd rent a boat to dump St. James's body on Olivia's beach." Jane growled in frustration. "Ugh! Nothing is clearer today than when I left Oyster Bay, and the party starts in a few hours."

"I'm going to get in touch with Henniger and Locklear to tell them that unless their local drug dealer killed Mr. Hoyt, they need to look at other angles, and fast. I'll call you with any news. Until then, keep your chin up."

It was too early to dress for the party, so Jane went down the hall to the surveillance room. Sinclair and Sterling were there, monitoring the screens.

Jane quickly filled them in on Alex Hoyt before adding his name to the whiteboard.

"All along, we've been wondering what motivated Justin St. James to base his books on Angel, Winston Heather, and Olivia. We never found a common denominator between St. James and this group, but maybe that's because we were looking at the wrong man. What if Alex Hoyt is linked to these four people?"

Sterling turned to Sinclair and said, "I'll keep watching. You do your thing."

While Sinclair turned to the laptop, Jane grabbed a legal pad and started making a list of names of all the people she'd encountered in Oyster Bay. When she was done, her eye kept returning to one name in particular.

"What is it?" asked Sinclair.

"Francis. When we first met, he mentioned he'd stayed at Storyton Hall several times. As manager of the

Admiral's Inn, he had access to all the guest rooms and would've known exactly what Rachel was up to. *And* he owns a boat. Maybe he's related to Angel Sanchez. Maybe he has money problems and tried to blackmail the stepbrothers."

Sterling swiveled in his chair. "Call the inn—see if he's there. If he's in Oyster Bay, he's probably not involved."

"Good idea."

When Francis answered the phone, it was clear that he was pleased to hear from Jane.

"I was just thinking about you," he said, his voice infused with warmth. "How are you? And how is Edwin? Healing, I hope?"

"He won't be dancing at tonight's ball, but he's managing pretty well on his crutches. He's lucky the barb on the right foot didn't penetrate as deeply or he'd still be in a wheelchair."

She heard a woman's voice in the background, and Francis whispered, "I'll be right with you."

"Sounds like you're busy. I was just calling to check in on you, but we can catch up another time."

Francis groaned. "I'd love to chat, but one of my best employees just quit on me and I'm scrambling to keep up. Talk soon!"

Jane was about to hang up when her phone beeped, signaling an incoming call. Ending the call with Francis, she said, "Sheriff?"

"We struck pay dirt with Alex Hoyt. Chief Donahue found drafts of every Justin St. James manuscript, including drafts with notes from the editor. Donahue also found printed contracts, royalty statements, and a folder of receipts for writing-related tax deductions. Payments from Alex's literary agent are deposited directly into

Alex's checking account. Alex paid Justin a monthly stipend as his PR liaison. Justin was the face of their brand. Alex was the wordsmith."

Swallowing hard, Jane said, "Did he find a draft of the new book?"

"The password program on Alex's computer was disabled, so Donahue was able to see his files. There's one called *The Sharpest Turn.*"

Jane let out a humorless laugh. "That's an awful title. Is Chief Donahue going to send you the file?"

"Not without getting a warrant first." He took a breath and continued before Jane could protest. "Alexander Hoyt is dead, but he still has rights. Donahue had cause to enter his home because Mr. Hoyt is a murder victim in an open investigation. However, the police need a warrant to do a thorough search. Sharing computer files wouldn't be a cursory search."

"I know it's important to do things by the book, but—"

"Don't worry. Donahue already called a judge, and he should be able to get us what we need in the next few hours. There's nothing else to do but wait."

As soon as Jane got off the phone, she sent a text to Butterworth and Lachlan, updating them on the situation. She then messaged Olivia and asked if she or her late husband had ever met Alex Hoyt. Olivia replied that while the name wasn't familiar to her, she'd get online to see if they'd crossed paths.

Jane and the Fins spent the next ninety minutes learning all they could about Alexander Hoyt, but when it was time for Jane to go home and get ready for the ball, they were no closer to understanding what had motivated Hoyt to write novels based on Angel, Heather, Winston, Olivia, and Jane's personal tragedies.

At home, Edwin helped her apply white makeup to her neck and shoulders. She covered her entire face with the opaque white cream makeup, which gave her skin a frost-kissed look.

After braiding her hair into a crown, she dusted it with powder until it was a silvery, icy blond that reminded her of Olivia's shade.

As she teased strands of her hair and then used holding spray to stiffen them into spikes, she told Edwin about Alex.

"He looks like the Woodsman from *Little Red Riding Hood*—a quiet man with kind eyes who works with his hands and spends lots of time outdoors. I mean, he breeds bunnies, for crying out loud. He creates sculptures. He's devoted to his dad. How can the same man deliberately choose to profit from other people's suffering?"

"Maybe he didn't think he was in the wrong. He changed the original stories just enough to make them unrecognizable to all but a handful of people."

Jane glared at him in the mirror. "But those people already went through hell! Isn't one time enough?"

"I'm not saying what he did was right. I'm just trying to figure the guy out." Edwin picked up the crown of icicles sitting on Jane's bureau and held it over her head. "May I?"

"Yes."

Edwin gently lowered the circlet onto Jane's silvery hair and watched her secure it with bobby pins. She dusted her cheeks with blue blush, added a shimmery pale blue shadow to her eyelids, and rubbed a shiny silver gloss over her lips. She finished the look with white mascara. To complete her transformation, she tied on her mask. The delicate, minimalistic material was covered in small rhinestones and didn't restrict her vision in the slightest.

At last, she stepped into the incredible gown Mabel had created for her. It was the color of moonlight on snow, with a snug, faux fur–trimmed bodice and a wide, flowing skirt embellished with rhinestones and lace snowflakes. When she moved, her gown drank in the light. It evoked images of glaciers or the iridescent sheen of a frozen river.

"You're magnificent," Edwin said, taking her in.

"I told Mabel what I wanted, and she made it twenty times more amazing than my original request."

Leaning on the back of a chair, Edwin performed a low bow. "Your majesty."

Jane handed him his mask. "The Snow Queen can't perform her wicked deeds without her malevolent goblin, and you're too handsome to be a monster."

"That's because you haven't seen my crutches. The boys helped me transform them. I now have another set of arms. But these are green, with black claws. Aren't they creepy?"

Edwin tucked the crutches under his arms and, rounding his back slightly, took two steps forward. Because the crutches now looked like long, thin limbs, the impression was of a creature putting its weight on its front legs.

"Oh, that's good!" Jane said, admiring how easily Edwin morphed from a man in a green suit to a menacing goblin.

If he can transform with just a mask and a few accessories, our guests can too.

Catching sight of her expression, Edwin put a steadying hand on her lower back. "Sweetheart, it's going to be okay. Between the Fins, your book club ladies, Olivia, and the two of us, there are nineteen people watching the guests tonight. Nineteen people will monitor the fifty attendees who aren't neighbors or previously vetted guests. And it's not just us either. We've got undercover deputies and the sheriff too. Deputy Emory is with Uncle Aloysius and Aunt Octavia. The twins are hanging out with their classmates and a dozen parent chaperones. The trap has been laid in the library. We're ready for whatever may come."

"And whatever that is, at least it'll finally come to a head. This time tomorrow, we won't be wondering anymore."

The doorbell rang, and Edwin arched a brow. "Are you expecting anyone?"

"No."

Jane slipped a folding knife into the hidden pocket near the top of her skirt and headed for the stairs.

"See who it is before you open the door," Edwin warned, hobbling down the hall behind her.

After a quick glance through the peephole, Jane immediately relaxed.

"It's Eloise!" she called, and opened the door.

Eloise's eyes went wide as she stared at her best friend. "Wow. You are . . . just *wow*."

Jane smiled. "Mabel works magic, doesn't she?"

"You're breathtaking," Eloise murmured.

"I see your dress poking through your coat. Can I get a preview now, or are you waiting to reveal yourself at the party?"

Eloise shook her head, as if to clear it. "You have me so dazzled, I almost forgot why I came here. I needed to talk to you before the ball because—"

Suddenly catching sight of her brother, Eloise reared back a little.

He laughed. "That's exactly the reaction I'm going for! I know you thought I was a goblin for most of our childhood, so it's a fitting costume, don't you think? It was rough finding a suit this shade of sickly green, but . . ." Trailing off, he reached for his sister. "Eloise? What's wrong?"

"I just heard from the bookstore owner in Charlottesville. Heather O'Grady rushed through her signing and drove away like a madwoman." Eloise's gaze shifted from her brother to Jane. "She told a fan that she and her boyfriend had broken up the night before, and that she was about to do something rash—something that would change her life forever. She was smiling as she said it too, and the fan thought she sounded a little unhinged."

Jane grabbed the phone from the hall table. "I need to tell the sheriff."

Eloise took hold of Jane's arm. "There's more. Winston Hall canceled the dinner he was supposed to attend—the one with the mayor. He told the owner of Fountain Bookstore in Richmond that he had a better offer. And then he asked if she knew of a place close by where he could buy a mask."

Chapter 18

After imparting her news, Eloise hurried back home to retrieve her mask, which she'd left sitting on her kitchen table.

"I'll meet you in the lobby," she called over her shoulder as she sped up the path leading to the carriage house.

Jane and Edwin entered Storyton Hall through the loading dock door. They knew it would please Mrs. Hubbard to be the first person to see their outfits but hadn't meant to startle her as she was stepping out of the walk-in fridge.

"*Oh!*" she cried. Her whole body went stiff, except for her arms. Those went limp, and the flat of eggs she'd been holding fell to the ground.

All three of them gazed down at the floor. Brown shells had flown outward like shrapnel, and yolks oozed over the sides of the container onto the floor. Mrs. Hubbard's black shoes were speckled yellow.

"Oh!" she cried again, pressing her hand to her chest. "You gave me a scare!"

Jane gazed at the mess of the floor and felt terrible. "I'm so sorry."

Mrs. Hubbard made a shooing motion. "I don't want you stepping in this and ruining your gorgeous gown. Go to the cookbook nook so I can have a better look at you two."

A member of the kitchen staff appeared with a mop and a bucket and told Mrs. Hubbard that he'd clean up the mess while she took a well-deserved break.

"Thank you, Luis, but there's no time for a break. Not when I have twelve skull cakes to finish decorating. But I *will* get a few photos of my favorite couple."

Jane and Edwin posed in front of the bookshelves while Mrs. Hubbard chattered on about how other-worldly they looked, and how they were sure to out-shine everyone else at the ball.

"The boys stopped to see me before they left for their party. They looked so grown-up." She let out a wistful sigh. "I tried to take pictures of them too, but the little devils wouldn't keep still."

A sous chef poked his head into the room and asked Mrs. Hubbard if she'd taste his béchamel sauce.

"Duty calls," she declared, following the sous chef back to the kitchens.

Sheriff Evans had already texted Jane to say that he was waiting in the lobby, so she and Edwin met him there.

At first, Jane didn't see him standing in the shadow of the grandfather clock, but then he turned, and she smiled in delight. He wore a black doublet, pants, a sword belt, and a long jacket. A chain of faux silver hung around his neck and his hands were encased in gloves of black leather. His salt-and-pepper hair was dyed a dark shade of brown and slicked back from his forehead.

"Sheriff of Nottingham. It's a pleasure," Jane said.

Evans had no hat to doff, so he gave Jane a deferential dip of his chin. "Between the suit coat and cape, I have plenty of hiding spots for my shoulder holster, phone, and flex-cuffs."

"And your deputies? Are they characters from the same book?" asked Edwin.

The sheriff pointed to the other end of the lobby, where four men stood talking to Butterworth. "It's hard to see them from here, but they're musketeers. Like me, they're armed. Like me, their batons are hidden in their sword scabbards. We're prepared for violence, but I'd rather this investigation ended without it."

"You and me both," said Jane.

The sheriff wandered off to check in with his deputies, and Edwin joined Lachlan near the front door. It was too early for guests to arrive, but no one was going to risk having a stranger enter Storyton Hall. Not tonight.

Jane took a moment to savor the quiet. She'd been too hyperfocused on what might occur in the next few hours to appreciate how the staff had transformed the lobby. The space was still elegant, but the elegance now had a gothic twist. With its rows of candelabra and roaring fire, Jane could've been looking at the grand hall from Northanger Abbey or Thornfield Hall.

Wandering over to the mantel, she examined an arrangement of black roses and feathers set in a silver vase, a trio of crow sculptures, and a pair of engravings from an old anatomy book in ornate frames.

The furniture in the conversation areas was haphaz-

ardly draped in lengths of red or purple velvet. Picking
up one of the throw pillows, Jane saw that it had been
covered in a black fabric studded with crimson roses
and white moths.

The insect theme played out on the coffee tables.
Bugs encased in glass domes sat next to resin skulls of
small mammals or a taxidermic rodent. Jane knew the
stuffed rats and squirrels weren't real, but the candlelight reflected in their glass eyes and gave them an air
of sentience that she was beginning to find unnerving.

But then Eloise appeared, looking resplendent in a
cherry-red gown and a golden circlet. A gold sash was
cinched around her waist and she carried a handful of
artificial buttercups.

"How cool! Storyton Hall has its own cabinet of cu-
riosities!"

Jane smiled at her friend. "Look out. Prince Humper-
dinck could be hiding nearby."

Eloise gave her gown a pat. "Don't worry. This
Princess Buttercup is armed."

Considering Eloise was the gentlest person Jane had
ever met, it was hard to imagine her wielding any kind
of weapon. Not even a book.

"My Dread Pirate Roberts wanted me to be prepared." Eloise's gaze slid away from Jane. "And I'm not
the only one. Here comes our reinforcements."

Jane turned to see four masked women walking their
way. Violet was the easiest to recognize because she
wore a gauzy, face-framing veil instead of a mask. The
rest of her costume consisted of purple harem pants, a
fitted purple-and-gold top, and gold slippers.

"Scheherazade?" Jane asked Eloise.

"That'd be my guess. I didn't know that Phoebe,

Anna, and Mrs. Pratt were teaming up, but I love that Anna is the Queen of Hearts and Mrs. Pratt is Alice."

Jane waved at their friends. "Phoebe's the prettiest White Rabbit I've ever seen. Everyone's going to be tempted to touch that gown."

Eloise suddenly grabbed Jane's arm and cried, "Look! Is that Mabel?"

The woman with glittering, iridescent tentacles attached to a deep purple gown was indeed Mabel. The green stole around her neck was made of intertwining cotton eels.

"Ursula!" exclaimed Mrs. Pratt as she opened her arms to embrace her friend.

"This witch is not a hugger," Mabel declared. When Mrs. Pratt's face fell, Mabel boomed out a laugh and planted a kiss on her cheek. "I'm just messing with you, Alice. Oh, Jane. Seeing you in the gown with the makeup and the hair? You're beautiful. And terrifying."

Jane grinned. "As are all the best villains. I'm glad you're on the dark side too. Is Betty with us, or is she a good guy?"

"My salty sea lips are sealed."

While they waited for Betty to arrive, the Cover Girls continued to admire one another's outfits and pose for photos. They also showed Jane the veritable arsenal they'd collectively assembled.

Jane ticked off the weapons on her fingers. "Just to review, we have two pepper sprays, a switchblade, a pair of knitting needles, a letter opener, a hatpin, and a stun gun."

Mabel pointed to the other end of the lobby. "Here comes Betty. I think she went James Bond and filed her umbrella into a shiv."

"Is she Mary Poppins or Scarlett from *Gone with the Wind?*" asked Phoebe.

Anna shrugged. "Dunno. They both had white dresses."

"Mary had an umbrella. Betty's carrying a parasol and her hair is in ringlets. I vote for Scarlett. Which is it, Mabel?" asked Phoebe.

Mabel told Phoebe that she was correct and motioned for Betty to hurry up.

"We need to take a group shot before the guests show up," she said, ushering Betty into place between Eloise and Mrs. Pratt.

By the time a good-natured staff member took a dozen photos, the first guests staying at Storyton Hall began to trickle into the lobby.

Jane asked her friends to huddle up. "Okay, this is it. Remember, your goal is to keep track of Winston and Heather. Just watch them. Do not engage. And if you see any suspicious behavior, tell the sheriff, one of his deputies, or me."

Glancing around, Betty whispered, "The sheriff's here?"

"He's the Sheriff of Nottingham tonight. Deputy Phelps is Robin Hood, but he hasn't come in yet. Those four over there? Dressed like musketeers? They're all deputies. Deputy Emory is upstairs with Uncle Aloysius and Aunt Octavia." Jane gestured to the door leading to the Great Gatsby ballroom. "Don't forget to enjoy yourselves, okay? Mrs. Hubbard went all out with the buffet and there'll be dancing after dinner."

"Don't you worry, we can have fun *and* watch your back," Eloise assured her.

The rest of the Cover Girls murmured their agreement.

"Where will you be?" asked Violet.

"I'm going to take up my position at the welcome table, which is where Edwin, Butterworth, and I will check the identities of our ticket holders. Each guest will then receive a raffle ticket for a chance to win a deluxe spa package. The raffle tickets look like laminated poker chips, and some of these chips have nano trackers inside them. Anyone we don't know well gets a special chip. Lachlan and Sterling will monitor the whereabouts of these people for the entire party. Once they have their raffle tickets, the partygoers will be directed to one of four drink stations."

Mrs. Pratt elbowed Phoebe. "*I* could use a cocktail. How about you, Rabbit?"

"Let's hop to the closest bar," Phoebe said, linking her arm through Mrs. Pratt's.

The rest of the Cover Girls trailed after them, and Jane joined Edwin and Butterworth by the front door.

"Where's Olivia?" she asked Butterworth.

"Putting the final touches on her costume. There was an incident with the iron, which meant she had to abandon her Red Riding Hood costume in the eleventh hour. However, I believe she adapted quite splendidly." His eyes lit up. "Ah, here she is now."

Jane turned to find Edgar Allen Poe walking in their direction. Olivia had donned a black suit and a vest over a white shirt. She'd tied a black chiffon scarf around her neck and a black bird, similar to those on the mantel, was pinned in place to her right shoulder. A quill pen stuck out of her left breast pocket, and she'd used makeup to create a mustache and the semblance of a black mask around her eyes. Jane assumed the tousled black hair was a wig.

Extending her hand, Jane said, "Mr. Poe. It's an honor."

"I wish my pen was mightier than the sword, or that I could've dressed Haviland as a very large raven, but I figured this look would let me blend in with the shadows."

The front doors opened, and four guests rushed into the lobby, along with a burst of cold air. In the ballroom, the Storyton Band struck up their first song of the evening. The All Hallows' Ball had officially begun.

As Jane greeted her guests, she was amazed by the creativity of their costumes. Partygoers came as characters from children's books and fairy tales, from classic literature and sci-fi. There were couples from Greek mythology, Shakespeare, *Outlander,* and *Pride and Prejudice.*

A pair of locals came as Poirot and Marple. The Hogg brothers from the Pickled Pig Market dressed as Holmes and Moriarty. Roger, Mrs. Pratt's beau, came as Doctor Dolittle, while Sam of Hilltop Stables was the Tin Man from *The Wizard of Oz.*

Between the locals and those guests staying at Storyton Hall, Jane felt like she recognized the majority of the revelers, but there were still plenty of strangers. Jane couldn't help viewing each and every one as a potential murderer.

Her suspicions were only exacerbated by their masks and makeup, and she wondered if the man dressed as Frankenstein's monster was really a monster, or if the witch with the large nose and yellow teeth had killed two men. She mustered a smile for a truly terrifying devil and was genuinely unnerved when he didn't smile back.

"He'll smile once his fangs are back in," his date whispered to Jane. "They came unglued in the car and he's pouting."

The pretty angel grabbed the devil by the tail and led him to one of the bars. Jane was still watching them when she heard a familiar voice.

"Olivia? Is that you?"

"Tonight, I'm Edgar. I had no idea you'd be at this ball. Did you drive here from Richmond just so you could channel Count Dracula for an evening?"

Act casual, Jane told herself. *You'll never know if he and Heather are working together if you scare him off right now.*

Moving to Olivia's side, she thrust out her hand and smiled in welcome. "Hello, Mr. Hall. It's lovely to see you again. You might not recognize me in this outfit, but I'm Jane Steward. I met you in Oyster Bay."

He took her hand and shook it gently. "I didn't recognize you at all. You look like a completely different person." Glancing between Oliva and Jane, he said, "I've got to be straight with you both. I didn't plan on coming here. I don't have a ticket because I didn't know a thing about this shindig until Heather told me about it. Is she here, by the way?"

His eager gaze roved over the lobby. Jane saw desire in that gaze. And when he turned back to her, the zealous light in his eyes continued to burn.

"She isn't. I don't think she's on the guest list."

Winston shook his head. "Neither of us are, but we were hoping to buy tickets at the door. Please. I'd be grateful if you'd let us join the party. I know this sounds insane, but this could end up being the most important night of our lives."

Jane forced a little laugh. "Not even the Snow Queen

would send you away on such a cold Halloween night. If you'd just register here, I'd be happy to welcome you to Storyton Hall."

Winston wrote his details in the book Edwin presented, and then Butterworth gave him a raffle ticket.

"I hope Lady Luck is with me," he said, slipping the poker chip into his pocket.

Olivia offered to give him a quick tour of the main floor, and as soon as they moved away, Jane looked over Edwin's shoulder to see how many attendees had yet to check in. The number was low—less than twenty—so she decided to mingle for a bit.

"Text me when Heather gets here," she told Edwin.

He brought her hand to his lips and said, "Yes, my liege."

At the bar just outside the ballroom, Jane ordered a Necromancer cocktail. The dark red liquid was full of tiny bubbles, and when Jane took a sip, she tasted blackberries, prosecco, and something else.

"What is that other flavor?" she murmured to herself.

"Thyme," said Eloise. She showed Jane her nearly empty glass. "I asked the bartender. I don't like it quite as much as my first drink, which was a blood orange martini, but I'm not going to have anything else until I get some food in my stomach. If I have one more drink, I won't be able to tell the difference between the Big Bad Wolf and that Cruella de Vil on the dance floor."

The two women joined several of their friends at the buffet, and though Jane was hungry, she couldn't concentrate on the amazing dishes the kitchen staff had prepared long enough to savor any of them.

She popped a bite of roasted mushroom crostini in her mouth and chewed. Her taste buds appreciated the hit of butter and garlic, but her brain was focused on locating Winston Hall.

As he was one of five vampires and the room lights were turned down low, he wasn't all that easy to spot.

"So many capes," she muttered, and then decided to text Lachlan and Sterling.

Lachlan's reply came back seconds later.

Trackers are working. WH is in line for drinks near the grandfather clock.

Jane asked if any of the other guests had left the designated party areas, which included the lobby, the ballroom, the restrooms, and the Ian Fleming Lounge.

Not yet. Just heard from Butterworth. Heather O'Grady is checking in. She's a black cat.

"Be right back," Jane told her friends.

She made it to the lobby in time to see Butterworth offer Heather a raffle ticket. She waved it away, but he offered it to her again. She smiled, thanked him, and closed her hand around the poker chip. She then walked toward the drinks station where Winston Hall waited in line.

Jane followed her.

Like many of the other partygoers, Heather wore black. Her shirt dress was a bit casual for the occasion, and her minimalistic costume was comprised of a cat mask that covered the top half of her face. Her red hair hung down her back in a single braid and she'd drawn whiskers on her cheeks.

As Heather passed by a man dressed as Professor Plum, Jane saw her drop the poker chip raffle ticket into his pocket without breaking her stride.

Nice try, kitty, Jane thought.

None of the guests seemed to take notice of Heather, but they all cast admiring glances at Jane.

Why didn't I come as the evil witch from Snow White*? I can't blend in at a Halloween party looking like a walking icicle!*

Jane didn't really wish she'd chosen a different costume. She loved everything about her look and was suddenly irritated that she couldn't enjoy the ball because once again, she'd become entangled in a murder investigation.

Two teachers from Storyton Elementary School came over and asked how the twins were doing. The first woman was channeling Fancy Nancy, and her coworker was Laura Ingalls Wilder. Jane talked to them while simultaneously watching Heather make her way over to where Winston Hall stood, gazing into the fire as if hypnotized by the dancing flames.

At the touch of her hand on his arm, he swung around and cupped her by the elbows. For a long moment, Winston and Heather simply stared at each other. Then Heather said something, and Winston's face broke into a huge grin. He pulled her roughly to him and kissed her.

It was not a kiss between friends. It was a kiss a long time in the making, and they clung to each other like two lovers reunited after years apart.

When they finally broke apart, they were both smiling.

Winston whipped off his mask and then gently removed Heather's. Gazing at her with open adoration, he traced her whiskers with the tip of his finger. Jane saw a tear slide down Heather's cheek.

"Be still my heart," said one of the teachers.

"Do you know those lovebirds?" the other teacher asked Jane.

Jane fixed her attention on the teachers long enough to say, "They're guests. I haven't welcomed them yet, so I should go do that now. Enjoy the party."

Winston saw her approach and took hold of Heather's hand. Pressing it over his heart, he beamed at Jane and said, "Lady Luck was with me. And now, my lady love is too."

Heather flashed him a warm smile before turning to Jane. "I know what it looks like, but I'm not cheating on Greg. We broke up yesterday, and even though it was mutual and totally friendly, I wasn't sure if it was too soon to meet Winston here. But I was in the middle of my bookstore event when all my doubts just disappeared and I knew I had to come. I've been falling for this man since we first met. He understands me in a way no one else ever could."

That made perfect sense to Jane. Heather and Winston had experienced life-shattering traumas. It was easy to see how the bond they shared as survivors and writers had grown into a friendship and, later, love.

Studying them now, Jane asked, "How does Storyton Hall fit into this picture?"

"We heard about the resort from Olivia," Winston explained. "She made it sound like such a magical place. And when I went to your website and read about the ball, I knew I wanted to ask Heather to meet me here." He shot a tender glance at Heather before adding, "I knew her tour schedule as well as my own, and I knew she and Greg had been talking about calling it quits."

"Winston wrote me a letter when we were in Oyster Bay. He told me that he loved me and that he'd drive here after his event in Richmond and wait for me. He said that if I was ready to admit how I felt about him, I should drive down from Charlottesville and meet him at this ball. It sounds ridiculous, but both of us want to create new memories. And not just new. To balance out the bad ones, we need them to be fantastical, powerful memories."

Winston's eyes were shining. "Like dancing with the love of your life in a roomful of strangers."

"Or drinking cocktails by candlelight. With the most captivating vampire in the castle."

They kissed again, making Jane feel like a third wheel.

But she couldn't walk away from them just yet. Indicating the sofa, she said, "I need to circulate, but there's something I'd like to ask before I go."

Once they were all comfortable, Jane looked at Heather. "Did you mean to give your raffle ticket to Professor Plum?"

She blushed. "I'm only here because you let me in. I wasn't going to take advantage of your graciousness by entering to win a spa package too. I've already gotten my prize, and all I had to do to win was buy a cheap mask and find the courage to walk through your front door."

Is it possible they mean what they say? That they arranged this meeting to create storybook memories for themselves?

"Did either of you know Alexander Hoyt?"

Their expressions were blank as they shook their heads. Neither of them exhibited the slightest tell, and Jane was inclined to believe them.

Winston said, "Who is he?"

Jane could have told him but decided not to. There weren't enough moments of pure happiness in life, and she didn't want to corrupt theirs with talk of murder.

"Another writer," she replied casually, and got to her feet. "Enjoy yourselves tonight."

"We will," Heather said. "And thank you again for including us."

Before returning to her meal, Jane wanted to send a group text updating everyone on what she'd just seen and heard, so she ducked into her office.

Sheriff Evans responded by saying he and his deputies would continue watching Winston and Heather. Lachlan reported that he and Sterling hadn't seen any unusual activity on the security monitors, and that the last two guests were checking in now.

A message from Edwin appeared next.

Butterworth is giving these folks the third degree because they bought their tickets from a pair of locals. They even used their names to check in, but they are NOT Mr. and Mrs. Porter from High View Farm.

Jane wrote, **Who are they?**

Edwin explained that they were acquaintances of the Porters and had offered to buy the tickets when they heard that Mrs. Porter had fallen and injured her knee badly enough to require surgery.

Sinclair looked them up. **They appear to be who they say they are, so we've given them raffle tickets and sent them in. Check-in is officially over.**

The party was now in full swing. Jane returned to her table and tried to eat, but after picking at her food, she pushed the plate in Edwin's direction.

He shook out his napkin with a flourish and said, "I'm happy to eat your leftovers, but I'd like a few of those Korean beef wraps. Eloise was on her way to get some when she was intercepted by a customer. The two of them are talking books by the dessert table, which means I'll never get those wraps."

"I don't think there are any left," said Betty.

Edwin looked so crestfallen that Jane almost laughed.

"I'm sure there's more in the kitchens. Mrs. Hubbard wouldn't want her favorite goblin to miss out, so I'll go check. Be right back."

As Jane wove her way through the ballroom, the band struck up "Halloween Waltz in Five," and couples flocked to the dance floor.

The skirts of the ladies' dresses swirled around their ankles and the men's capes billowed outward like flags in the wind. Overhead, the chandeliers glittered. Around the perimeter of the room, candle flames joined the dance.

Music and laughter swept through the room. Everywhere Jane looked, she saw movement. People milled about the buffet tables. They talked, ate, drank, and danced. They smiled and laughed. They circulated with their cocktails, touched friends on the arm or shoulder, or leaned in to listen to someone's story.

All is as it should be, Jane thought.

Still, she couldn't relax. She sensed that someone was waiting in the shadows. Their moment had not yet come, and so Jane's stomach remained knotted.

As she stepped into the staff corridor, she heard footfalls on the stairs leading to the second floor.

There was nothing unusual about the sound. The staff was constantly moving around the hotel behind the scenes, but this person's tread was off. It was the hesitant gait of someone who didn't know where they were going.

Taking the stairs as fast as she could, Jane ascended to the second-story landing and came face-to-face with a woman wearing a server's uniform. Her name tag was missing, but Jane had no trouble recognizing her.

Here was the person who'd been waiting to step from the shadows into the light. And now that the pivotal moment had finally arrived, Jane felt a strange and powerful sense of calm.

Clasping her hands in front of her, she let out a breath and said, "Hello, Sammi."

Chapter 19

Sammi gave Jane a look of cool appraisal and said, "I really like your place."

"Thank you." Jane made a sweeping gesture with her right arm. "This isn't your first visit to Storyton, is it?"

"No. I came here to see Alex Hoyt. It was over a week or so ago, but it feels like a year. So much has happened since then."

Jane was tempted to scoff at the understatement. Instead, she leaned against the wall of the stairwell and tried to give off the impression of a woman with nothing to do and no place to go. "I don't know your story. Why don't you tell it to me—from the beginning?"

"My name is Samantha Doyle. My parents are Nick Doyle and Angel Sanchez. They weren't married, and my dad took off when I was nine. That's when my mom started writing. And drinking. She'd get home from work and lock herself in her room with her computer and a bottle of wine, leaving me to take care of my little sister. I made sure Bella had food and clean clothes to wear to school. I helped her with her homework and read her books at bedtime. For the next few years, Mom barely noticed us. She only cared about three things: writing, drinking, and men."

"It sounds like you had to grow up very fast."

Sammi snorted. "*Someone* had to be the adult in our house. Even when Mom started making good money and was able to quit her day job, things didn't get better. They got worse. She forgot to deposit checks or take out cash so I could buy groceries. She started having her booze delivered. I found out the PIN of her debit card, and by the time I was thirteen, I was paying the bills and hiding cash in a lockbox in case of emergency. That was our life for the next four years. Mom wrote. Mom drank. Mom entertained men in our house. I took care of Bella and kept putting money in the lockbox."

Jane could picture Sammi as a girl, pushing a cart around the grocery store, folding laundry, and tucking her sister into bed. It pained Jane to compare Sammi's experience to her sons' carefree childhood.

"Bella was lucky to have had such a strong and devoted sister."

Sammi's placid expression shattered. "But not strong enough to save her."

Seeing the agony etched on the younger woman's face, Jane longed to comfort her. "You tried. The fire wasn't your fault."

"That night, my mom was partying with her new man. He was a writer too. Our house was near Myrtle Beach, and a big tropical storm rolled in earlier that day. Lots of streets were flooded, and the wind knocked out the power. Mom had candles everywhere. Candles and liquor."

Jane winced.

Sammi's gaze went glassy. She'd traveled back to that night, and when she spoke again, her voice was hollow with grief. "The two of them drank and fought, which was nothing new. Mom's boyfriend called her books trash. She said he was jealous because he couldn't get published. They screamed at each other until they finally passed out. I don't know when the fire started. I just woke up coughing. My sister wasn't in her room, so I went downstairs and found my mom passed out on the sofa. I dragged her outside and left her in the grass. Then I went back in for Bella. But I . . ."

A sob rose in her throat and she dropped her chin to her chest. Though Jane felt compelled to put an arm around the hurt and haunted woman, she remained where she was.

Sammi was a killer. Jane had no doubt of that. She had done terrible things. But all Jane saw before her was a tortured soul. She saw a child who'd been broken by heartache at a tender age and had never recovered.

Taking a step in Sammi's direction, Jane said, "You didn't fail Bella. For sixteen years, you gave her all you had. She knew she was loved. Because of you."

"I couldn't find her," Sammi continued as if she hadn't heard. "There was too much smoke. I was in the kitchen. I looked down and . . . my shirt was on fire."

Slowly, Sammi unbuttoned the top two buttons of her blouse. Jane caught a glimpse of puckered skin and angry red scars before Sammi refastened the buttons.

That's why she always wears turtlenecks.

Sammi continued her harrowing story. "I ran out into the rain and dropped in the grass. That's when I saw him. Mom's boyfriend. He was standing by his truck, watching the house burn. Then the roof collapsed. And he drove away."

Jane's hand flew to her mouth.

Balling her hands into fists, Sammi whispered, "All I knew about this guy was that his name was Alex and he raised Harlequin rabbits, but I was going to find him. He was going to pay for letting my sister die."

Her quiet words rose in the air. They didn't dissipate but lingered like ghosts. Sammi had summoned the memories of her mother and sister, and now Jane felt their presence too. She felt them in the slump of Sammi's shoulders and the pain swimming in her eyes.

"I read about the fire," she said softly. "The article said that Angel Sanchez's daughters, Luz and Bella, died that night. Did you change your name?"

"Samantha's my middle name. Only my mom called me Luz. Bella always called me Sammi. There wasn't much left of the house by the time the fire and the rain were done with it. Just mud and ashes. When the cops finally came, my mom wouldn't stop screaming that we were dead, so that became the truth. After Alex's book came out, I thought someone might find me, but no one did. That's when I knew it was safe to punish the man who'd left us to die."

The weight of Sammi's words pressed heavily on Jane. If they weren't standing in the stairwell right now, she'd sit down.

"After the fire—where did you go?"

"To the shed, to get my bike and the lockbox of cash. I broke into a rental house I knew was empty. I took a shower. I used a first aid kit I found in the bathroom. I ate food I found in the pantry. I don't remember anything except for that. A few days later, I stole a shirt off a clothesline, bought a bus ticket, and went to my dad's."

Jane gaped. "And he never told anyone that you survived?"

She shook her head. "He felt guilty for leaving us with my mom. He wanted to be my dad again, and my price was his silence. I never went back to school. He went to work and I took care of the house and studied at home. He lived near a nice library, and I'd always loved to read. I checked out *Burn Down the House* a few days before my mom overdosed."

"And then all the rage you felt the night of the fire came back."

Sammi blinked in surprise. "Yeah. It did."

Now Jane did sit down. "I've felt that kind of rage. The people who hurt my husband—I wanted them to suffer for what they did to him. He saved me from it, though. He saved me by sacrificing himself, by showing me that love is greater than hate."

"I only had my dad, and he had a heart attack when I was twenty. After that, all I cared about was getting to Alex. It was the only thing that kept me going."

Sammi explained how she searched for breeders of Harlequin rabbits. Once she'd located Alex, she applied for a job working at the assisted living community where Alex's father lived. Her duties including cleaning rooms and delivering meals to the residents.

"Alex didn't recognize me. He'd talk to his dad as if I wasn't there. He'd tell him about the chapter he was working on, ideas for his next book, how the rabbits were doing. He'd take his dad for a walk around the grounds and leave his laptop open. I'd close the door, turn on the vacuum, and read his files. I'd see what he had on his calendar. I'd look in his notebook. That's how I knew where he'd be and when. Where Justin would be and when."

"Was this before or after he wrote the book about Olivia?"

"After. I wanted to kill him before he could finish it, but I was afraid of getting caught. I needed to make sure there was no way for people to connect me to him, so I had to leave the assisted living job."

"When did you start working at the Admiral's Inn?"

Sammi said, "In May. I started in the kitchen and pitched in with housekeeping when I needed to. Reggie, the other bartender, taught me how to make drinks so I could cover for him when he was in school."

Jane frowned. "If you wanted to punish Alex, why didn't you just go to his house?"

For a moment, it seemed like Sammi wouldn't answer. She sank down to the ground, her knees folding into her chest, and let out a soft sigh.

"I almost did. Lots of times. But I had no way of controlling what might happen there. It was his turf. I had to wait," she said wearily. "I read an email from Justin to Alex, talking about the Triple Thrills event. Justin didn't want to do it, but Alex made him. He wanted to twist the knife a little more. And in Olivia's bookstore too. He couldn't resist."

Jane shook her head. "What did your mom, Heather, Winston, and Olivia do to Alex to make him so hateful?"

Sammi held up two fingers. "First, they got published before him. Second, they won some kind of writing award. He didn't. They all went to the same writing workshop in Georgia. I don't remember what it was called, but they were there at the same time. Alex was obsessed with those three writers. He kept tabs on their awards, speaking engagements, best-seller lists—you name it. He sold ten times as many books, but that didn't matter. He never got an award. No one praised him for his talent. He used to complain to his dad about how everyone always loved Justin because he was good-looking and cool. He said Justin's mom never liked him, which is why he wrote stories about how she emotionally abused him. I think that was a big lie. I think he used his writing to make her look bad, and that led to the divorce. That's when he figured out he could hurt people by writing fiction."

"That sounds petty and ridiculously immature." Jane pointed at herself. "But how do I fit in? I'm not a writer."

"He had an article bookmarked on his computer about the best Southern writers of our time. There was a bit about Olivia, the book that won the award, and how she got through writer's block because of Storyton Hall. I guess that put you on his radar. When I looked it up, I was pretty interested too. I mean, this place is a hotbed for crime."

Jane's face flamed. She hated that her family home had such a long and colorful history of violence. She wanted nothing more than to make it a peaceful haven for readers, but year after year, she'd failed in that endeavor. She put her hand against the cold, concrete wall and wondered if she would fail again tonight.

"Alex Hoyt was a disgusting human being," continued Sammi. "Instead of trying to save my family, he drove away. He drove away and turned their deaths into a book. It worked so well that he did it again. And again. He was addicted to it. He thought he was this master manipulator. This God of the Keyboard. With every book, he got richer. But he didn't want money. He wanted power over his characters. Who were *real* people. And he would've kept on hurting people if I hadn't stopped him. I had his password, and I could still log on to his email, so I knew that he'd rented a cabin here. No one could tie me to his death in this town, so I waited until he left his rental cabin and shot him up with ketamine."

Jane suddenly remembered dropping by Mabel's shop last week and hearing two customers complain that someone was walking around Storyton, whistling the same song over and over again. She knew, without having to ask Sammi, that the song had been "Paperback Writer."

"I had to take out Justin too," Sammi went on. "Otherwise, the publishers would just hire a ghostwriter, and he'd keep pretending to be St. James the author. Alex had a list of authors he was going to write about—all of them had been in a workshop or at a conference with him and had survived some kind of hell. He was never going to stop ruining people's lives."

"And Rachel? How did she figure in?"

Sammi wrapped her arms around herself and stared down at her shoes. "I paid her to get me the ketamine. She knew I planned to use it on Justin. After it was done, she asked for more money. It was a crazy amount, which I didn't have, but she said she'd tell the cops about me if I didn't give it to her. That's how she was— always pushing people to give her more. I didn't want to hurt her. She gave me no choice."

There were many questions Jane could ask Sammi, but they no longer seemed important. At twenty-four, Sammi had known more grief and sorrow than most people experienced in a lifetime. Though Jane didn't condone her actions, she felt pity for this sad and broken young woman.

"I can see that you're tired," she said very gently. "Are you ready for it all to be over?"

Sammi's whole body drooped. "I thought I'd look for it—your secret room. I thought I could get money from you and Olivia and then disappear. I made those men pay for what they did. And now, you can stop the last book from coming out. There's tons of proof that Alex was writing about you on his computer and notebooks."

"If you had the money, where would you go?"

Tears filled Sammi's eyes, and a noise, half sob and half shout, burst from her throat. "Nowhere! I have *no one*! I'm all alone and I'm *so* tired . . ."

Jane moved over to where Sammi sat and dropped to her knees beside her. She put her arms around Sammi and held her while she cried.

She was still holding her when the door leading to the guest hallway opened.

"Everything okay down there?" asked Sheriff Evans.

She saw Edwin standing behind the sheriff. Turning her head to the right, she saw Butterworth and Sinclair on the stairs.

"I could use a handkerchief," she said.

Butterworth passed her one and then retreated.

"Here you go," Jane whispered, pressing the cloth into Sammi's hand. "You can rest now. It's all over."

Without warning, Sammi rocketed to her feet. The movement was so abrupt that it knocked Jane backward.

"It's okay," Jane said, holding up both hands. "No one's going to hurt you."

Suddenly, there was a syringe in Sammi's hand. She held it up to her own neck and hissed, "Get back."

"Do as she says," Jane told the men.

Butterworth and Sinclair descended to the first floor. When the sheriff hesitated, Jane said, "She won't hurt me, and I don't want her to hurt herself. Please."

Reluctantly, the sheriff stepped back into the hallway. The door slammed shut with a bang.

Jane clambered to her feet and locked eyes with Sammi. "If you use that on yourself, you'll be surrendering to Alex. *Your* story will be all about *him.* It'll be about how he left you the night of the fire and how you got back at him. Everything people write about you will include his name. You'd be lost. Bella would be lost. *You* need to live. You need to tell your own story."

Sammi lowered the syringe and murmured, "I'm scared."

"Sheriff Evans is a good man. He'll treat you well. And I'll hire the best lawyer around to represent you. But only if you go peacefully. Because I'm tired too. I'm tired of violence."

Sammi looked into Jane's eyes for a long moment. Whatever she saw there convinced her to hand over the syringe.

Closing her fingers around the warm plastic, Jane whispered, "Thank you."

"Before they take me away, can I see it? The secret room?"

Jane didn't owe this woman a thing. Sammi was a murderer who had to face the consequences of her actions. She would spend many years behind bars. Years she could have had living the life her sister never had the chance to live. Years she'd stolen from Rachel Wilcox.

And yet Jane kept thinking about all that Sammi had

lost. Her sister. Her mother. Her father. Her childhood. It felt right to give her something—just a few minutes of wonder—before she lost her freedom too.

"Yes. I'll show it to you."

Jane called the sheriff and told him what was about to happen.

"It won't take long, and Sammi will go with you as soon as we're done."

She ended the call and gestured for Sammi to follow her. She explained how the secret library was reached through a hidden door inside her great-aunt and -uncle's apartment, and how the china cabinet would swing away from the wall, revealing a narrow space.

Sammi trailed her into Aunt Octavia's closet and watched as Jane turned the key in the lock and activated the lever. She didn't say a word when Jane turned on a battery-powered lantern, led her up the narrow staircase, and pushed open the heavy door at the top.

"This is it." Jane beckoned Sammi into the room. "This is the secret that's caused me so much turmoil for so many years. But no more. By Christmas, this room will be empty. These treasures will be gone, and Storyton Hall will no longer have anything to hide." She touched Sammi's arm. "Some secrets are too heavy to carry."

Sammi leaned against the doorframe and said, "I'd like to come back here one day. As a guest. I'd like to have tea and walk in the garden. I want to hold a falcon. Would you let me stay here? Even after everything?"

"Yes. I would." Jane gave Sammi a minute to collect herself. Then she held out her hand and whispered, "Are you ready?"

As she felt Sammi's hand close around hers, she knew there would be no violence tonight. No bloodshed, no sirens wailing, no panicked screams. The All Hallows' Ball would continue until well after midnight. The guests would eat and drink and dance long after Sheriff Evans helped Sammi into the back of his car. They'd continue celebrating as Jane sat in the lobby, nursing a cup of coffee and counting the minutes until she could escape.

Edwin joined her on the sofa and put his arm around her. The two of them sat in silence while the party roared on around them. Later, when Jane said that her icicle crown was giving her a headache, Edwin carefully removed it and ran his fingers through her hair until the ache in her temples was gone.

Finally, he kissed her powder-pale cheek and said, "I'm taking you home now."

Jane didn't argue. Her staff would make sure the guests had everything they needed. Lachlan would tell Eloise about the arrest, and Eloise would share the news with the other Cover Girls. Jane would talk to her friends tomorrow.

Right now, she just wanted to go to bed. She wanted to pull the covers up to her chin and stare at the shadows the moonlight painted on her ceiling until sleep came to claim her.

She didn't want to be the Snow Queen anymore. Or a Guardian. She wanted to be Jane. That was more than enough.

The Friday after the ball, Jane and Eloise sat in the bookstore's kitchen. Eloise poured hot apple cider into mugs.

"How was your meeting?" she asked, pushing a plate of pumpkin cookies closer to Jane.

"Long. I was a little intimated by all the paperwork, but Christie's is known for their thoroughness."

Eloise dunked her cookie into the hot cider and took a bite. "And the Library of Congress reps are coming Monday, right?"

"Yep. After that, the secret library will no longer exist."

"It must be bittersweet. This ending."

Following Eloise's example, Jane plunged a cookie into the cider. She watched the hot liquid eat away at the round edges.

"Whenever I feel sad about it, I think about the money I'll be putting away for the future," she said. "I can set aside funds for the boys' college tuition and for the endless maintenance and upkeep that a place like Storyton Hall requires. On top of that, Edwin and I decided to create a charitable organization. We're calling it the Golden Bookmark Foundation."

Eloise cocked her head. "Are you giving away more free vacations?"

"We're still going to do a few of those a year, but this is different. We want to offer an all-expenses-paid retreat for writers. Our foundation will award a stipend to aspiring writers who need time and a quiet setting to work on their novel, children's book, essay collection, volume of poetry, or whatever. Sinclair, Butterworth, and Aunt Octavia have volunteered to oversee the application process."

"I love that idea." Eloise ran a finger around one of the cookies. "It feels like the closing of a circle. After selling or donating so many stories, you'll now be encouraging the creation of new ones."

Jane smiled at her friend. "Exactly. The guest cottage

Olivia used last year will officially be known as Author's Cottage. I've already ordered the plaque."

"Speaking of Olivia and cottages, she's definitely made herself at home in Butterworth's. I pass by it every morning, and he doesn't have curtains in his kitchen windows, so I can see her at the table with her laptop. She looks like she belongs there."

"I'm glad they found each other. And now that Olivia will be spending the winter here, I hope Captain Haviland's behavior rubs off on Merry and Pippin. They ate my favorite pair of boots, you know. Shredded them like they were made of cheese."

Eloise laughed. "It must be hard to reprimand them. They're so cute."

"People used to say that about the twins too," Jane said with a snort.

The women sipped their cider and continued chatting. Eloise told Jane what she planned to do for her holiday window display, and Jane shared the news that the attorney she'd hired had already made headway with St. James's publisher.

"They're willing to make the necessary changes to the plot and have agreed to let me read the revised version," Jane said. "I can't tell you how relieved I am that Fitz and Hem won't be exposed to a twisted version of their father's story, and neither will anyone else. William deserves to rest in peace. As does anyone who died because of the secret library."

Echoing Jane's somber tone, Eloise said, "I have a few books for Sammi. How's she doing?"

"As well as can be expected. Her sentencing hearing is next week. I told her I'd be there. She really doesn't have anyone else. Her father's family wants nothing to do with her."

They finished their cider, and Eloise carried their empty cups to the sink. Beckoning Jane into the bookshop, she showed her some of the new releases she'd gotten in earlier in the week. When she unboxed a mystery featuring a bottle of poison on the cover, Jane said, "Sammi read about ketamine poisoning in a book. Some police procedural that came out two years ago. She knew she could get Rachel to buy it from Trent Little, and it wasn't hard to figure out how much she needed for a dose to be fatal."

"I can see how it would be easy for her to get close to Justin St. James and convince Rachel to meet her outside your hotel room, but how was she able to stick a syringe into Alex?"

Jane ran her hand over the glossy cover of the mystery novel and said, "She deliberately ran into him on the trail near his rental cabin. He recognized her from his dad's assisted living facility, and they started walking together. At one point, Sammi pretended to stumble, and when Alex reached out to stop her from falling, she clung to him. The needle went in, and that was that."

"Was Alex in Storyton to learn more about you? For his book?"

"It seems that way. Based on what he wrote in his notebook, he wanted to describe how the village looked around Halloween, and to get a sense of what the locals thought of me. He also needed to see inside Storyton Hall, but Sammi kept that from happening." Jane shrugged. "She never stepped foot on our grounds. She killed Alex and then turned around and drove right back to Oyster Bay."

Eloise touched her temple. "I can't imagine what was going on in there on her way home. Was she a basket case at work?"

"According to Francis, Sammi never missed a shift. She was always on time, friendly, and a total team player. He was floored when he found out she'd killed three people. He said he often wondered why she always wore shirts with high necks, even in the summer."

Eloise touched the fragile skin between her collarbones. "She was trying to hide her scars."

"Among other things. But that's all over now." Jane picked up a cozy mystery and admired the cute cat on its cover. "Speaking of scars, Edwin's going to have a nice set on the bottom of his feet."

"You have to admit, his dreadful luck makes for a good story."

Jane laughed as she slid a new book into its designated shelf space. "It totally does."

A few days later, after the representatives from the Library of Congress drove away with the last of the secret library's collection, Jane waited for Aunt Octavia and Uncle Aloysius to join her and the twins for afternoon tea.

Aunt Octavia arrived first and had barely sat down before trying to convince Jane that she should turn the attic turret into an exercise space for Muffet Cat.

"We could build cardboard trees for him to climb and plant cat grass for him to eat. He's getting long in the tooth, and it'd be so much easier if he stayed in the apartment from now on. I'm sick to death of letting him in and out every time he scratches on the door. He can be very demanding, you know."

"I haven't thought much about the future of that space, but I'll keep your idea in mind," Jane said as she poured tea into Aunt Octavia's mug.

"I can't imagine what's keeping Aloysius," she grumbled. "He was messing about with that train set again. Boys and their toys."

Uncle Aloysius was in his study, but he wasn't fiddling with his model railroad set. The wheeled table covered by train tracks, buildings, and greenery had been moved from its usual position, flush against the wall, so that Uncle Aloysius could access a hidden panel.

The walls of his study were made of paneled wood that smelled of lavender beeswax. However, the bottom-most panel in the center of the wall concealed a hollow space large enough to contain a man. All Uncle Aloysius had to do was press on its center with both hands to release its hidden mechanism. He could then slide the rectangular piece of wood to the side, as if he was opening a window at a drive-through restaurant.

"I nabbed a few more of your friends," he told the stacks of priceless books inside the clean, dry space. "The Library of Congress got enough, and the Stewards have always guarded a literary treasure. One day, Jane's children, and their children's children, will thank me. Until then, no one else needs to know about my little collection."

Grinning at the books, he closed the panel and laid his hand over the polished wood.

"It'll be our secret."

Chapter 20

Three days before Christmas, Jane stood at the back of the church, waiting to start her procession down the aisle.

She wore a 1950s-inspired, tea-length tulle gown with a jewel neck and sheer sleeves. The lace flowers covering the bodice came from Aunt Octavia's wedding gown. Mabel had lovingly stitched each flower onto Jane's dress, wishing her friend health and happiness with every pull and dip of her needle.

Jane didn't carry a bridal bouquet because her hands were loosely wrapped around the forearms of the two people who'd raised her. Standing between Uncle Aloysius and Aunt Octavia, she felt like a book hugged by a pair of bookends.

"Are you ready, my girl, or should we make a run for it?" her great-uncle asked, giving her a conspiratorial wink.

Jane smiled at him. "I'm ready."

"What a relief." He mimed wiping his brow. "I'm not

wearing my running shoes, and I've grown rather fond of your young man."

"He's very lucky to have found you, our beautiful angel," Aunt Octavia whispered. "Our lovely, sweet girl. You've brought us such happiness, and there's nothing else we want in this life other than your happiness."

The organist struck up "Jesu, Joy of Man's Desiring," and the smiling trio began their march down the aisle.

The church sanctuary was dressed in its Christmas best. Greens garlanded the ends of every pew and a galaxy of white poinsettia plants were clustered like stars on the altar steps. An arrangement of red and white carnations mixed with sprigs of holly festooned the altar table. Glowing candles sprouted from the greenery, and the lights from the Christmas trees flanking the table cast a gentle glow over the red carpet.

As Jane walked past the empty pews, she looked straight ahead to where Edwin waited. Edwin and her sons.

Today was not just a marriage ceremony. On this day, Jane, Edwin, Fitz, and Hem would become a family before God and the people they loved most.

There was no bride or groom's side at this event. All the guests, and there weren't many, had squeezed into the center pew. When Jane reached them, she paused to blow a kiss at the Fins and the Cover Girls.

Everyone's eyes were misty—even Butterworth's— and Jane had to struggle to maintain her composure. But when a tear slipped down Eloise's cheek, Jane couldn't stop herself from leaning over and embracing her best friend.

"My sister," Eloise whispered.

Jane didn't dare speak. If she opened her mouth, all the love she felt for her oldest and dearest friend would escape her as a loud sob, so she kissed Eloise's petal-smooth cheek instead.

When she straightened, she dabbed at the corners of her eyes with her pinkie finger and murmured, "Oh, boy."

Though the quiet outburst eased the wave of emotion crescendoing in her chest, she knew she wouldn't be able to keep her feelings in check for long.

In this sacred space, she felt enveloped in love. Surrounded by so many precious faces. Their shared memories and the memories yet to be made filled the air like a silent song. How could she not be overwhelmed by such an abundance of blessings?

"Who gives this woman to be married to this man?" asked the minister.

This patient, soft-spoken man of the cloth had once held Jane over the baptismal font and dribbled water over her tiny head. He'd baptized her sons and watched them grow from newborn infants into tall, wide-shouldered boys. He'd invited Aunt Octavia and Uncle Aloysius to serve as elders and sat at their bedsides during times of sickness.

Aunt Octavia put her hand over her heart and looked at her husband as he proudly declared, "We do!"

Grasping Jane's hands in theirs, her great-aunt and -uncle led her to her groom. Then they pressed Jane's hands into Edwin's.

Uncle Aloysius said, "Never let go. That's the secret."

"Just hold on, no matter what," added Aunt Octavia.

Jane looked into Edwin's eyes and saw the rest of her life laid out before her.

She saw mornings at the kitchen table, summer evenings on the patio, walks in the woods, grocery lists, movie nights, washing dishes, whispers in bed, heated arguments, boarding airplanes, planting gardens, pouring wine, flopping on the sofa to watch TV, dancing at parties, sending texts, laughing at jokes, reading in bed, and a countless exchange of kisses, hugs, and small touches. And always, always, she saw the joining of their hands.

She pictured time aging them, as it had Aunt Octavia and Uncle Aloysius. She saw Edwin as an old man, still rakishly handsome, with waves of silver hair contrasting with his dark eyes and brows. She envisioned smile lines fanning out from his eyes, deep furrows on his forehead, and wrinkles bracketing his mouth.

She saw all this and felt deeply grateful for the days to come. She and Edwin would walk through life together. Hand in hand.

The wedding ceremony continued with prayers and readings. The couple chose traditional vows, but when it was time for the exchange of rings, they turned to Rumi's poetry. Edwin had wooed Jane with the Persian's romantic verse, so it seemed fitting that their marriage begin with his words.

Edwin held Jane's wedding band in the air near her ring finger and said, "'The minute I heard my first love story, I started looking for you, not knowing how blind that was.'"

He slipped the ring on her finger.

Picking up where he'd left off, Jane said, "'Lovers don't finally meet somewhere. They're in each other all along.'"

She eased the ring over his knuckle smiling through her tears.

The minister pronounced them man and wife, spoke a final benediction, and invited Edwin to kiss his bride.

As he took her in his arms and kissed her long and heartily, their friends and family jumped to their feet and applauded.

Above the din, the minister pronounced, "It is my joy to present to you Mr. and Mrs. Steward-Alcott."

Following another round of applause, the minister signaled for quiet.

"Today, we're not only celebrating the union between Edwin and Jane, but the union of a family. Hemingway and Fitzgerald, please come forward."

The two boys shuffled closer to the altar, looking bashful and uncomfortable in their three-piece wedding suits.

To Jane, they looked like fairy-tale heroes. They were Jack shimmying down the beanstalk or Arthur pulling a magic sword from a stone. They were her charming, shiny-haired, precocious, and precious sons.

Though their biological father was no longer living, Jane knew that this moment would make William happy. He'd want a good man to look after his sons in his stead, and Edwin loved the boys with all his heart.

"At their confirmation this coming spring, Hem and Fitz will become members of this congregation. However, they would like to be recognized by their new names, with you, their family and friends, as their witnesses."

The minister had to move to a higher step in order to raise his hands over Fitz and Hem's heads. After speaking a prayer over the boys, he lowered his hands to their shoulders and said, "It's my pleasure to introduce Hemingway and Fitzgerald Steward-Alcott."

Reddening with pleasure and embarrassment, the boys accepted hugs from Jane and Edwin.

In the middle of this display of affection, the organist struck up the first chords to the Beatles "All You Need Is Love."

Hem bounded over to Aunt Octavia and offered her his arm. After wiping both eyes with her handkerchief, she wrapped her arm around his.

Fitz bowed low to Uncle Aloysius and took him by the arm.

As the oldest and youngest guests filed to the back of the church, the organ music grew louder and more playful.

Jane and Edwin were supposed to follow behind the twins, but Jane didn't want to leave just yet. She wanted this moment to stretch on for much, much longer. She wanted to store this bliss in her heart for the rest of her days.

As she couldn't freeze time, she had to settle for hugging the guests. She moved down the row, embracing Eloise, Mabel, Betty, Mrs. Pratt, Anna, Violet, Phoebe, Sam, Lachlan, Sterling, Butterworth, and last but not least, Sinclair.

The music swelled through the church, its exultant strains echoing from the organ pipes. As it pirouetted over the carpet and spiraled toward the rafters, its energy growing with every note, it became impossible not to sing along.

"All you need is . . ." sang the Cover Girls.

"Love," sang Sam.

The Fins chimed in next, "All you need is . . ."

The organist nodded at the minister and together, they belted out, "Love, Love, Love!"

As the chorus repeated, Edwin took Jane's hand. "Wife of mine, we have a party to get to."

The twins were waiting by the front doors with Aunt

Octavia and Uncle Aloysius. All four were bundled up in winter coats.

Fitz held up a beautiful, faux-furred lined coat. "Mom. This one's yours."

Jane had never seen the beautiful, blush-colored coat before. "Are you sure this is mine?"

Helping her into the coat, Aunt Octavia said, "We wanted you to be warm and toasty on the ride home."

"Is there something wrong with the car's heater?" Jane asked, confused.

Ignoring the question, Aunt Octavia patted the pocket of Jane's new coat. "Your gloves are in here."

Hem stepped up to Edwin and said, "Your turn, Dad."

Edwin's face broke out in a huge smile that had nothing to do with the handsome wool coat his son was holding out for him. He slipped it on and clapped Hem on the shoulder.

Behind them, the organist was in her own world. Her feet and hands roved over her instrument. Her head swayed in time with the music and her eyes were squeezed shut.

By this point, the guests had joined the newlyweds by the door. They were all wearing coats and gloves.

"Where'd Sam go?" Edwin asked Lachlan.

Lachlan responded with a sly smile. "You'll see."

Butterworth and Sinclair moved to the double doors and grabbed hold of a handle. At Butterworth's nod, they pushed open the doors, inviting a rush of wintry air to rush in.

Jane heard the high, excited whiny of a horse, and when she looked outside, she saw the horse-drawn sleigh parked at the end of the path.

Sam had somehow managed to exit the church, slap on a Santa hat, and climb into the driver's seat.

A tinkling laugh bubbled up Jane's throat as she and Edwin half-walked, half-ran to the sleigh.

"How did you know we'd get hit by that snowstorm three days ago?" Edwin asked Sam.

"The horses. Forget science. Animals are the best predictors of weather." Pulling down his hat over his ears, he said, "You two get comfy under that blanket and we'll go over the river and through the woods to the biggest block party this town has ever seen."

After helping Jane into the sleigh, Edwin hopped in and tucked the blanket around their legs. Their friends and family waved goodbye as Sam clicked his tongue and told the horses to walk on.

The sleigh started moving over the snow, and the bells on the horses' harnesses jingled merrily as they quickened their step from a walk to a smooth trot.

Storyton was so quiet that Sam was able to drive down the middle of Main Street. There were barely any cars parked in front of the shops and the only vehicles on the road were traveling behind the sleigh.

After crossing Storyton River and taking Broken Arm Bend at a conservative pace, Sam steered the horses off the road and into woods.

The rest of the guests continued driving toward Storyton Hall, and when Sam slowed the horses to a brisk walk, Jane guessed that he was giving the wedding guests time to reach the manor house before the bride and groom arrived.

It was quarter to five in late December, and night wasn't far from falling. The last light from the setting sun draped the bare trees and virgin snow in rose gold. Overhead, the stars began surfacing like fishing bobbers in a deep blue lake.

"I guess we're taking the long way 'round," Jane said, snuggling up to Edwin for warmth.

Sliding an arm around her, he pulled her close and kissed her cold lips. "I wouldn't mind if we got a little lost. Then I could keep you all to myself."

"You have me for the rest of your life. Isn't that enough?"

He shook his head. "I want to be with you always. I don't ever want our story to end."

Jane laid her gloved hand on his cheek and said, "Then let's make every chapter count."

They spent the rest of the ride in companionable silence. The only sound was the ringing of the harness bells and the gentle whisper of the sleigh gliding over the snow.

When they exited the woods and entered the clearing at the base of the Great Lawn, Jane gasped in surprise.

"Is that a barn? In the middle of the lawn?"

Edwin chuckled. "It's more of a barn façade. A bunch of volunteers built it this morning, which is why we kept you busy at home and the twins turned up the Christmas music so loud. The barn front is built around one of Storyton Hall's wedding tents."

"When you said you wanted to be in charge of the reception, I never pictured this. It's crazy and sweet and totally unexpected."

"Wait until you see the chicken coop."

Jane shot him a sidelong glance. "You're kidding, right?"

Sam eased the sleigh to a stop in front of the faux barn doors, which were flanked by hay bales and glowing lanterns. Twinkling lights formed a curtain over the entrance. From inside, Jane heard upbeat music and boisterous laughter.

Jumping down from the driver's seat, Sam said, "Give me a minute to tell them you're here."

As he disappeared into the tent, Edwin hopped out of the sleigh and raised his arms to Jane. He grabbed her by the waist and swung her gently to the ground.

"Ready or not, here we come!" he called out.

Together, Edwin and Jane parted the curtain of lights and entered the tent.

They were greeted by an explosion of applause, interspersed with jubilant hoots and shrill whistles.

Jane glanced at all the familiar faces and realized that over half the village had congregated in the tent.

Fitz and Hem materialized from behind a group of Storyton Hall staff members and joined Jane and Edwin. Eloise tapped a microphone three times, signaling for quiet.

She threw a huge smile at Jane and shouted into the mic, "Congratulations to the Steward-Alcotts!"

The response from the guests was thunderous.

Eloise made a sweeping gesture around the tent and yelled, "Welcome to your country Christmas wedding!"

It took the newlyweds a long time to receive congratulatory hugs and remarks from their guests, but eventually, Jane was able to take in the oak barrel tables, the centerpieces of baby's breath and flowers made of book pages, the battery-powered lanterns and candles, and the buffet tables stuffed with food. Luckily, Edwin had been joking about the chicken coop.

"I know what you're thinking," Edwin said. "But Mrs. Hubbard didn't cook for the whole town. She only made the wedding cake. Everything else came from our guests. They all brought a favorite dish and a serving utensil."

As they moved closer to the food, Jane realized that their wedding tent was actually two wedding tents.

"The bar and dancing are in the other tent," Edwin explained.

"Do you want to handle all the wedding bookings from now on?"

Edwin picked up a clean plate and handed it to Jane. "Actually, I've been thinking about going into business with another woman."

Jane stared at the dishes in front of her. There was no rhyme or reason to the arrangement of bowls and platters. A bowl of rainbow pasta salad was sandwiched between a cheese ball and a tray of sweet-and-sour meatballs. There was green salad, sausage rolls, mini-quiches, roasted veggies, baked brie, salsa and chips, buffalo chicken sliders, hummus and pita bread, deviled eggs, and a melon medley. And this was just the first of four food tables.

"Another woman, eh?"

Edwin put a chicken slider on his plate and said, "Yep. Here she comes now."

Olivia Limoges looked dazzling in a satin, champagne-colored pantsuit. She held two crystal flutes in one hand and a bottle of bubbly in the other. After offering her congratulations, she said, "Sorry I missed your entrance, but I had to run back to Alistair's to get this. You need the good stuff for your toast."

"I was just about to tell Jane about our joint venture," said Edwin.

Olivia gestured at Edwin with the hand holding the flutes. "I happened to mention wanting a project to

work on while I'm in town—other than my writing—
and your husband suggested that we join forces. He
wants to transform the Daily Bread into something
new."

"If we convert my old apartment into dining rooms,
we can use the main floor as a wine bar. I thought we'd
call the new restaurant the Library Bistro. Everything
on the menu will have a literary name."

"The Library," Jane repeated. "I like it."

Olivia showed them to their table on the far side of
the tent. After putting down their plates, Jane and
Edwin walked over to where Mrs. Hubbard stood guard
over the wedding cake.

"I've been thinking about this cake since you two fell
in love," she said. Her lower lip wobbled, and she pressed
a napkin to her mouth.

Jane was too enchanted to speak.

The all-white cake was five tiers high, with a spray of
delicate dogwood blossoms spiraling down from the
top tier to the bottom. The flowers looked so lifelike
that Jane could almost smell their sweet, springtime
perfume.

Fondant versions of Jane and Edwin perched on top
of the cake. They stood upon an open book, holding
hands and smiling at each other.

The book had a gold cover and gold-edged pages. A
line of elegant script on the left page said, "*All You Need
Is Love.*" On the bottom of the right page, inside a pair
of dainty parenthesis, was the text, "*And books.*"

Jane pulled Mrs. Hubbard into an embrace and whispered, "This is a cake made of spun sugar and dreams.
Thank you."

Through her tears, Mrs. Hubbard beamed.

After toasts and eating, there was dancing and more

eating. There were tears and laughter and the cutting of the cake. There were jokes and more hugs.

And when it was finally time for Jane and Edwin to say good night, the guests walked them to the entrance of the tent. The music was muted, and every man, woman, and child turned to look at Aunt Octavia and Uncle Aloysius.

Aunt Octavia raised her champagne flute, and her movement was mimicked by all the guests.

In one voice, they toasted the couple with a version of Storyton Hall's motto.

"Your story is our story!" they cried. "Here's to the next chapter!"

Jane put her hand to her heart, too moved to speak. All she could do was smile through her tears and blow kisses to her friends and neighbors. Edwin thanked their guests for sharing in their joy before sliding an arm around Jane's waist.

Then the couple stepped out into the winter night. The sky was a riot of stars. The moon was a shiny coin hanging directly over their heads. As they followed the lantern-lit pathway to their honeymoon cottage, the clock at Storyton Hall began to ring out the hour.

It didn't normally ring at night, and the low, resonating gong swept over the snowy ground like a thunderous wave.

Jane turned to the man she loved. "It's like the house is saying that even though our magical night is ending, there's no need to be sad. Because we have tomorrow. And every tomorrow after that. Every day is a new beginning. A fresh page."

"What a book we're going to write," Edwin said.

And then he kissed his bride.

Author's Note

Readers often ask me if Storyton Hall is a real place. I wish it existed exactly as it appears in the Book Retreat Mysteries, but unfortunately, it doesn't.

However, the series was inspired by the magical setting of the Omni Homestead Resort. I've stayed there several times and never tire of its elegant rooms, delicious food, and beautiful surroundings. If you're looking for a little peace and pampering, make your way to Bath County, Virginia.

Thank you for visiting Storyton Hall time and time again, and for all the lovely things you've said about the series in reviews, social media posts, and personal messages. You're sweeter than Mrs. Hubbard's finest creations, and I'm forever grateful.

Yours,
Ellery

Visit our website at
KensingtonBooks.com
to sign up for our newsletters, read
more from your favorite authors, see
books by series, view reading group
guides, and more!

BOOK **CLUB**

BETWEEN THE CHAPTERS

Become a Part of Our
Between the Chapters Book Club
Community and Join the Conversation

Betweenthechapters.net